'Barkworth is excruciatingly good at encapsulating that point in life where Mia and Lily stand – on the edge of growing up . . . Intense and claustrophobic, this is an impressive first book'
OBSERVER

'Painfully real, and so beautifully written I wanted to stay within its pages forever. *Heatstroke* is unsettling, challenging and utterly immersive'
CLARE MACKINTOSH

'A sultry, stifling debut exploring power, consent and womanhood'
COSMOPOLITAN

'Tense, sultry, unsettling, sweaty and evocative . . . A thrilling look at mothers and daughters, adolescence, sex, suburbia and secrets'
NELL FRIZZELL

'Stylish and sensual'
KIRAN MILLWOOD HARGRAVE

'Gripping and intensely atmospheric . . . beautifully explores the complicated relationship between mothers and teenage daughters'
HEAT

'Compulsive, sticky and full of gorgeous writing'
KIRSTIN INNES

'I am addicted! A gripping, dark and twisty read with beautiful, poetic writing'
EMMA GANNON

'An atmospheric read that will draw you into its tangled web'
WOMAN & HOME

'Raw, unsparing and almost unbearably tender. Perfect sentences swim gracefully across every page, overlaying a narrative that delights in wrong-footing the readers' assumptions. I couldn't tear myself away'
ERIN KELLY

'Dark and unsettling'
RED

HEAT STROKE

HAZEL BARKWORTH

REVIEW

First published in 2020 by
Headline Review
An imprint of HEADLINE PUBLISHING GROUP

First published as a paperback in 2021 by
Headline Review
An imprint of HEADLINE PUBLISHING GROUP

Cataloguing in Publication Data is available from the British Library

ISBN 978 1 4722 6562 3

Typeset in Dante MT by CC Book Production
Printed and bound in Great Britain by Clays Ltd, Elcograf S.p.A.

MIX
Paper from
responsible sources
FSC® C104740

Headline's policy is to use papers that are natural, renewable and
recyclable products and made from wood grown in well-managed forests
and other controlled sources. The logging and manufacturing processes are
expected to conform to the environmental regulations of the country of origin.

HEADLINE PUBLISHING GROUP
An Hachette UK Company
Carmelite House
50 Victoria Embankment
London EC4Y 0DZ

www.headline.co.uk
www.hachette.co.uk

For Paul

'It's always been, so it's no surprise.'

'Cola', Lana Del Rey

'I am important to her. She comes and goes.'

'Mirror', Sylvia Plath

1

Languid. The word that formed in Rachel's mind was languid. The figure on the lawn was languid. Its limbs were loose, its joints fluid. Its hands and feet seemed too heavy for the bones that held them. It was draped over the sun lounger, dripping from its edges. Not a single muscle seemed tensed. Rachel knew she was staring.

The sun was so high that everything in the garden was bleached. The grass was brittle and the patio slabs blinding white. Rachel's feet were cool against the kitchen tiles and it felt indulgent. It had been too hot for days but was only mid-June; there were still five weeks until the school holidays began. The temperature had crept into the high twenties every afternoon, and Rachel had woken tangled in the sheets every morning.

She stood at the sink, squeaking a dishcloth into mugs. One by one, she rubbed the stains from their nooks then placed them on the draining rack. The outside brightness made the inside gloomy. She leaned forward, her eyes never leaving the torpid figure. Even this close to the window, Rachel was still in the shade. There was no way she could be visible from the garden.

A towel made the lounger soft. Rachel had owned that beach towel for eighteen years. She remembered buying it in a Cornish surf shack she'd felt too hip for. It bore a now-faded dreamscape, a technicolour sunset with *Aloha Hawaii* scrawled in pink. The towel was three years older than the body that lay on it. There she was, in her lime-green bikini. Her head tilted so her metre of hair waterfalled over the side of the lounger. Her drink was only an arm's length away, but she moved so slowly it seemed to take enormous effort. Just reaching down to the grass was apparently enough to exhaust her.

As Mia settled back, the left strap of her bikini top fell from her shoulder. There was a shock of white where the material had been. The rest of her was slick with lotion, but turning a warm pink that would blossom to brown. She was baking her body perfectly. She stretched to her full length; the wing-span that seemed impossible, the bubble-gum painted toenails. Her eyes would be closed behind those plastic sunglasses. She arched her back, forcing her breasts upwards, pouting as if she was being photographed.

Rachel stepped further back into the dusk of the kitchen. The window would form a mirror in the sunlight. Mia slouched back again. Supine on that towel, nothing could be troubling her. There were no hairs on her legs, not even little golden ones that might glint on her thighs. Not a single bristle would snag any palm that stroked them.

Rachel found her eyes lingering on the shadow where those green bikini bottoms met the skin. It was just as smooth there. Rachel wondered what blade or wax or lotion had removed the hair. Had Mia holed herself up in the bathroom and waited whilst noxious cream burned every follicle away? Had she held the skin taut and dragged a razor against the grain? Had she booked an appointment to have it ripped out of her? Rachel wanted to know who it was designed to impress. Who else did Mia expect to see that patch of flesh? Rachel longed to hold that body she'd known so well. The clavicle she'd kissed so often. The ribs she'd once xylophoned.

Mia lifted an arm to swat something from her thigh, some insect or pollen spore, some floating dandelion seed that had dared to tickle her. Rachel worried it was instead her own gaze made solid. She worried her daughter knew she was watching.

The stillness didn't last long. As the sun began to ease, the house began to fill and, by six, the kitchen was crammed with teenage bodies. Mia was playing hostess. Three girls arrived, laden down with sleeping bags and backpacks. Between them, there could only possibly be eight arms, but they flailed into every corner. It was incredible they didn't cause damage. The pizzas Rachel had bought were wolfed straight from the oven.

'I'm such a cow.' Ella's voice rose above the others.

Keira deepened hers. 'Ah, *la vache!*'

'Accurate.' As perfect as their eyeliner flicks were, as dainty as their ankles might be, the girls ate like boys – folding slices, dipping them in ketchup, then gulping them down in seconds, standing up.

Rachel hung back, eager not to look eager. They all knew her from school. She'd taught half of them, and wanted to avoid anything that might smack of desperation. She kept her greeting swift.

'Evening, ladies.' A curt nod in their direction, then she lingered in the garden – tilting her head backwards, pretending to relish the early-evening sun, miming the bliss of it seeping into her skin – and let them colonise the living room. They'd scoured Netflix and chosen a film that had been popular when Rachel was only a few years older than they were now.

'Shut up. He's totally cute. He is!' To hear them watch it felt like mockery. Teenage laughter crescendoed into hysteria so easily; that wracking wheeze. *Don't, don't.* To them, it could only be ironic to lust after that stubbled actor, to crave those clothes, those hairstyles. How Rachel had coveted Winona's full-length floral dress, her clumpy Mary Janes. She'd never tell them to quell that laughter. In a year's time, they'd be deep in the mire of their GCSEs, and this lightness would be a memory.

Rachel's hands itched to open the bags of popcorn she knew were in the cupboard. She could pour them into pastel plastic bowls, then perch on the arm of the sofa, chipping into the edges of their conversation. She resisted. Methodically, she tidied the carnage of the kitchen – rinsing plates for the dishwasher, folding the pizza boxes into neat piles for recycling. She was grateful for the plausible occupation. Afterwards, she settled at the kitchen table with the few remaining slices, nibbling the crusts as she worked through a ream of marking, leaving greasy fingerprints down the margins of essays. She was used to eating alone, but leaned upon the companionship of work. The girls were on their feet now, dancing to a song from the film. The living-room door was open, and she could see them wiggle their heads in pastiche as they sang. *Running down the length of my thigh, Sharona.* They stumbled over the lyrics of a song they'd never heard before, rewinding to shriek it again.

The girls had risen early. All four of them had showered, dressed and left to catch the bus before Rachel ventured downstairs. Mia had sent a text rather than call out her goodbye. *Gone to town, back by four-ish.* Then the emoji of a steaming coffee cup. There were too few words to interrogate.

After the thrilling whispers that had punctuated the night, the house felt hollow. Rachel poured a cup of tea. They'd be in Starbucks by now, cooled by the air-conditioner breeze, each making a Frappuccino last for two hours. They'd be squealing at the slightest quip, posing in case boys they knew walked by, still young enough to glean sophistication from their drink's Italianate name. They'd be sipping at their green straws, tasting a coffee with no hint of bitterness.

Rachel wandered back upstairs. Mia's usually immaculate bedroom was in disarray. Three sleeping bags still crosshatched the floor. Their sleepovers were usually for five. It was rare to see the group divided, but Lily hadn't been able to make this one, cancelling at the last minute. Rachel assumed only illness could keep them apart. The bedding swallowed up every nook of the room. When Rachel lay down, Mia's duvet was still warm, even warmer than the air. She nuzzled her face into the pillow, wriggled her limbs right down, soaking up the heat that had been left. If she placed her head on the dent where Mia's head had been, she wondered if she would hear the thoughts that had formed there.

Rachel inhaled, trying to catch anything of the remaining scent, but there was no human smell there, no sweat or spit, just the synthetic honey they all loved so much. Those girls were like hummingbirds; they had to swallow twice their body weight in sugar every day just to survive. Their tongues must be thick with glucose. They sipped Diet Coke every second they were allowed to, popped Haribo, sprayed perfume that smelled of an opened sweet jar. Rachel breathed it all in. It made her light-headed, dizzy with that vanilla.

Rachel wanted to open the window, to shake their crumpled sleeping bags until they were crisp and clean, but she moved nothing. The five girls had formed a tight circle before they started school. They'd already clocked up a decade of fierce loyalty. Whatever sticky truths they'd breathed into that ether were safe.

The mornings were a brief respite from the heat, but Rachel was too late. The sun had already hit the exact angle that flooded the back of the house, turning the kitchen into a greenhouse and thickening the air. The stack of essays wouldn't diminish by itself, but Rachel couldn't settle. She couldn't bring herself to sit down in the blazing light and work through them. Tea was too hot to drink, ice cubes vanished before they could be any use, and her phone was silent. Rachel composed messages, trailing her fingers over the screen, letting the technology predict her words, but never pressed send.

She hadn't arranged to see anyone, and the sun was too bright to contend with. There was no other pulse in the house, and her breaths were all that stirred the air. That black slab was her only portal. Rachel toyed with it, passing it from hand to hand, coaxing it to bleat. The tiny green light would change everything. But Tim wouldn't call. She could fathom the time difference without arithmetic now. She didn't even need to check the digits. He would still be asleep.

The telephone rang at exactly two. Rachel was cross-legged on a kitchen chair, a slice of avocado inches from her lips. The shrill ring made her start. Not her mobile, but the landline that lay dormant in the hallway. She didn't want to answer, but the bleats were so demanding. The receiver felt alien in her hands, heavy, and seemed to require a different sort of greeting. *Hello, Rachel Collins speaking.* It was Lily's mother, Debbie.

She'd never called the house before. She had Rachel's mobile number, her email address – they were linked through a WhatsApp group of mums – but she'd chosen the land-line. The number must have lived in an address book, a floral Christmas gift from years ago.

'Sorry to bother you, Rach. I just wanted to check that Lily was still there.'

'Lily? No . . .'

Debbie's voice cut her off, her tone too bright for the shadowy hallway. 'She said she'd be home a few hours ago, but I know how these things can be. I wondered if she maybe needed a lift, or something.'

The words were out before Rachel considered how to form them. 'No, Debs, Lily couldn't make it. I thought she was with you.' The syllables hung in the air, sounding stupid at first, then – as the silence ticked into full seconds – horrifying.

Rachel could hear Debbie swallow on the other end of the line. 'No. No, she walked round yesterday afternoon. She said she'd be home in time for lunch today.'

Rachel knew she should say something, but her mouth jarred. She was caught in a spasm. It would fade. In a few seconds it would fade; they'd realise their silly mistake and get on with their day with just the memory of that shudder to haunt them. It happened all the time when you were a mother. Facts got mixed, confused, terrifying. It never lasted.

Before Rachel could exhale, Debbie made a small noise. A hiccup. A yelp. Then a gush of words. 'I've been trying her phone for the last few hours, but it keeps going to voicemail, I thought it had probably just run out of charge, she never remembers to plug it in and they have such short battery lives, don't they? I was going to try Mia, but I didn't want to seem like I was nagging. I've left Lily messages, but she hasn't got back to me yet. I'm not really sure what to do.' The last words trailed off.

Rachel grabbed her own mobile. 'Mia will know. Mia'll know where she is, Debs.' Her numb fingers were somehow able to unlock the phone, to manipulate its digits. It seemed wilfully capricious. That was why Debbie had chosen the landline. Mobiles were tricksy; always at risk of being lost, silenced, ignored. If the robot voice spoke instead of the person you wanted, you could draw no conclusion. It could be out of range, drained of energy. Rachel's thumb dialled Mia's number. It only took a few swipes; her daughter was nearly at the top of her favourites list.

The metallic ring pulsed, the seconds between each burst stretching longer and longer. Debbie was silent on the end of the landline. Rachel held both receivers to her ears, clumsy and ridiculous. Their weight doubled, tripled, straining her wrists. Mia answered after five rings, achingly long given her phone was never more than an inch from her hand. Her voice was thick with irony. She'd seen the caller ID; she was playing to the audience around her, poutingly put out at the interruption.

'Hey, Mother. What is it?'

Rachel slid the untouched rump of avocado into the mouth of the Brabantia bin. There was nothing else to do. Mia was being dropped home by Keira's dad. There was no use in all the parents driving to town to pick them up. They'd be better off together. They'd be scared. Mia would be home in twenty minutes, twenty-five at the very most. Rachel wiped the kitchen surface with a dishcloth, then wrung it out under the tap, wrenching so hard her fingers turned red, then white. The tap was streaked, blotchy with the dull breath of limescale. Only bleach would lift it. There was a bottle in the cupboard beneath the sink, and Rachel poured a viscous line down the stainless steel. Her eyes watered, but she left it to work its enchantment, to make the silver pure again.

The gleaming taps cast the rest of the kitchen into relief. How could she have ignored the watermarks on the hob, the sticky patches and drips on the cupboard doors where they'd been careless? Rachel began to scrub. Lily would call home soon. This awful hour would become the stuff of stories. Lily was probably with a boy, some smarmy twat in the year above who had persuaded her to go to a party. She might be feeling worse for wear, but nothing a long bath and a Nurofen wouldn't sort out. Teenagers could be like this. No one ever said otherwise.

Rachel scrubbed the wooden units with a sponge scourer, digging her fingers into the forest-green bristles, feeling them force their way under her fingernails. Mia would be home soon. Inside, safe from anything that might snatch or lure her away. Rachel scrubbed hard, pushing down into the grain, into the pebble pattern of the kitchen surfaces. Once they were clean, she scrubbed the grey slabs of the kitchen floor, the ones she and Tim had chosen when they'd moved in. They were the first owners; they'd selected the shade of every carpet, every detail of the finishings. Mia had hardly known any other kitchen floor.

The sponge was disintegrating under the effort. Rachel threw it in the bin, and grabbed a fat, unopened packet of wipes from the cupboard. She broke the seal with too much force and sent all eighty wipes spilling over the floor, then snatched handfuls of them. They came away filthy. The floor looked clean, but the grime must have been all around them, filling their lungs with every breath. Rachel couldn't bear it. The house needed to be clean for when Mia came home. She scrubbed. It was too hot for that kind of vigour, but she scrubbed anyway, ignoring the dizzy blackness that fogged her head. She scrubbed until her knuckles were raw, until sweat dripped into her eyes; scrubbed without stopping, without thinking, until Mia's key grated in the lock.

Rachel squeezed teabags against the side of the mugs they hardly ever used: the ones that were a gift from her mother, the ones that matched. She placed the spent bags into a china dish. Her hands were weak. It was too hot for tea, but she'd offered and they'd accepted. The kitchen shone. She stirred in their milk and one sugar, chinking a teaspoon and setting her face to mild.

Rachel perched on an armchair as they spoke, nothing but a chaperone. She curled her hands around the unbearably warm mug of English Breakfast to keep them from shaking, forced her feet to stop tapping. This was not supposed to be happening. The police officers were not young, not the mavericks of television shows, but a man and woman in their mid-forties who were unerringly calm and polite.

'Thank you so much for your time, Mia, we really do appreciate it.' They punctuated their steady questions with sips of tea. It hadn't cooled, and must have scalded the soft flesh of their tongues, but they didn't flicker.

Mia was meek at first; eyes down, voice small. Rachel had scarcely addressed the situation with Mia before the police arrived. They'd hugged so tightly their bones had clashed, but Rachel hadn't articulated her fears. She didn't want to hear them out loud. Mia answered the first few questions – about who she was and how she knew Lily – incredibly carefully, as if she might be tripped up, calibrating her age to the month. She looked exhausted. Lines ran from the inner corners of her eyes down to her ears, as if her face had been folded with tiredness. She could scarcely have slept the night before, and the news of Lily seemed to have depleted whatever reserves of energy were left.

'Okay then, Mia.' The woman spoke most often, brown hair tucked behind her ears, resting her mug on the round of her knee. 'We do need to know if Lily seemed different to you over the last few days.' Her tone was light, as if she was talking to a much younger child.

'She was the same. She was fine.'

'She didn't seem worried at all to you, Mia, like maybe she was nervous about something?' Each of her questions followed the same sing-song pattern of intonation.

'No.'

'Did she mention any plans she had to you, anything she was looking forward to?' That same flimsy rhythm.

'No, she didn't. Can you just tell me where she is?'

'We're not sure at the moment, Mia.' The woman, who'd introduced herself as DC Redpath, kept saying Mia's name, cooing out those two syllables – *mee-aah* – like she was stroking her, luring her to tell more. 'Were there no hints or anything at all we might need to know?'

'No.' Mia was definite. 'I really don't know what you're talking about. Just tell me where Lily is.'

The philtrum of her lip was curling upwards, a sure sign she was trying to stop herself from crying. Rachel knew that lip. It curled the same way Tim's did. That same patch of flesh she'd kissed so often had been lifted directly and transferred to her daughter's mouth. Rachel couldn't stand to see it twitch. She wanted to stop them, make them wait. Mia needed to process the news before being interrogated. DC Redpath's manner didn't stop it from being a grilling. But they'd been adamant. They wanted the girls' first reactions, unsullied by too much thought, with no chance for them to conspire. They were making an exception by not asking them to come to the station. Rachel had been grateful for the gesture, but now she wanted to stand up and order them to leave her daughter alone, to leave her house immediately and not come back. She wanted them to take their thoughts with them. She knew the grisliness of what they'd been trained for, of what they were imagining. The smells and the textures. Rachel wanted their statistics, their likelihoods, their blood-soaked practicalities far away from her home. She could only sit with her cooling mug of tea and watch.

The man, DC Scott, finally broke his silence. 'Mia, whatever you tell us now, however insignificant it seems to you, could be crucial in finding Lily and getting her back home. Did she say anything that we need to know? Do you know where she might be? Do you know who she might be with?'

Mia didn't answer.

Rachel wanted to hold Mia's face, focus their eyes on each other and tell her it was okay, that she didn't need to worry, that Lily would be fine, that no one was in trouble. But Rachel had been superseded by a higher authority. Even in her own home, they were both under a different jurisdiction. She wanted to look into Mia's eyes close up, not clouded by even a few steps. She wanted to see if there was anything Mia had to tell.

'Lily has been missing for over twenty-four hours now. This is very serious.'

Rachel tried to blank his words and their implications. It wasn't serious. It was a mistake. As they questioned her from different angles, repeating the same enquiry over and over, Mia lost her stiff calmness. As they kept trying to winkle out a fresh reply, she became every inch fifteen; stroppy and outraged, raking her hands through her hair. Her voice was louder now. Higher. Faster.

'Why do you think I know? I don't know anything. You don't even know. *Why* don't you know where she is? How do you even know if she's okay?'

The roof of Rachel's mouth throbbed. Seeing Mia's distress, but not being able to ease it, was painful. It was all meant to be over by now. Lily was supposed to be at home, tearful and apologetic, tucked up in her purple duvet and eating platefuls of toast made by her mother. There was meant to be nothing left but relieved exhaustion and a hackneyed lecture. Instead, two uniformed officers were sitting on Rachel's sofa, their black shoes square on her cream carpet.

'Can you come back?'

It was Sunday where he was too, lunchtime, but she'd still had to summon him from a meeting. She had never interrupted his work before.

'I'm back in just over week, Rach. It's not long.'

Rachel paced the kitchen. Three steps one way, then three

steps to retrace them. 'It's twelve days, Tim. We need you back. She's frightened. I'm frightened.'

There was a time lag between every utterance. A stutter of silence that hindered their flow. It was technology stretched to its limits, struggling to keep up, or Tim stumbling to form his sentence.

'I know, sweetie, I know. But I can't do anything. My being there won't make her any safer. It might just freak her out more, make it seem more urgent.'

Rachel had to modulate her voice. 'Tim, her best friend has vanished. She could be anywhere. She could be dead. This is urgent.'

After the blank beat of time, his tone was saccharine. 'Rach, honey, she'll be fine. You know that, don't you? She'll be back tomorrow and it'll all be over.'

Rachel let his platitudes coo down the line, eking their way across four thousand miles, barely registering as sounds by the time they reached her ears.

The television was on. It was an HBO drama they'd never watched, deep into series seven. There was a courtroom scene, a woman with immaculate lipstick, then thumping music. It was too bright, too loud. The remote control was on the other side of the room. The screen people began to shout at each other. Rachel had no idea who they were, or why they were upset. She and Mia both watched. They didn't play with their phones, just faced the screen. It was after ten, but neither of them had made any move to go to bed. Rachel swallowed. Words formed in her mouth, swelled to fill it, then sat leaden on her tongue.

The figures on the screen were kissing now, suddenly pawing suits and shirts off each other. Rachel looked at Mia without moving her head. Mia didn't respond. Rachel remembered the creeping awkwardness of her own parents' house during a television sex scene – the silence, the personal prayer not to make an inadvertent sigh, the hard stare straight at the floral curtains. She and Mia had always turned it into a joke. Even when Mia was very young, they'd shriek at each other, *Don't look, don't look, it's rude.* They'd hide their faces in their hands, cover each other's eyes. They'd squeal if the characters merely shared a chaste peck. *It's rude, don't look. I'm being corrupted,* Mia would yell, *I'm morally ruined.* She'd been so much fun.

Rachel coughed. The little bark echoed around the living room. Mia didn't even shift her gaze. 'You tired yet, Mi?'

Seconds passed before her reply. 'Not really.'

Rachel wanted to talk. She wanted to turn the television off and sit with her daughter, to hold her, to ask her every question that was clogging her thoughts. But it was so precarious. A single word badly pitched could throw the whole evening. Rachel didn't know which phrase would make Mia jink like metal on a filling. Mia was curled into the corner of the sofa, tiny in her leggings and hoodie. When she stood, she seemed all limbs, but tucked around herself, her knees hugged to her chest, she was so little again. She was huddled despite the heat, her hands stuffed into her top's marsupial pouch, her hood up. The circle of her face was the only skin on show.

Rachel wanted to push herself up from the armchair, take the two steps across the room and hold her daughter. She wanted to wrap her arms around that grey hoodie and whisper into the soft of Mia's ear, coo right into her thoughts, whatever they were, wherever they took her, and tell her she was safe. If she spoke right into her ear, Mia couldn't slink away. She'd have to hear her mother's fierce words. Rachel didn't need Mia to speak; she just wanted to feel her daughter's shoulder blades dig into her collarbone as she held her. She wanted to push her face into Mia's hair, and smell the warm salt of her scalp.

With Tim away, Rachel was left to steer every vital conversation, quell every silence, soothe every concern. It used to be so easy. When Mia was small, Rachel had read the articles, heard the whispers at toddler groups. She knew all about the despair other mothers struggled with, the malaise they fought. It sounded terrible, but Rachel had experienced nothing of it. She'd loved those clammy, milky days, that blanketed bubble. She'd loved shutting the door and revelling in the hours alone with her tiny cub.

She tried again. 'I might head up soon.'

'Okay.'

She could never pinpoint the day, the exact moment it had altered. They'd sailed through thirteen, and Rachel had grinned with smugness. It happened so gradually, so subtly that it seemed invisible. She noticed it like a new piece of furniture she had no memory of buying. Mia, one day, stood level with her. When they spoke, Rachel's eyes faced forwards. She could no longer see the crown of her daughter's head, no longer examine that whorl where her hair began. Suddenly, there were two women in the house. There was a tall, demanding stranger, an interloper who ate her food and flopped over her sofa. Her little comrade had gone, and Rachel felt it as grief. She ached for her girl, and struggled to get used to this new person. Words became complex around her, movements too clumsy. Even now, even when they needed each other.

'Do you want anything else to eat?' She spoke the lines of the bland mothers she'd sworn never to be. She cringed as the words landed. 'Cup of tea?'

'I'm fine.' Mia stood up, unfurling those endless legs and arms. Rachel tried to reach her as she left the room, tried to stroke the marl of her hoodie, grip the flesh beneath it, but Mia wisped by and vanished upstairs. Her phone was in the folds of grey material, and she'd text her friends, her boyfriend, as soon as she was alone. Rachel wanted to follow her. She wanted to keep her in sight. They used to curl up together in the evenings Tim worked late, a pile of snacks on the coffee table, watching films Mia was far too young for. Rachel had always been proud of being permissive. They'd plait each other's hair as the movies flashed in front of them. Rachel would carry Mia up to bed when she inevitably dropped off.

There must have been a night in that dark room – Rachel struggled to conjure back the sense memory – when she'd placed Mia down and never picked her up again.

With Mia upstairs, Rachel was alone. The house had far too much space when it was just them. It seemed mocking in its airiness; only two figures to fill its family-sized expanses. The boundaries of Rachel's body felt too definite. No hands had touched her skin for so many days. She'd spend too long in the shower just to feel its spray on her muscles.

That night, the house echoed; its shadows loomed deeper. Nothing felt familiar. The woollen throws they draped over the sofa felt cloying; their curtains seemed to trap the air. Heat brewed in every room with no escape. The house felt foolish – a charade of safety. It was just an insubstantial construct of bricks and wood. Just because the door needed three keys to be opened didn't mean it couldn't be torn from its hinges in a second. Mia felt too far away to protect. Rachel had to be upstairs with her. Lily was out there somewhere, not safe in her bed. Rachel stood outside Mia's room. She sank slowly to her haunches, until her back pressed against the door. Was Mia awake on the other side of that painted wood? Was she wide-eyed and terrified for her missing friend? Was she frightened of what might come splintering through the glass of her window and drag her away for ever? Or did she sleep soundly? The floor was the coolest place in the house, and the air felt easier there. Rachel didn't blink. In that position, in that dark, she spent the whole night, silently guarding Mia's door.

Rachel dropped Mia off before school for the first time in years. The night had blurred into Monday morning, and Rachel's eyes pulsed with lack of sleep. The temperature had already risen to irritable levels. Rather than let Mia walk, they drove to Keira's. There would be no other pupils at school for an hour, and she couldn't leave Mia alone, not until Lily was safe. Keira's house was in the neighbouring cul-de-sac, almost identical to theirs. Rooms in the same places, bricks laid in the same year, the same honeysuckle trailing over the doorway. The smell was thick even so early in the morning. When Keira's mother, Marianne, opened the door, Rachel had an overwhelming desire to hug her, to sob in her arms. Instead, they exchanged stiff smiles.

'You'll call if you hear anything at school, won't you, Rachel?' Their voices were tight, acting the roles of calm adults with nothing to fear.

'Absolutely. Of course. If I hear anything at all. I'm sure Lily'll be in touch today, and feel terrible for putting us all through this.'

Marianne's grin had no light. 'Then we can have her guts for garters.' They both flinched at the image.

The girls nodded, solemn. Their faces were unusually free of make-up. They were bare of their perennial crayoned eyebrows and sculpted cheeks, and it made them look peaky.

Rachel tried to catch Marianne's eye when the girls weren't looking, to allow them a flash of the horror they both felt, but Marianne stared straight ahead.

Rachel's days were front-weighted. She grabbed at the crisp hours to plan. It was the only chance she had to gain mastery over her workload. And she hated the school at night; hated being alone in a dim corridor. She'd do anything not to leave last. Steps echoed more in the darkness, after the cleaners locked up and turned off the buzzing halogen lights. Schools were full of unexpected noises – trainer squeaks, coat friction, books slipping from shelves. It could be terrifying. The daytimes had their own form of mania, and mid-June marked their high point, as exams drew to a close. Even the pupils who stood years away from their GCSEs seemed irritable, a premonition of the stress that would descend. The whole school seemed fractious once that first bell had rung, and the heat just ratcheted it up.

The early mornings were different. Seven-thirty could feel like dawn. Pale light would fill the corridors; great shards of light, so perfect their edges could cut, would fall from the upper windows. There was peace. The eucalyptus detergent used overnight lingered, masking every other smell that would later taint the place. That morning it felt like a benediction. Rachel inhaled the scent as if it could strip away the terror, the hideous thoughts she couldn't fend off; as if it could clean her lungs, cleanse her thoughts, and make everything pure again.

★

The head walked in and stood, hands steepled, until the room eventually scuffled to silence. It took nearly a minute.

'Thank you for coming in so early today.' They'd been called to the staffroom before registration. Rachel stood near the back wall, close to the door, where she hoped it might be cooler. The room had filled quickly, bags littering the floors and papers spilling across every table. The last weeks of summer term should feel like respite, a simple counting-down of days, but the tension of those teenagers infected everything. They walked around, pale and taut. The sun felt like a bad spirit, urging them to lethargy just as they most needed alertness. It left everyone jittery.

A handful of teachers, mostly maths and science, were using the end-of-term class schedules to attend training courses, but everyone else was crammed into the same room. They were gathered in small clutches, speaking in low voices with wide eyes. Rumours had already whipped around, but no one knew anything solid. Rachel didn't speak. At eight o'clock, the heat in that packed room was already punishing. The men were still in shirtsleeves, the women in full shoes. The windows were not opened.

The head was young for his role, maybe only a year or two older than Rachel, and seemed perpetually concerned with being likeable. He asked the sixth-formers to call him *Graham*, and kept his face in a constant, tense Tony Blair smile. It made him oddly unapproachable.

'We've spoken to the police.' His voice cut through, and the

23

silence was genuine now. Rachel could hear her own breath. Graham straightened his burgundy tie. He'd come from the corporate world, and wore a dark suit every day. He paused for seconds too long – it was Blair again, those three-beat breaks in the middle of an utterance – then continued like it was a new topic.

'They've let us know some . . . vital information.' Rachel twisted her onyx engagement ring in full circles with her thumb.

'Lily Dixon, of our Year 10, is now being treated as a missing person.' His words began to flow more readily. 'They're beginning their full investigation today. I've agreed that our students can be questioned in school time and on school property. We'll liaise with them and, of course, offer every support possible.'

Rachel felt her weight slump against the wall behind her. Hearing him say those simple syllables made it real. She let the handles of her bag drop. She pressed her palms against the wall to support herself. The paint was smooth, shiny, so slick it was hard to gain traction. Lily was missing. This was no overblown teenage strop. Lily was gone. She hadn't come back. It was real and serious and terrible. The adrenalin juddered through Rachel's body. The white noise of the room seemed to dial up – the whirr of somebody's laptop, the clink of spoon metal against china, the scuff of rubber-soled shoes in the corridor outside. Rachel wished that closing her eyes could stop sound as well as light, that it could deprive her of enough senses to breathe freely.

'Oh, dear God.' Rachel watched as Sandra from the History department was comforted by colleagues, arms around her shoulders. She buried her face in a handkerchief.

A sob then came from Cressida, the Modern Languages NQT, shaking her head through shuddering sighs. 'That poor, poor girl.' Her pale eyelashes were so damp they became transparent, and blue veins peeped through at her temples.

Rachel wanted to scream at them, *She's not dead, don't act like she's dead because that's how you'll make it true*, but her face stayed neutral.

Graham also kept his composure. His voice was steady. 'We'll host an assembly later this morning to keep the students up to speed. We have no interest in triggering any undue alarm, but we do have to make sure everyone is being vigilant. We don't know where Lily is, or if any danger is still present. Students will be advised about not walking home alone, and reporting anything that seems unusual. We absolutely need to think about safety, but we also need to keep everyone calm. The final few Year 11 exams will continue as planned this week, and nothing will be disturbed at this stage.'

The crowded room seemed vacant to Rachel.

'We need everyone to be safe, and to behave as normally as possible. Please stay alert, but keep teaching and stick to your usual schedules.'

Rachel sat in the empty classroom and closed her eyes. Her thoughts were too cluttered. Only days ago, in this room, she'd worked with Lily, their copies of the text bent over at the spine, key phrases highlighted in pink, blue, green. Lily had learned her lines before any of the others. Her dedication had been a surprise. Her ability had been a surprise. Rachel had expected to turn her down with a few encouraging words, but her audition had been astonishing. Her usual eagerness had fallen away, and she'd become a delicate, tremulous creature. Her words had faded to a wisp; her face had grown fragile. Rachel had hardly recognised her.

She approached the role with rigour, arriving earlier than the others, writing every blocking note neatly. But it wasn't just enthusiasm; she'd carved something lovely from the role of Laura Wingfield. Her eyes were wider and bluer than Rachel thought possible.

At the start, she'd been all concern. 'Laura's grown up, isn't she?'

Rachel had known that Lily knew the answer. 'Yeah, early twenties, I think.'

Lily had spoken in a voice so tiny, Rachel had barely been able to make out words. 'I don't know if I can do that.'

'What do you mean?'

'I don't know. I don't always feel like I'm even fifteen.'

Rachel had tilted her head, but said nothing.

Lily had turned away as she spoke. 'The others seem so much more, you know, mature. I feel like a kid sometimes. What if that means I can't play Laura properly?'

Rachel had shuffled along so their bodies touched. 'Lily,

love, I'm afraid you're wrong on two counts. Firstly, Laura is in her twenties, but she has such an innocence that she seems much younger. You'll nail that. Better than anyone else could. And secondly, those girls who seem so much older? Do you see them on this stage? You're the only one who can do this. This takes guts, and it takes a hell of a lot of maturity. Don't ever forget that.'

Lily's head had stayed turned away, but Rachel had felt the muscles of her back relax.

We need everyone to behave as normally as possible. That was the edict, but there was nothing normal about this. Lily was missing. Lily, who had been here, right here, all flesh and energy and light. Lily, who Rachel could imagine the warmth of, the smell. The police were launching their investigation; every avenue was being pursued, but it still felt shamefully remiss. They shouldn't be staying calm, doing a shaky impression of normality. They should be stamping the streets, screaming Lily's name into the sun, into the black of the night, screaming until their throats rasped, until their breath ran out, until they found her. They should be searching every shed and bush and ditch. Every garage door should be prised open with bare fingers; every loft and cellar should be upturned, scoured, combed. Even if it was pointless, they should be looking. The child was out there somewhere and she should know that they were doing everything to reach her. If it was Mia, she wouldn't be able to stop. If it was Mia.

Rachel gripped her copy of the play until the spine cracked

in her hands. Lily's own copy was somewhere. It could be safe on her bedroom desk, marked with fingerprints and pencil. Or it could be destroyed, ripped and bloodied, left to pulp in some damp, unknown place.

In the first period after assembly, Rachel was looking after Mark Webb's Year 9 physics. She rarely ventured to the science block, rarely covered another teacher's lesson, but the skewed summer timetable demanded it. As the class entered the room, it was the noise Rachel noticed. A sort of animal whimper, the sound of thirty teenagers struggling at once. When the news had been announced in the hall, there had been yelps from some of the girls, tears springing in an instant. They'd been instructed to silence, and obeyed, but once they were in their classroom, a rumble took hold, a low-level buzz as they gathered in small groups. They were frightened. Rachel watched a huddle of girls near the window, holding each other's arms and stumbling through the clichés of peril: '. . . *could be dead . . . not walking home . . . could get snatched . . . any of us . . . strike again . . .*' She couldn't bear where imaginations were leaping.

'Girls!' They jolted as one, primed for a scare. The whole class hushed. Rachel spoke quietly and slowly. 'Listen. None of us know what has happened to Lily Dixon, and this kind of childish speculation isn't going to help one iota.' They looked down, eyes still wide. 'Now sit in your seats, and I don't want to hear a single word more.'

They did as they were told. Rachel stood behind a desk that wasn't hers, feeling her breaths arriving twice as fast as they should.

She put my arm about her waist / And made her smooth white shoulder bare. Rachel stood at the front of her Year 10 class and inched them through the poem. Line by line, she nudged them to the responses they'd need to parrot in their exam a year from now, hitting every bullet point on her lesson plan. She'd taught the poem every summer for five years. She knew exactly which parts to emphasise, which to gloss over, which they'd need to write down and remember. But that day, it was appalling. Rachel couldn't process the images, couldn't interpret the words. Her eyes were ringed with salt. The scorch of no sleep was not eased by caffeine, just made into a shriller sting.

She turned away from them – those twenty-seven sets of eyes – and gulped water from the two-litre bottle of Evian she kept on her desk. She breathed consciously, counting the beats as her lungs filled – *two, three, four* – and the beats as they emptied. It was only second period, but there was no air coming from the windows, and the class was shaky. Their distress was expressed through fidgeting: hooking their feet around the legs of their chairs and tilting backwards, teetering for minutes before crashing forward when it got too precarious. The girls occasionally grabbed their hair on top of their heads, twisting it around their fists, letting the marginally cooler air hit the skin of their necks, before tumbling it all down again with a sigh. It was only ten past eleven.

Rachel turned back. *And all her yellow hair displaced.* She enjoyed reading aloud in her classroom. If she stood in the right spot, an echo would ring, and make the words sound ancient. But that day the Browning poem – looming behind her on the interactive whiteboard – repulsed her. The assembled teenagers seemed undisturbed by the image of the beautiful, inert girl. *Perfectly pure and good.* Rachel assumed they simply weren't listening, weren't reading the words. Despite their red eyes and occasionally shaking breath, they seemed blind to the delicate corpse at the heart of the text. *Blushed bright beneath my burning kiss.*

Rachel drilled them to trot out their responses, fleeting over rhyme patterns and key metaphors. *A sudden thought of one so pale.* She'd prepared for the lesson three days before, when it was merely a smart way to engage Year 10 on a Monday near the end of term. Now, the images were too real. The black, dead eyes of the poem-girl, the hair clinging around her neck. *Three times her little throat around.* Rachel couldn't stop seeing it when she closed her eyes. The blush on her cheek faded, her skin mottling greener with every minute. *The smiling rosy little head.* The weight of her thighs and arms, the cold flab that might now just be meat. The minute dwelling on the flesh of the dead woman. The crawling gaze. Where was she? That lovely, pretty girl with her yellow hair and pale skin. Where was Lily now? What had happened to her, and who had taken her away? What kind of monster had snatched her, and what was he doing to her? Was she crying out into empty air for help; was she sobbing with no one to hear?

Rachel felt it like a fist on her windpipe, a punch more than a grasp. She found herself in the corridor. The door thud resounded. There were no eyes to see her there. They were all still back in the classroom. Had they even seen her leave? She let herself slump to the ground. The linoleum was gritty, and her trousers and shirt and her ballet pumps would be filthy with the scuffs and grime of the morning, but she didn't care. Her throat was brittle. She fought to breathe. Rachel felt calcified, as if she was gasping through stone.

Rachel could feel the warmth pulsing from the passenger seat. The smell of black bean sauce, of chicken and mushrooms, fugged through the car, and the polythene bag was already sweating. The meal didn't feel like a treat.

Mia sat on the back seat, protecting their more precious cargo. Rachel had waited in the school car park for long minutes, watching the doors, scanning every face until Mia's had finally leapt out. The car park had been choked, with every parent finding a way to leave work early. The pavements had remained untrodden; every pupil was safe within a family saloon. Rachel had waited whilst Mia kissed Aaron, her boyfriend of a few months, goodbye. She'd considered changing their plans, delaying, but the doctrine of normality had been too well imposed. She didn't want to scare Mia. The Prom was just over two weeks away, and her dress was zipped pristine in a grey garment bag. It sat propped up, like a passenger in its own right, rigid and vacant. Mia had tried it on months before, but the tiny, crucial alterations to the neckline and hem had only just been perfected. The lilac dress had cost nearly double what Rachel had ever spent on a single item of clothing, but Tim had insisted Mia have whatever she wanted, so Rachel had smiled blithely as Mia tried on dozens of frocks, each one frothier and more revealing than the last. Next year would bring the same performance. Year 10 as well as Year 11 were invited to the event, making the girls squeal when they heard the news. The bagged dress was the bulk and height of a person, and peeked at the edges of Rachel's peripheral vision as she drove. Its blankness spooked her.

Rachel's hands felt uneasy on the wheel. The vinyl was too hot to hold firmly, and her palms slipped with sweat. They'd been driving for ten minutes with little conversation. Every time she could pass it off as vigilant road safety, Rachel snuck a glimpse of Mia in the rear-view mirror. Her job had taught her nothing if not the transformational power of silence. She just had to hold out. Rather than swing onto the ring road, she turned left, taking a winding route through the back lanes. The car felt safe; its case of metal more protective than any other space. Rachel wanted to linger there with Mia only feet away. She didn't turn the radio on. The only noise was the white blare of the air-con.

Rachel caught Mia's eye, finally, and held it, raised an

eyebrow. She knew she had to concede, had to speak first, but did so in a whisper. 'You okay?' Mia only shrugged. It took grit, but Rachel let the silence swell until one of them had no choice but to break it. Mia shuffled, tugging at her seat belt, pulling it away from her neck as if it was strangling her, then settled. Rachel bit down on the inside of her lower lip.

'Mum?'

'Hmm?' Rachel counted the fat seconds until Mia spoke again. Her voice was high.

'She'll be okay, won't she?' Mia's lips twisted. 'She didn't tell me she was going anywhere. She didn't say anything.'

Slopped onto plates, the food looked repulsive. Thick sauces and hot meat seemed inedible. They both picked with forks, but lifted little. Rachel's throat had not yet relaxed. The house, closed up all day, was stifling. Every window had been flung open, but there was no breeze to beckon in. Rachel tried to talk.

'How are your friends feeling?'

Mia shrugged, a tiny movement.

'Are they scared? Is anyone upset?'

Mia's lips pushed together, her head twitching in a near-nod. Rachel didn't know how to respond. Then a phone trill. Rachel grabbed it from her pocket, her body jolted by its vibrations. A name flashing on the screen. Marianne. She swiped it open.

Marianne's voice was as steady as ever, even more soothing so close to her ear.

'We've got some news.' Her tone gave nothing away.

Rachel felt her head grow light, a buzz in her hands, her skin.

'It seems that Lily took more than they thought.'

Marianne paused, but Rachel could gather no words to respond. She just waited for the news to make sense.

'Debbie just called me, I've just hung up from her this second. At first, they could find nothing missing except Lily's school bag, with her wallet and a few other bits, but they've apparently looked more closely.'

Rachel could only murmur, 'Mmm?'

'An overnight bag has been taken from their loft, something they hardly ever use, tucked away right at the back, they've only just realised.'

The words formed meaning and Rachel felt her body come back to her. 'Oh, God, she chose to go. She planned it.'

Mia jumped from her seat, all alertness, and stood so close to Rachel she'd be able to hear every word of Marianne's in miniature. Rachel couldn't see Mia's face, but could feel her hands on the back of the kitchen chair, tapping with no rhythm at all, an insistent random beat.

'So it seems, so it seems. Debbie's relieved, of course, as much as she can be.'

Rachel felt her own shoulders release and the thrumming under her skin ease. She exhaled. 'Oh, lord.'

'But the little madam went further than that.' Marianne's voice was measured, too calm for the news it delivered. 'She took a few pieces of her mum's make-up, and something quite personal of Debbie's.' Marianne was being overheard too. It was there in her voice. The restraint. The signal to Rachel that there were words they couldn't say.

Rachel needed to ask. 'Personal?'

'A lace teddy from her drawer. Debbie says it's years old, from before Lily was born. She had no idea Lily even knew it existed.'

'A teddy? Like a nightdress?'

'A little more intimate, from what I can gather.'

Mia's tapping stopped. Rachel wished she could talk to her friend, that other mother, share their reactions far away from their daughters. With Mia there, she had to stop the conversation.

Before the phone was away from Rachel's ear, Mia was talking. The silence had shattered, and she was all words. 'It's good news, isn't it? It's good. It means she's okay.' She was jabbering. 'It means she wasn't taken, she wanted to go.'

Mia hopped from foot to foot, as if unable to still her insides. Rachel watched her daughter's jig on the kitchen's grey slabs, and saw the food cooling and congealing on their plates.

When Mia was in bed, and the house was still, Rachel shut herself in the downstairs toilet. She closed the door behind her, sat on the lid. Being behind a door, in the smallest room possible, felt necessary, urgent. Lily had chosen to go. There was no shadowy villain stalking their streets. No other girls were in danger. Mia was safe. The relief was nearly physical. Rachel reached over to lock the door, needing another layer of distance from anyone else. Her hands could barely turn the bolt, her weak fingers fumbling, unable to twist the metal. The lock finally clicked, and she slumped to the floor, as near to alone as she was able to be.

She pulled her knees up and rested against them. The plastic floor she sat on mimicked wood, its intricate lines designed to show an age it didn't bear. Rachel sat, silent. There were no arms to hold her, no chest to crush herself against. It was still within Tim's working day. He hadn't even managed to reply to her messages. Rachel dragged the hand towel from its round loop and pressed it over her eyes. Behind that closed door, on the laminate floor of that tiny toilet, breathing in the scent of their vanilla reed diffuser, Rachel wept. Mia was in her bed, and no one was planning to wrench her from it. Rachel had to comfort herself. Her arms hugged the top of her knees, gripping them for support, and she let herself cry, desperate for the built-up grime inside her to flow out. Every muscle she'd held so taut needed to release. Lily had chosen to go. No one had forced a handkerchief of ether over her mouth and nose; no one had bundled that sweet, guileless girl into the empty boot of a car. She'd planned to go; she'd wanted to go. Rachel stroked her own arms.

She aimed her tears right into the fibres of the towel, not letting them hit her cheeks. By the time her breath calmed, she felt hollowed out, unable to gather the energy to lift her head, to stand up. It felt as if nothing but milk flowed in her veins.

Rachel knew Mia's password. She'd watched her type it in so many times, it was impossible not to memorise the pattern. Top, then bottom three times. *2000*. The year of her birth. Rachel had watched that flick of her daughter's fingers every day for months. She'd locked the knowledge away, but now she had to use it. It was protection more than betrayal. It was necessary; she needed to know what was in there.

Lily had chosen to go, but they still didn't know the destination. They didn't know who her companion was. That lace teddy had been for someone's eyes. Mia's glee was misplaced. One fear could dissipate, but a dark other was just rearing. Lily wasn't on her way home. Rachel's eyes were now dry.

She took the phone whilst Mia slept. It was long past midnight. She snuck in to drop a kiss on Mia's forehead, then eased the jack from the charging socket. It was surprisingly acquiescent. Rachel clutched the phone in both hands as she stalked out of the room. Her steps were tentative, but once the door was closed, her fingers flew. She could waste no time. Vital information might only be a few taps away. Once she'd submitted the four-digit code, it was all there for her to see; the treasure trove of her daughter's world. The phone had the same layout as Rachel's own – the bright icons in nearly the same places – but it felt alien. She panicked for a moment, unsure where to look. No teenager used emails, so she went straight to social media. Her fingers were too frenetic to navigate the deft systems. She stumbled, pressing the wrong buttons, double-clicking so profile pictures filled the screen and had to be retracted. Her movements were so frenzied that the phone slipped, wriggling free from her fingers. Rachel caught it before it hit the laminate. She closed her eyes. It was too risky. She made herself tiptoe downstairs and sit.

She had to tread softly; it was vital that she left no traces. It required intricate care to avoid slipping and liking a picture from weeks before. Her limbs weighed dense with the guilt of it, with the leaden thud of hypocrisy. The idea of Mia doing the same to her own phone was unbearable. Rachel's fingers were numb, but she had no choice. It was her duty.

She knew the sites, which buttons to click, but the content was all novelty. Their profiles were set to private, or under pseudonyms she'd never have sniffed out. A whole universe opened up. In those posts and messages, she learned more about her daughter than a month of conversation could muster. Mia came to life in the pixels. Rachel saw the idioms she repeated. The little French phrases they bleated. *C'est la vie, ma cherie. Arrête ton char!* The way she rarely crabbed words like her friends did, but wrote out every syllable. She saw the emojis Mia favoured in her comments. The exploding fireworks, the two black-clad dancers. She saw the stylised universe Mia created. Where her friends were enthusiastically slipshod, posting haphazard pictures of any enjoyable moment, Mia was slick. She'd evidently taken cues from major influencers, and replicated their content with poised competence. Her grid of pictures was co-ordinated: pale pink, black, pops of mustard-gold. It was considered. She had over two thousand followers.

Rachel flicked back through weeks of conversation, and time fell away. She learned Lily's style too. Sweet Lily with her penchant for unicorn emojis. Lily who told the other girls how gorgeous they were at every opportunity. Lily who created pictures of Hollywood stars with their names scrawled in gold over their faces, their décolletage. She posted few images of herself, and never with the filters and edits the other girls so clearly favoured.

Rachel scoured every picture of Lily's, pinching her fingers apart to zoom into every corner, but there was no one else there. No boy from the year above, no lingering Lothario. Mia's pictures often showed Aaron, usually facing away from the lens. Aaron gazing into the middle distance, Aaron hunched over his phone. Aaron washed in pink or black and white. He was as much a prop as the cactuses and painted nails and coffee cups she favoured. But Lily was always alone.

As she explored their words, their pictures, Rachel's finger stopped. There were no new updates. She scrolled back through every app, checked three or four different profiles – Ella, Keira, Abby – but there had been nothing new since Sunday afternoon. Not from any of them. She flicked back and saw their check-ins at the shopping centre, the hazy pictures of their Frappuccinos. Ella was the most confident. *Delish drink with my delish girls*. Her tongue stuck out towards the lens. A few swipes further showed their selfies from Saturday night, arms raised in dance moves, eyes crossed in front of the Netflix logo. Abby was goofier. *Wtf am I doing with my life? Faire l'andouille!* Fingers in the peace sign obscuring their faces. *Get ugly, you freak*. Their mouths full of pizza in her kitchen. Keira tried for dramatic wit. *I'm obsessed with this margherita. Dr. Oetker should basically impregnate me now.*

Their faces, only hours before, looked unbearably young. Despite their thrusting hips and flirty comments, they looked like children. None of them had posted anything since Sunday afternoon, since Rachel had received the phone call that had twisted the day. The silence felt solid. The chirping little birds in their hands never shut up. Over a day without noise was implausible. Did they have nothing to say, or was what they had to say so unutterable? Rachel hadn't thought to check the call log; she'd ignored the phone's original function. Did they ever use it for audible words? There were no red numbers; Mia had missed no calls, and had received only her mother's. Rachel's finger tapped the warm screen one more time. Lily's number had been dialled at 14:07. 14:11. 14:24. 14:52. Twenty-four times since two o'clock on Sunday, and she hadn't once picked up. 15:09. 15:32. All of Monday, at every moment of opportunity; before school, in breaks and lunch. 8:32. 11:34. 11:37. 11:49. 13:04. 13:26. And all night. 19:46. 19:58. 21:03. 21:54. The blue and white of the screen suddenly burned

Rachel's eyes; the brightness seemed to blare. So many calls with no answer. Such desperation to hear her friend's voice.

He had smeared glitter on her cheeks. It came from a plastic pot he took from his pocket. Tiny sparkles of gold. He had spoken, in between strokes, right into her ear, so close that if he rose louder than a whisper it would leave her ringing for hours, but he never uttered a word in more than a breath. He said her name, hushed, like it was a precious thing, lingering over both syllables, making them prettier than they'd ever sounded.

He'd dipped the pads of his thumbs into the little pot of sparkle, then pressed them gently into the soft spaces beneath her eyes. She'd thrown her head backwards, letting the light of the moon or the streetlights catch the smudges and make them gleam. He'd lifted her high, and watched as she laughed. He'd held her jaw in his hand, and tilted it back and forth so she glimmered.

2

'Oh, God. She'll hate it. She'll hate it.' Mia stroked the picture of Lily's face that sat on the bottom right corner of the front page of the *Daily Mail*. As soon as Mia had roused from another restless night, she'd begged to go to the One Stop. Rachel had handed over her whole wallet. Mia came home minutes later with a fat wodge of papers. Her arms were loaded with a haphazard mix of broadsheets and blazing red tops – anything that might feature Lily's face.

'She'll hate it. She'll think she looks fat.' They'd seen the picture online, but it only seemed to register to Mia as real when she could touch it. The print had rubbed onto the pads of her fingers and left grey stains in the crook of her arm. She'd bought all the papers, but Lily's face was only on the front of two. With the others, Mia had to flick through, licking her fingers for traction, finding Lily on page six, page nine. She spread the papers across the kitchen table. Eight Lilys stared up at them. A choir of Lilys, eyes blue and mouth grinning. In the grainy dots that formed her, she looked gauche. Her cheeks and chin were round, her hair scraped back into a tight ponytail. It was her most recent school photograph, but she looked several years younger. Rachel couldn't remember when she'd last seen the girls smile for a photograph – images of them were all cheekbones, tongues pushed out with no flicker of mirth, eyebrows raised until their brows wrinkled. Lily's newspaper grin was so broad her nostrils flared. There was such a chasm between fourteen and fifteen.

Rachel hadn't noticed Mia's face pucker, but the hair-trigger had flicked, and a tear fell from Mia's cheek onto the image of Lily's, puddling the ink. The glee of the previous night had faded. Lily just stared back, eager and diligent. Rachel put her arm around Mia, their skin pressing together.

Rachel had expected the story to gain nothing more than local interest. Maybe it was the season – that swathe of summer when the stories dried up – maybe it was Lily's clean blonde hair and pink smile. She was in her school uniform in every picture. She looked no more like Lily than a witness identikit. The image must have been picked with precision, if not by Debbie, then by the Police Liaison Officer. That beaming face was deliberately innocent. The blonde girl pictured couldn't have deceived everyone with such sly ease; she couldn't have crept up to the back corner of the loft, couldn't have rummaged in her mother's knicker drawer. She had the clear eyes of a child who couldn't possibly have plotted for weeks.

'Do you think she's seen it?' Mia wiped her eyes, but Rachel didn't let go of her. 'Do you think she's seen a newspaper, where she is?'

Rachel pictured Lily at a motorway service station or a cramped hotel room. There was no way of knowing where she was, or how far she'd gone. She could be holed up in some remote place with no phone reception. And there was someone next to her. A man. A man or a boy. A faceless figure who had her in his grasp. 'I'm sure she has, Mi. She'll feel so awful that we're all worrying. I'm sure she's on her way home.'

Mia's phone buzzed in her pocket. She swiped it and held the screen out to Rachel. It was Keira. *Put the TV on now. BBC News.*

It wasn't cold, but his lips had been chapped. Clots of dry skin had made them thick and bitten. The corners of his mouth had looked sore. She'd known what to do. The stick of lip salve lived in her pocket all year round. She'd had to hold his head; her fingers on the back of his neck, her thumb pressing his jaw still, as she slicked on the balm. His eyes didn't leave her as she focused. He didn't know the pout that women learn, the particular grimace that turns the flesh rigid, so with every stroke the skin of his lips tugged and puckered. When she'd finished, the peeling shards had softened, and the redness soothed. She'd pulled back, still holding his face, proud of her handiwork. The sheen on his lips lengthened as he smiled.

*

'Lily, love, we're not angry with you, darling. We're really not. We just want you to come home.'

Rachel had to quash the momentary thrill of recognition. She swallowed back the gasp of adrenalin that comes when something familiar fills the space reserved for the important. It was Lily's father, Gary, in close-up. He looked odd; his face seemed swollen, the flesh pushing his skin to stretching point, but you could still discern the genes that had gifted Lily her prettiness. The softness, the wide eyes, the mobile mouth. Rachel wanted to reach out and touch the screen.

Debbie was sitting next to him. She was holding a tissue under her lashes to stem the flow of tears. She moved it from eye to eye every few seconds. 'We love you, Lils.' Her words came out as sobs.

Their faces were lit with flashes so frequently the screen seemed to flicker.

Mia stood in front of the television, one hand cupped to cover all her face except the eyes. She chanted to herself. 'Oh my God, oh my God, oh my God.' Her phone was already in her other hand, dialling Lily's number. Rachel could hear the dull tone from across the room. It didn't ring, but Mia kept pressing the button.

Every whisper of Lily's technology would be tracked. Rachel knew that behind the analogue story – the printed pictures, the face-to-face interviews – must be a frantic digital search. They weren't pacing the streets, but must surely be scouring every CCTV image, every beep of her phone, every spark of her face on a screen. It was impossible to stay hidden with so many devices primed to capture. They must have clues: a sense of which direction she'd headed in, of who might be holding her hand. They must be getting closer. They must.

A tissue box was just visible on screen, a protocol nod to compassion. Gary's fingers worked on his tissue as he spoke, twisting and worrying it into thin rolls. He must have known how he'd be seen. Rachel felt her stomach tense. The bag and the teddy. A few lipsticks. That was all they had to go on. She'd left no note, made no contact. It could be faked. Gary's face was tight. He'd know how his words would be given that cadence of unreality, how every gesture would be scrutinised. He'd know the role he'd be cast in. There was a sigh between every phrase.

'We don't care where you are, love, or why. We just want you to get in touch. A call or a text or a Facebook message. Anything.'

Mia repeated the word in agreement. 'Anything.'

Gary's head on the screen was bigger than Mia's in the room. His whole body shook with each breath. Formal name-plates sat in front of them. *Gareth Dixon. Deborah Dixon.* Those names, in their shortened forms, lived on Rachel's phone, in her email address book. That face, now contorted in distress, was the same one that always checked from the car window that Mia had gone through the front door safely. Now, it was beamed in perfect HD onto her thirty-six-inch television. The zoom was so close you could see the pores of his cheeks.

'Mia, come here, sweetheart.' Mia remained inches from

the screen, her phone pressed against her ear. 'Give me your phone, Mi. You need to sit down.'

Gary pulled another tissue from the box, and pressed it against his lips, his forehead. He supported the weight of his head with his fingertips. Beside him, Debbie seemed to suddenly wake up. She went from slumped to wildly alert in seconds. Gary's microphone picked up his whisper. 'It's alright, darling, you're doing amazing.' Debbie's chair scraped against the floor as she stood, and the camera zoomed onto her. She was holding something up to the lens. It was a small stuffed toy, a once-plush animal from the Disney Store. It looked damp in her grip.

'Lily, love, you've got to come back, please. You've got to.' Her voice cracked, and then dropped. She stared right down the lens, to no one but Lily. It felt intrusive to even look at her. 'Kanga misses you, Roo.'

Gary stood up to support his wife, his arm around her, guiding her back to her seat.

Mia made a noise, somewhere between a gasp and a sob. Rachel felt her cheeks flash, her scalp tingle with sweat. The heat they'd all withstood for so many days was suddenly aggressive, clawing at her. Mia stood almost touching the screen, as if her proximity could lend urgency to the appeal. She added her voice. 'Please.'

Rachel grabbed for the TV handset, abruptly aware that it was too much for Mia to see, but Mia's grip was firm.

'I want to watch it. I want to see Lily's mum.'

Rachel wrangled the black plastic from Mia's sweaty fingers and clicked it towards the television. The sudden silence was thick. Mia's sobs were now the loudest sound. Rachel sat down next to where she'd slumped, on the warm leather of the sofa, and leaned her head on her daughter's racking shoulders, so they moved as one.

'I want to see Lily.'

He would always buy the alcohol before they met. The bottles would clink together in their flimsy blue plastic bag, and the stickers on their necks – £5.49 printed on a yellow tag – would peel away. They'd always been picked up at some minimart or corner shop. It was always cider or alcopops or syrupy fruit liqueurs. Drinks that hid their kick behind spoons of sugar. They'd down them straight from the bottle, never in a glass and never inside.

He'd drive twenty minutes away from where she lived, from the catchment area of the school. There were eyes everywhere. He'd play music as they drove. He never asked what she wanted to listen to, but crafted compilations of the songs he loved. He knew every line, she knew snatches of melodies, and when the words came to her, their voices would meld. They'd sing with the windows closed tight, drunk before they'd even popped the lids from those bottles. *She is a changeless angel, she's a city, it's a pity that I'm like me.* His voice was deep and sweet, and his stubble caught the light as he sang, those bristles that never felt harsh.

The hairs that grew just above his wrists glinted as he gripped the wheel, as his hand reached over to rest, casually, on her thigh. The weight of it was glorious. It was early spring, but she didn't feel cold in the slightest. She pulled her legs up, so her Converse trainers rested on the upholstery of his car, driving until the streetlights came on in roads they didn't know. Floodlights on a tiny playground. The denim clung to her as she sat cross-legged on the gravel, and her hair whipped across her face. They stood on the swings, hands white on the chain links, both flying manically high, as high as the metal would let them go. His grin in the light. 'Higher. Push higher.'

Then sinking down onto the seats and rocking gently as they sipped from the same bottle, their mouths tightened around the same circle. To drink from those bottles was a sort of kiss: lips on the glass, tongue stoppering it. It created the kind of drunk that transports, makes the world an entirely different place. It was the kind of drunk that made her able to dance.

She could leap there; she could turn cartwheels by the bright, false lights. Streetlamps had never looked so glamorous. She pulled herself up onto the climbing frame with strength she didn't know her arms had; heaved her whole body skywards, hooking her legs over the metal rods, letting herself hang, impossibly, in the night. His voice reached her upside-down ears, singing every word of 'Spaceball Ricochet'. Then straddling the frame, her thighs taut, her arms up in the air at the beat of the soundtrack coming from his car. *She is a changeless angel, she's a city, it's a pity that I'm like me.*

Her hair was loose, and tangling in the breeze, and every song was written about her. He was looking at her; he was watching.

Then they lay, sprawled on the asphalt. No one in the world knew where they were. The night crept darker, and the tarmac was cool against the backs of her legs. She could taste the antiseptic tang of alcohol on his mouth. Her fingers, filthy from the ground, were in his hair. They barely spoke, but kissed. His hands on her face, her waist, her legs. They kissed like adults can't kiss: where the kiss is everything there is; where there is no thought of whatever might come next.

Rachel headed to the gym on nothing but autopilot. She only ever had forty-five minutes. Three times a week. She'd contort her already jammed days to fit it in. It had to be regimented: twenty-five minutes on the treadmill, then twenty on the static bike. Afterwards, she'd shower, dab on lipstick and eyeliner – smudging both to make them look worn in – then head straight to school.

She made the most of her time that morning, eschewing a warm-up and starting as close to full pelt as possible, pumping her legs up and down. Up and down. It was sluggish at first, slow and uncomfortable. She debated stopping, leaving, getting a coffee instead, but then it eased. Whatever stickiness lay in her muscles turned to oil, and the movements suddenly flowed naturally. As soon as it was fluid, she pushed herself harder. Hard enough that it hurt. Harder than she'd ever pushed. Her body was hers now. No other eyes saw its hidden parts; no other hands moved over it for weeks at a time. Her body, once so touched, so cherished, was now alone. Its shape and scent and taste belonged to no one else.

For forty-five minutes, Rachel focused on nothing but her movements. She played no music, tuned into no podcast, no television programme. She didn't let herself think. Just move. Faster and harder until it felt like her veins would burst and her lungs might flood with blood. Sweat gathered on the crown of her head. She bowed her face down and closed her eyes. She could see nothing but the red behind her lids. When it reached the tipping point, when the weight of the pooled sweat was enough to send drips coursing down her nose, it felt like victory.

As Rachel drove into the car park, the school seemed invaded. It wasn't yet eight, but two large vans sat squarely in the centre of the tarmac, logos proud on their sides, satellite dishes perched on top, crossing several parking bays each. The story had become juicy: the blonde girl, the distraught parents, the missing underwear. Lily Dixon was no longer a friend, a pupil; she was public property. Her name was known hundreds of miles away.

The people busily charging between the vans were all men. They looked different from the men who usually walked around the school. These men wore thick-rimmed glasses, lanyards round their necks, black T-shirts. They had stubble that sometimes thickened into beards. The equipment they held on their shoulders, or positioned on tripods, was enormous and professional. These images would be beamed all over the country. It looked like a film set. It was almost exciting.

Rachel slalomed her Corsa around them to get to her usual spot. There were at least ten men in the car park, and she'd have to wade through a throng to get to the door. She didn't know how to greet them; should she smile, nod, stoically ignore? As they came into focus, she felt acutely aware of the peek of bra strap that was showing under her shirt, the painted toenails in her sandals.

She nudged the arm of a camera-carrying man as she squeezed by. 'Hey, watch it.' As he turned, the camera swooped to stare at her with its unblinking mechanical eye. Rachel felt the blood redden her cheeks.

'Can you guys back off a bit?' Rachel cringed at her use of the word 'guys', but the man just looked at her blankly. 'The kids are freaked out enough.'

'I'm sorry, but we've got permission. It's totally legit.'

'Permission to be here, not to be intrusive.'

He backed away from her, his one free palm raised in a gesture of mock-surrender. 'It's not my call, I'm afraid. We're Sky News.'

Rachel knew how to talk to errant teens, but the same tone of voice deployed on a grown man sounded absurd. The slick of MAC Ruby Woo that usually gave her such swagger felt gaudy now, heavy on her lips.

'A girl's missing. Can you show some fucking respect?' She spat the words out, then walked towards the school, every step placed carefully, so she didn't stumble.

'Have you seen this?'

It was all Rachel could do not to grab the paper from DC Redpath's hand. The police detectives were the same, but the location was very different. DC Redpath. DC Scott. No longer nursing mugs in her living room, but stationed behind the deputy head's desk with glasses of water placed officiously in front of them. With new evidence, they needed to question Lily's friends further. Rachel was cast again as the chaperone.

She was eventually passed a copy. It was a printout of an Instagram screen. The blue strip at the top, the love hearts to show who had double-tapped their approval. The digital made physical looked uncanny. The image was a still from an old movie: black and white, a woman with pale, wavy hair that fell over one eye, sitting in a car with a scruffy man in a hat. Rachel didn't know either of their names. Scrawled over the top in mock-handwriting, too perfect to have flown from human movements, was one word. *Wanderlust*. It had 129 likes.

'Have you seen this before, Mia?' The sing-song tone of their last meeting was gone.

Mia only shrugged. Her face was calm, but her breaths were jagged. 'Yeah. It was on Lily's Instagram the other week.

She's always putting crap like this on.' Rachel could sense her daughter's thrill at the mild swear word, and felt almost proud.

'Did it seem significant to you?'

'It's the sort of thing she loves. She's always making stuff like this.'

'Do you know where the image is from?'

'Some old film, I don't know.'

DC Redpath coughed slightly, clearing her throat. 'We haven't found a note from Lily, as you know, Mia, but we do know that she packed a bag and took it with her. Her mum thought she was heading to your sleepover, but she never turned up, did she?'

It was barely a question. A flash of guilt jabbed Rachel's veins. Should she have known something was amiss? Should she have called Debbie to alert her? The girls had seemed unconcerned, and hardly commented on Lily's absence. But they were only fifteen.

'We need to know where she might have gone instead. Do you know what "wanderlust" means?'

Mia's eyes closed. 'Wanting to travel.' Rachel was impressed. She had no idea where Mia had picked up the concept.

'Yes. Exactly. It means a strong, innate desire to travel.' In the detective's mouth it sounded mechanical, like she'd learned it by rote. 'Does she ever talk about running away?'

A sigh now, heavy, shaking. 'She talks about wanting to go places, but we figure she means after sixth form.'

'Who is we?'

'All of us, we all talk about things like that. We talk about everything.'

'Where does she want to go?'

'Hollywood, I suppose. She's always posting pictures of films.'

'Do you know where she might have gone?'

Mia shook her head ever so slightly. She was giving nothing away, if there was anything at all to give.

'Do you know who she might be with?'

Another shake. Rachel knew they had checked every register. No boys from their school were absent without reason. Everyone had arrived at every lesson, every exam. But there were other boys, and other ways to meet them. Lily had been in plays outside of their drama studio.

'Does she have a boyfriend?'

Mia's head shook again. Rachel felt the disappointment; the breath she held still couldn't be released. A boyfriend would answer everything. Some boy from another school she'd met at Friday-night theatre club. Some boy she'd been seeing secretly for months. Some older boy who'd convinced her to sneak away for a few days; some boy she wanted to impress with her bravery, her spontaneity, her lingerie.

'Is there any boy she talks about?'

Mia swallowed. 'Lily isn't really like that.'

A brisk nod. 'Is there anyone she particularly likes, though?'

'She isn't like that. She doesn't talk about boys she fancies.'

DC Redpath's voice was deeper now. 'Mia, do you have any

idea at all who Lily might be with, or where she might be?'
The questions, asked again, stuck in the air.

Mia shrugged, her shoulders flicking up and down. 'I really
don't. I don't know where she is.'

He had spun the metal that night. He'd heaved it with strong
arms, gripping the railings, then releasing, to lurch the rounda-
bout into ragged circles. She had forced her eyes to stay open,
and caught a flash of him with every cycle. Him. Him. Him.
Him. The whirling had caused the earth to jink on its axis
over and over. Stop it! Stop it! She'd screwed her eyes tight,
and there'd been no way of knowing which was up or down.
Everything had blurred.

When the speed seemed almost frightening, he leapt on
with her, propelling himself in one movement. They both
clung to the metal and faced each other. The rest of the
world had faded to a dizzy, sickening whirr, and she was
unable to see anything but his face, grimacing against the
speed, the centrifugal force. The neon whirl of the world
eventually slowed, in wobbling revolutions; slowed to the
speed of his records, thirty-three and one third rotations
per minute, the speed where the needle could dip into the
grooves, bobbing and nodding until sound miraculously
formed, until plastic turned to noise. They'd looped slower,
slower, slower, then circled to a close, a halt that shocked
them with its stillness.

*

'What can we do without Lily?'

The drama studio was dark, and several degrees cooler than the rest of the building. After a morning of lessons, Rachel felt the relief of being around only two other people.

'Will someone else play Laura?'

Rachel felt her shoulders relax for the first time in days as she told the truth. 'You know what, I don't know, Dominic. I really don't know. I suppose we're going to have to give it a few days. See what happens.'

'Yeah, this might all be nothing, right?'

Last year's summer show had been a fifty-four person, all-singing-and-dancing spectacle of *Oliver!* that Rachel had assisted the head of drama in staging. She'd spent long weeks sourcing scores of butcher-boy caps and drilling the cast in awkward *pas de bourrée*. When it was her turn, she'd opted for something more intimate. This year didn't need a major event. A cast of four was enough. Briony Havering in Year 11 did such an accurate southern drawl in her audition that the part of Amanda could go to no one else; Ross Pike was a solid, handsome Tom, and the other two roles were students Rachel knew well – Dominic, Keira's brother, as Jim, the Gentleman Caller, and Lily as Laura Wingfield.

When Briony and Dominic turned up at lunchtime as scheduled, Rachel could scarcely contain her gratitude. The room felt almost normal.

'As you guys are both here, do you want to run lines? We

can only really do scene seven, but it might be worth a go?'
They had barely opened their battered, highlighted texts
before Graham strode in. Rachel had never seen him in the
drama wing before.

'So, actors, how goes the "menagerie of glass"?' His eyebrows added the quotation marks around the words. Rachel
sensed the phrase was rehearsed but hadn't come out quite
how he'd intended. His face rearranged as he seemed to realise
the tone he'd struck was all wrong. He was suddenly grave,
turning to face Dominic and Briony. 'Well done, you two,
well done. You really are doing exactly the right thing. We
need to keep going, to keep our chins up.' They both nodded
without smiling.

He steered Rachel a few steps away, his hand glancing her
elbow. She could feel the warmth from his skin.

'How are the students holding up?'

Rachel couldn't muster the energy to lie. 'They're rattled.
What else can you expect?'

'Of course. I understand. Your response seems spot on.
We have to steer them through this in the right direction.'

'But we're all rattled as well. And how do you know if
you're picking the right direction, or steering them down one
that will seem fucked up in a week's time?'

He seemed to stiffen at the challenge, at the language.
Rachel knew she'd gone too far. She didn't wait for him to
reply.

'How are the police doing? Have you heard any more?'

'No, nothing. They're doing everything they can. We're just hosting, to be honest. You'll be the first person I contact when we hear from them. I know you were close to Lily. This must be very hard for you.'

Rachel felt her throat tighten at his words.

Rachel could see the screen, but not clearly. Five or six of them were crowded around Cressida's laptop in the staffroom. The footage was on the BBC News website. It was only a few seconds, but Cressida kept clicking it to repeat.

The screen filled with black and white at first, as if the connection had been lost. Then a ghostly figure danced across the top right corner. It was CCTV footage. Cressida made it perform those same steps over and over. The images had been taken from the security cameras of a small shop in a ferry port, hours away. Lily was walking towards the counter to pay. She had an armful of bottles and packets. Rachel knew for certain it would be Diet Coke and Starmix.

'It's her.' Cressida had watched it scores of times, but still sounded awed.

Lily was alive in those seconds of film. Her strong, vital legs were pumping across the screen, propelling her forwards. She was wearing black leggings and ballet shoes. Despite the heat, her coat was slung over one arm.

Lily had been in a ferry terminal. She would be hundreds of miles away now, an ocean away. Rachel leaned over and stopped Cressida's hand.

'Let it play to the end.'

The newscaster spoke for a moment, solemn words Rachel couldn't make out. Then another burst of footage. It was as flecked and grainy as before, but there was a figure by the door, holding it open, waiting for Lily. A figure in the shadows, unidentifiable, but clearly male.

Cressida emitted a stifled gasp. Rachel rested her hands on the younger woman's shoulders, on the thin, green cotton of her blouse. She was grateful for someone to comfort.

Lily had been timid around Briony and Ross. They were in the year above, and Rachel had noticed how Lily rarely approached them. She'd sit on her own at rehearsals, staring at lines she'd already memorised until Dominic arrived. Sometimes she'd hardly speak in her own words, relying entirely on Tennessee Williams. Her own accent would be silent for the whole evening, but Laura's drawl would arrive at all the right moments. It was a blessing that her most charged scenes were opposite Dominic. The interchanges between Laura and Jim were the hardest to nail.

'I wanted to ask you to – autograph my programme.' Lily's voice was soft as Laura.

'Why didn't you ask me to?'

Lily would ask questions just to Rachel after each run-through.

'He's older than her, isn't he?'

'Jim? No, I think they're the same age. If you remember, he talks at one point about being twenty-three, and she says she's twenty-four soon.'

'But she seems younger.'

'Okay.'

'It's not always just about actual age, is it? And she's so impressed by him.'

Lily's eyes had been wide with an odd kind of intensity. Rachel had made sure not to disregard her. 'How do you think that might make her feel?'

'Intimidated, maybe?'

Lily had paused, but Rachel hadn't wanted to interrupt her thoughts.

'I actually think she feels really flattered. That this impressive man is paying her so much attention. He doesn't have to, does he? But he can obviously see something in her that her family or her friends don't. There is something about her he really likes. That must feel nice for her. It must make her feel special.'

It was the most Lily had ever said in a rehearsal. The others had stopped to listen. Rachel had felt a prickle on her skin, under her skin. Sweat had pooled in the mass of hair held at her nape. She'd nodded at Lily. Then, she'd dismissed the unease as no more than heat and stress; no more than the tickle of sweat as it made a slow journey down her spine.

★

'You need to relax, Debs, you need to sleep. You must be exhausted.' Rachel cooed the words, extending the vowels, stroking Debbie's head with every phrase, combing fingers through her hair. It left an oily sheen on Rachel's palms. Showering must be the last thing on Debbie's mind. Rachel eased the coffee mug – pink, a cartoon girl dancing by a cartoon rainbow – from Debbie's hands.

'Settle back, now. I'll be here. Don't worry.' The Police Liaison Officer had gone out with Gary, to give Debbie a few hours of quiet in the early evening. Rachel had agreed to stay with her, to keep her company and to monitor the now-tapped phone.

Debbie looked shattered. Not just tired, but broken, as if the whole she'd once formed had splintered. Debbie had never been the sort to glide through life. She walked as if the air was viscous, her left arm always pumping heavily. Rachel had spent so many cumulative hours with Debbie – dinners with the other mums, book group meetings, doorstep conversations around the details of netball fixtures, jumble sales, dates of inset days – but they'd never become close. Debbie favoured the trinkets that were designed to beguile five-year-old girls: circlets of plastic around her wrists, tinsel clips in her hair. Rachel would mentally make her over as they chatted, staining her lips ruby instead of pastel, chopping in a fringe, warming her bleached ends to rich honey. The last few days had blanched her even paler. Rachel didn't want to improve her now, just hold her. She couldn't bring herself to imagine the other woman's pain, to consider if it was worse to know that Lily had chosen to go, if it hurt more that she'd acted on her own volition.

'You'll wake me, Rach, if anything happens, if you hear anything.' Her voice was a scratch.

Rachel held Debbie's shoulder as she curled her legs up onto the sofa, resting her head on the cushion. 'Of course. Just relax. I'm here, I promise.' She could have kissed Debbie's forehead.

Rachel sat in an armchair and waited. The room was dim. The curtains might not have opened again since they'd closed on Sunday night. It was a fug that was deepened by the knowledge of the blaring sun outside. A slice of light crept in through a gap in the material and lit a vivid triangle. That shard of brightness picked out the dust motes in the air so they twinkled and danced. Just when Rachel thought she'd dropped off, Debbie's eyes flashed open, her hands jerking out, splayed and tensed, as if she was braced for a fall, as if her dream-self had been pushed to a plunging death. In time, she calmed again. Rachel sat for minutes and minutes, until Debbie's breath thickened, rhythmic and heavy, until the whole room seemed to sigh.

Rachel flicked on the light in Lily's bedroom. The click resounded, and she paused, but Debbie made no noise downstairs. Rachel needed to see the room for herself. She'd been in there a handful of times, once or twice in recent years: to collect Mia, to admire a dress. It looked odd now. Every object had been moved, photographed, toyed with. It felt violated.

There was a blank in the centre of Lily's desk where her laptop must have sat. It was being dismantled somewhere now, raided for clues. Everything had been ransacked for Lily's safety.

Rachel stood in the middle of the room. She let her eyes scan, let them rest on every object for a second. Lily's copy of *The Glass Menagerie* lay on the bedside table. The police must have scoured every inch of carpet, every scratch on the paint, but Rachel was sure she could decode it further. She'd spent over fifteen years watching teenagers. She could read their glances, detect their brags and their shifts. The police would have taken fingerprints and inventories, but they didn't know what to look for.

The room was heart-breaking. Its walls were the shade of purple that must have thrilled Lily six or seven years ago, and every corner was filled with the whispers of her childhood. Mia had already dispatched every potentially embarrassing item to bin bags and charity shops, but Lily was more sentimental. Amongst the hairspray and high heels were all the things she hadn't cast away; books that surely hadn't been opened for a decade, a lamp shaped like a bunny.

'They moved everything.'

Rachel's hands flew to her chest as Debbie's voice cut the air. She must have floated up the stairs, appeared from out of the dust. Rachel wanted to apologise, explain why she was there, but there was no reprimand in Debbie's voice.

'I couldn't even come in here for the first day. I just couldn't handle it.' Debbie went over to the window and ran her fingers over each of the milky blue and green gobbets of sea glass that glowed on the sill. 'She collected these at West Wittering. She was seven. She thought they looked like treasure.'

Cuddled up on her bed, sitting on a pile of cushions, were three stuffed bears. Debbie plucked the biggest one from the middle and cradled its rump on her arm like it was an infant. 'She loves this bear.'

Rachel didn't know what to do except smile. 'He's lovely.'

'She used to tuck him up into bed when she was little.' The fur had rubbed smooth on his body, but his face still looked fresh. Debbie pressed her nose against the soft fuzz between his ears. Rachel could see his plastic eyes stare plaintively as Debbie spoke. 'He must miss her.'

Debbie began to wander around the room, picking things up to examine them more closely. A pink feather boa that hung from the curtain tie. A series of black-and-white post-cards showing the golden age of Hollywood. A music box that tinkled a tune when it was knocked. Lily had inherited her mother's penchant for the glittered and fluffy, but it looked sweeter here. It was the taste of the little girl she once was, that she hadn't quite let go of. Mia and Lily could cover their faces in make-up, mimicking the women they might one day be, but this was the room Lily lived in once the door closed. Rachel had to squeeze her eyes tight. The girls were still so young.

Rachel kept her eyes shut for a moment, to silence her mind, to block out Debbie's movements, her words. She stood entirely still, but alert as a spiritualist waiting for a message to eke its way through; waiting for the glitch in energy that meant she could divine the truth. Her eyes opened, and her gaze lingered on a poster, printed on A4 and Blu-tacked onto the wall. A wash of pastels, with words in a sketched font.

'She made this. On the computer. She's ever so good with things like that.'

Don't waste sunsets with people who will be gone by sunrise. What could those words possibly mean if you were fifteen? Layered over the poster was a thin strip of photographs. They had not been caught by a digital device and held there, but were solid. They had been taken in a machine as big as a car and spat out to be kept for ever. They looked as if they came from another time. This generation were different. They didn't hoard endless scraps of paper, letters and notes and lists; nothing bled from a pen any more. Their precious memories were all locked inside their phones. They took more pictures of themselves than of their friends, and didn't keep them close, but displayed them to the whole world. But here was a tangible image. Five faces had squeezed together to fit into the frame. Lily, Mia, Ella, Keira, Abby. Four photographs lined up on top of each other. Mia was wearing a new top. The pictures were only weeks old.

Debbie pressed hot against Rachel's arm. 'They look pretty, don't they?'

They smiled in one, laughed in the next, gurned in the final two, pushing their fingers into their ears, their tongues into their cheeks to distort their faces.

'Mia's got your features, hasn't she? You must like that. Lily's got her dad's.'

Rachel held the pictures. She didn't look at Mia's face, but Lily's. Something had altered. The change was minute, but its impact was unambiguous. Rachel would watch the sixth-form girls as they sat in their semi-circle of desks, breathlessly parsing Plath. They were so round and bright in Year 12. Then, around the beginning of Year 13, the softness would judder. It was tiny: some delicate alteration in physiognomy, a weight loss of only an ounce, a faint line beginning to form. Lily's face in the pictures still looked plump. It still curved lavishly from chin to cheek as she smiled, but something near her eyes had sharpened. It would be easier to discern in person, but printed on paper, it was clear enough. There was that sudden definition around the edges. Lily looked knowing. Rachel swallowed hard, dropping the strip of images onto the desk. Lily was fifteen. It was too young. Did Debbie know? It must be someone they hadn't thought of, some drama club stud, some unknown older boy who'd lured her away. Someone had preyed on that pretty girl.

She'd never sat in an empty cinema before. On that Tuesday afternoon everyone else was busy, and the rows and rows of seats were unoccupied. It was deafeningly dark, as dark as she'd ever experienced. So dark the air seemed liquid. So dark they could lift off their chairs and turn slow somersaults.

He'd bought tickets based on timings, not content. They

had no idea what was showing. They didn't even look at the screen. In that flickering dark, wrapped in the warm smell of popcorn, they could be alone. Just her face and his. From a crinkled pink-and-white bag, he brought treats to her lips, each invisible to her eyes, unknowable until they were in her mouth. Spongy banana-flavoured sugar, jellied gems, discs of grainy chocolate. And the salt of his fingers with each one. It was the first time she'd ever felt like she was a body, not a person in a body. She wasn't trapped; she was whole. In that cavernous space, with the meaningless noise and light of the unwatched film, she was present. She was in her muscles and her sinews. She was her blood and her bones and her marrow. She was every inch herself as he touched her.

It was a piece of notepaper. That thing she hadn't known she was looking for. It wasn't a ripped-out page of foolscap A4, but special notepaper with a turquoise border and filigree patterns painted into each corner. It was covered in neat, curling cursive. It looked like a poem at first, with its jagged right edge, but as she stepped closer to the pinboard, Rachel recognised the words. *She is a changeless angel.*

Debbie moved towards her to see what she was staring at. Each letter had been formed with elaborate attention. This version was not the first. It must have taken Lily hours to get it this perfect. She must have thrown away page after page because one word sloped too much, was too small or towered above the others. Every word on this page was immaculate.

This had been painstaking. *She is a changeless angel.* It had been important to her.

Rachel snatched the paper from the corkboard. She knew those words. Debbie yelped as the corner ripped with the force of her tug. Lily could have copied and pasted the words into an app; a swift Google search would have laid them out before her. She could have made some cute meme with a bleached-out image of a meadow of flowers, a starlit sky, a beach.

> *She is a changeless angel*
> *She's a city it's a pity*
> *That I'm like me.*

Lily could have imposed the words over her own face. But she hadn't.

'What is it? Is it a poem?' Debbie leaned in to look, her breath warm on Rachel's neck. Printing it would be too easy. This had taken time. Lily had wanted it to take time. She'd dedicated hours to it, and she'd savoured them. She'd wanted to feel the shape of every word in her hands. And these weren't words she'd known before. They couldn't have been. They'd been entirely new to her.

The words would have meant nothing until he played the song to her. She must have sung it over and over as she wrote it out. She'd have memorised every breath. *She is a changeless angel, she's a city, it's a pity that I'm like me.* This page wasn't a meme to be shared. This was private. This was between the two of them.

Debbie pulled the paper out of Rachel's hands. 'Does it mean something? Rach, do you know it?'

Rachel felt her gut thud. She knew the song. It was 'Spaceball Ricochet' by T. Rex. It was an album track from *The Slider*, never released as a single. It was written nearly thirty years before Lily was born. Rachel held herself solid, although her blood had deserted her. Only one person she knew loved that song. He'd played it in his car the single time he'd driven her home. He'd clicked to make it repeat three times when he'd realised Rachel knew the words. She locked her knees to stop them from buckling. Mark had played the song to Lily. It was their song. They were together.

3

The next morning, Wednesday, hit twenty-eight degrees, and for once it felt like a blessing. The flush in Rachel's cheeks, the prickles of sweat on her eyelids and upper lip were made sense of. Everyone looked tired, puckered under their eyes where the heat had fought sleep. The weather had become a ritual, a punishment they were all growing used to. In the early days, the school field had been crowded every lunchtime, nearby parks littered with exposed flesh, but people now began to take refuge in the shade. Rachel was in no fit state to teach.

They were rarely asked to invigilate these days, but when the call had gone out, Rachel gladly accepted. Physical presence was all she could muster. Invigilation was ideal. Rachel sat, inert, as that huge room slowly filled up with tension, like water into an empty pool. Two hundred students filed in. The gymnasium was entirely reimagined for exams: drained of joy, with desks in regimented rows on the coloured lines that usually marked out play. Invigilation involved witnessing the moment of horror descend. That day, the screech of chairs, the growing rumble of fear, grated on Rachel. She watched as the room turned on those teenagers. She watched for the dawning of it on their faces.

The tension faded after five minutes, and the remaining hours became so dull it was almost meditation. All she had to do was sit there and make sure nothing happened. There were rumours of other supervisors playing invigilation games – racing to give out every piece of spare paper, playing chicken as they walked down aisles towards each other, concocting elaborate Battleships tournaments by pausing next to certain pupils. Rachel just stared.

His hair was cut short. It had been shaved all around the sides, inches above his ears, with a badger streak of longer, thicker hair on top. Half the boys in his year boasted the same style, mimicked from bands or television presenters. The school had previously upheld rules about hair cropped below a certain grade, but the sheer number of semi-shorn heads made it futile to police. It made them look uniformly ugly. The empty space where their hairline should be served to flatten their features, making their noses look boxed, and their cheekbones broad and dumb. You could see their scalps glisten beneath the speckles. The other fashions Rachel had watched flit through the school – tight jeans, pierced eyebrows – had made the boys look vainly over-styled, but this made them look like brutes.

As Aaron bit down on his wad of forbidden gum, Rachel could see the mechanics of his skull in action. Through some fate of alphabet, he was seated directly in front of her, his desk only a single step – maybe two – from her own. She'd never seen him this close up before. It seemed as if hundreds of tiny bones were flexing and unflexing under his skin, gripping together like cogs to make his jaw hinge. The exam was three hours long.

He looked down at his paper, so the full dome of his skull faced her. If she didn't blink, didn't deviate her gaze, could she penetrate the skin of his scalp, pierce the bone, and reach the tender coil of his brain? Could she read what he bred there? His hair was a length that was strokable. The sensation on her hand would be satisfying. The bristles would seem to move beneath her. Rachel wanted to drag her palm from the thick of his forehead, right across his scalp to the scruff of his neck. Had Mia done the same? Had her daughter run her hands along those prickles? Had she felt the coarse scrub of it under those purple-painted fingers?

Aaron wasn't the kind of boy Rachel would ever have gone for. He was too mainstream. Too conformist. Underneath that expensive haircut, that designer hoodie, there was no spark of real rebellion. It would never have been his head her hand had longed to touch. She'd have craved softer, lanker locks. It seemed odd that her poised daughter was drawn in by this lumpen ox, but Rachel knew why. It was the lumpen ox's moment. These were the months – fifteen months, eighteen months, thirty if he was lucky – when he would shine. When he could glow in the dark. When a raise of his eyebrow could change history. She'd never seen him this close up, but she'd seen him swagger down corridors, King of Year 11. His feet were encased in the most covetable nylon; his heart thumped red beneath his untucked school shirt. Rachel had glimpsed him on the football pitch. He barely broke sweat. The ball knew who he was; it knew to bend to his will, just like the cabal of boys who constantly shadowed him. He was sixteen and he knew everything. Rachel could see how that could be irresistible.

He was holding his pen badly, one crabbed fist around the biro. Rachel had never taught him, but she could see from feet away that his writing was a scrawl. There was nothing of sensitivity in those brutish hands. His fingers were like miniatures of his head. Had those fingers groped at Mia? Had those grubby-nailed stubs probed at her daughter's bra, at the pants she sorted in the washing basket? Had three sets of fingers toyed with those pink scraps of fabric – Mia's when she slipped them on, Aaron's when he tugged them off, and her own when she worked to make them clean again?

He stretched. Every ten minutes or so, he'd thump his pen down and pull one arm straight across his chest, using the other to wrench it tight. He'd reach both hands into the air, grasping for the ceiling. Those muscles must feel bulky. When his arms raised, Rachel could taste the sting of his aftershave and, underneath, something undeniably male. He was sixteen, but his body was grown. He was physically a man, even if not legally.

As he lowered his arms, he saw Rachel looking. Their eyes met. Rachel didn't allow her face to react. Aaron stared back, hands resting on his desk, his spine straight against the wooden chair. Rachel was suddenly aware of the dryness of her own mouth, the fabric of her skirt, the scoop of her neckline. Aaron didn't look away. His gaze was steady. Intentional. It flashed in Rachel like rage. These children were nothing of the sort. They knew exactly what they were doing. They held all the power, and they were fully aware of it. Rachel locked onto his stare and refused to flicker. She wished she could assert her authority. She wished she could report him, punish him for his flagrant insubordination. She wished she could upend the table she sat at, drag him out of the gym by his shirt collar and into the playground, where she'd knock the arrogance from him.

'How well do you know Lily Dixon?'

'She's my daughter's friend, and we've been rehearsing the school play for the last few weeks, but I've never taught her.'

'So, you'd say you knew her well?'

'Quite well, yes.' Rachel could feel the tendons of her neck throb. They'd forgotten how to relax.

'Okay, thank you.' He wrote something down in his notebook, tongue between his teeth, transcribing her dull response, even though she was being recorded.

'And what is Lily like? What sort of girl would you say she was?' He read the questions so carefully from his printout that the intonation patterns were all wrong. It gave everything a false note.

'She's a very sweet girl, always very polite and pleasant. Not too grown up for her age.' There was no sign of DCs Scott or Redpath this time, no sense of their mature composure, just a man so young and skinny he was scarcely formed; all elbows and Adam's apple. He tapped his pen against the page in front of him as he thought, or perhaps mimed the act of thinking. He could only have been in the force for months.

'What do you mean by that?'

They were in the airless, wood-panelled office of the deputy head. The room was as bare as a stage set; nothing to make it distinct, just a desk with a blank computer and an empty pinboard. Rachel knew the time to speak had arrived. She'd held onto the near-knowledge all night. It already felt too long. The facts sat heavily within her. This was the chance she needed to let them all come out, to say what she suspected. It was now. But she couldn't. There was so little to base it on; she'd look ridiculous. I saw some lyrics from the seventies, and now I'm convinced I know who took her. She'd be laughed at. No, she could say nothing. Not yet, anyway; she'd think about it more, fathom how to explain it, call it in as an anonymous tip-off. Not there, in the deputy head's office with this eager young man. His neck was prickled with red where he'd shaved too harshly. It looked painful. He wasn't expecting anything. It was just a routine chat, no different to the ones he was having with scores of other staff members.

'She's sweet, like I said, none of the brittleness of some girls. She always seems happy, and not afraid to show it. There's no posing with Lily, no front.' Rachel could hear the words, but wasn't sure how she was forming them. She had slipped into her work persona: the automation that was necessary in those endless afternoons, when her true energy had long drained, but she had to keep up the performance. So much of it was a performance.

The young man turned the page of his notebook to track down his next question. He was resting one ankle on the opposite knee in a stance of nonchalance, but his foot was jogging constantly. It hit Rachel. They knew nothing. They had no idea who Lily was with. No clue. How could they have missed it? Mark had been away, due to attend a STEM training course on Monday and Tuesday. He'd messaged to say he was ill both days and again on that Wednesday morning. The timing was glaring. But then, Rachel hadn't made the connection. She'd been distracted. They all had, with the toxic combination of heat and exams.

'Did she seem upset or in any distress to you?' He'd hit upon his next set question. There was no need to deviate.

'No, she actually always seems like a very upbeat girl, very smiley. She's not one of the ones you worry about.'

'How do you mean?' He was quicker now. Rachel's neck remained clenched.

'You keep a bit of an eye out for the quiet ones, you know, the ones with the black nail varnish and the tippexed band names on their bags, but Lily's always so sunny.' It was exactly what a teacher would say.

He nodded as he jotted something else down. Rachel had wiped her eyeliner off, combed her hair straight to create a note-perfect impression of a pleasant, middle-aged teacher. No one who had anything interesting to say.

'She's such a lovely girl.'

'Are Lily and your daughter close?'

'They hang around in a little group, I think they are all very close to each other.'

'Do you think your daughter knows where Lily might be?'

'I've asked her repeatedly, as have your colleagues, and she maintains that she knows nothing. I am therefore inclined to believe her.' It was exactly what a mother would say.

'Does Lily have a boyfriend?'

Rachel made herself pause. 'Not that I know of, and not that my daughter knows of.' It fell so simply from her lips.

'Do you have any thoughts at all, no matter how vague, as to where Lily might be, or who she might be with?'

'Absolutely not, I'm afraid.'

Rachel sat in her Corsa in the school car park that lunchtime. It was a windowed box, and every move she made would be visible, but it was the only place she could be alone. She was safe from any semblance of conversation. Rachel felt stuck between exhaustion and frenzy; she'd clocked up no more than three hours sleep, but her blood was frantic.

She sat back in the mock-leather of the driving seat and aimed the fan right at her face. The thrum of the engine blanked everything out. Mark. Lily was with Mark Webb. He had taken her away. They were on the other side of an ocean. Rachel was the only one who knew. Her thoughts were jammed, unable to do more than repeat the fact over and over. Her eyes were too dry to do anything but stare, and she didn't dare close them.

'Rachel!'

A knock on the window made her yelp – a scream that immediately seemed melodramatic. Cressida's face was only inches from her own. Rachel pressed the button that lowered the window and let in the outside heat.

'Sorry, Rachel, I saw you alone . . .' She was wearing a dress that could only be described as a frock: pale blue cotton with watercolour scenes of a windmill repeated across it, tied at the waist with a white belt. Her face grew stiff as the silence stretched.

'God, sorry, Cressida, I just needed a moment, you know.'

Cressida was instantly tearful, her eyes damp and red in seconds. 'I do know, I do. It's all just so awful. Every time I check my phone I say a little wish that there'll be a message telling me she's come home, but it's never there. And seeing it all on the news is so ghoulish, so ugly. She's fifteen. Fifteen.'

Cressida's emotions clearly sat just below the surface, just a scratch under her skin. Rachel only nodded. There was nothing said that she didn't agree with.

'I just don't know what to do with myself, Rachel.'

The way Cressida looked at her sometimes threw Rachel. Cressida saw her as an adult, a grown woman who viewed the world through clear eyes and approached every situation with certainty. 'I understand. I think all we can do is stay strong.'

Her words were meaningless, but the younger woman's hand was firm on her wrist. 'Thank you, Rachel. You're right. We need to stay strong for Lily.'

He'd clinked the two keys together. One for the gate and one for the door. He'd let the key ring dangle from his pinkie. He'd flicked a single switch, and the tinny pops of the lights waking up had reverberated around the enormous space. They'd been joined by the thwack and thrum of whatever machinery made the place function. Only one set of lights had come on. The deep end of the pool had remained eerie with shadow.

Mark's shoes were off before he turned to her. She'd never looked at his feet before. They were as pale and narrow as she'd expected. She folded her clothes neatly on a wooden bench like she was in a PE lesson, her eyes and nose already stinging with the bleach in the air. At the dark end of the pool, she could make use of the false dusk to undress. He dove in without making a splash. Surfacing, suddenly entirely wet, entirely naked and whispering. *Come in, come in.* The water was as warm as a bath, as warm as the air around it. It was the first time he'd seen her naked.

Every noise they made, every word uttered, echoed once, twice, three times, up to the vaulted metal ceiling and back down to the enamel tiles of the changing rooms. It had felt renegade. Trespassing in the school was an odd kind of daring. Breaking into a place they knew so well. They were inside a building they both walked by every day, with leather shoes and bags full of books, but every piece of their clothing was folded away. All it would have taken was a vigilant caretaker, or someone else with a key, and they'd have been caught, shivering and dripping.

Nothing about the place felt familiar. Mundane details became magical. The triangular flags suspended over the water fluttered slightly as they swam.

'You're like a mermaid. A siren. You'll make me dash myself to pieces on the rocks.' His voice was a whisper, but resounded to feel epic.

The blue-and-white lane dividers she'd seen so many times were now holding her weight, her tiny water-buoyed weight, as he swam, eyes straight, towards her. Their skin was lit to bright white above the waterline. Below it, a blur, just wobbling lines and streaks of colour. Her body was nimble in the water, nakedness making her lithe, turning somersaults, discovering the ways she could propel herself with just flicks of her feet, holding upside down for long seconds, completing a length of wide, perfect strokes without taking a breath.

Duck-diving to the very bottom, letting her hands run through the smattering of silt that had gathered there, the silt of the hundreds of other bodies who'd also danced in that water. Hundreds of wet teenagers. She left the traces of her touch in the deepest part, eyes open against the chlorine.

His hands had slid easily over her there. *Come here.* She was wriggling and silky as an otter – *you minx* – twisting in and out of his grip.

Rachel couldn't tell Debbie. She couldn't be the person to lob that grenade. She wouldn't be able to keep her face calm as she formed the words. She'd tell the police; tell the police and let them explain to everyone else.

The number was everywhere. Posters had appeared around school, full pages in the local, free papers. They were urged to dial it if they recalled the slightest detail that might help the investigation. Rachel had to tap the eleven digits in carefully. Typing numbers felt odd; everyone she usually called was already locked away in her phone's memory. She checked them three times. Her finger rested on the phone's casing, no more than an inch from the green icon on the screen that would trigger the dial, that skeuomorph of the kind of cradled telephone Mia had never used, that Rachel herself could hardly remember.

She sat on the edge of her bed, leaning against the plump cushions she repositioned in a carefully haphazard pile every morning, though no one so much as peeped their head around the door. The phone suddenly weighed nothing. It was crystalline; it could shatter in a second. Rachel passed it from hand to hand. She wet her lips, and stroked the screen awake again. She didn't even need to tell them her name; she could just share her knowledge as a hunch, a tip-off. If they asked anything more, she could just end the call. Lily would be returned home, and no one would ever know her involvement, but Rachel would be able to carry the knowledge with her, hugging that little glow of satisfaction close; she'd have done the right thing. Mark would be punished. He'd be imprisoned. He'd be vilified. Everyone would know his name. But it was nothing worse than he deserved. Her mobile felt like hollow tin. It couldn't contain anything. There could be no working mechanism inside it that could possibly maintain a line.

Rachel exhaled slowly, and placed her phone on the bedside table, face down.

Rachel could no longer bear the idea of sweetness. She wanted to taste salt, something deeper than salt, something darker. Anything that could cut through the cloying sugar that seemed to make up her own saliva. She craved something ancient and savoury. Something so adult that no young tongue could ever stand it. At the back of the drink's cupboard, behind the gin they shared out when visitors gathered, behind the dusty Christmas Baileys, was a bottle of Tim's. It sat there like a relic, some present he had never opened. It wasn't just whisky, but peaty whisky. Islay. Laphroaig.

Rachel sat at the kitchen table and took a mouthful straight from the bottle, holding it there, letting it sit on her tongue, soaking in, stinging her eyes, easing through the roof of her mouth and creeping into her bloodstream. The dark, difficult flavour filled her before she'd even swallowed. It sluiced her mouth clean, stripped the day's saccharine residue away. There was nothing naïve there now, just the tang of smoke and sweat.

She missed salt. When she'd followed Tim inland, she hadn't realised how being so far from the coast would feel. She'd never been so landlocked before they married. Even at university, she could take her housemate's car, park in a coastal layby and stand, breathing, until her hair was stiff. Their house was well over an hour of driving, over a day of walking from the nearest shore. The sea wouldn't enter her thoughts for months, then the ache would slam into her. The heat made it worse. The prow of every hill seemed to promise that glimmer of ocean. If you could just see over the top, just keep walking, the beach would appear and fill your vision, right to the very edges. It was a nagging, constant mirage. Rachel felt suffocated by the neat rows of buildings that inevitably spread out over every hill's real prow.

The whisky was nearly enough. Rachel had poured an inch more into a coffee mug before she saw Mia in the doorway. Rachel nodded towards one of the empty chairs and Mia sat without speaking. They'd eaten so many meals around that table. Rachel had chosen it just after Mia was born, when she and Tim had kitted out the entire home. Almost everything had been flat-packed, or off the department store shelf, but the kitchen table was different. Rachel had found it at a reclamation yard, and convinced Tim it would be clean enough, safe enough. He'd teased her bohemian tendencies, grabbed her around the waist, kissed the neck beneath her hair as she'd stroked the table's grained wood. It was rough, with corroded metal legs. It looked ridiculous in their clean, right-angled kitchen with its matching pale ash features and built-in fridge freezer, but she loved it.

Rachel walked to the cupboard, found a glass tumbler, and poured Mia her own inch of whisky. She pushed it across the table to her daughter. It was an invitation, but also a challenge. Mia reached for the glass and wrapped her thin fingers around it. Rachel let the moment hang before she spoke. What was Mia squirrelling away? What had Lily blurted out, too excited to hide? Did Mia know that Lily's stolen lingerie was to impress their physics teacher?

'Mia. Who is she seeing?'

Mia's response was immediate. 'I don't know why you think I know.'

Mia held the glass up and let the liquid touch her lips; she barely took a sip, but it still must have burned. She didn't wrinkle her nose, didn't grimace, just took another tiny taste and swallowed firmly. Rachel knew she was concealing her reaction. Even if she'd tried some sweeter, weaker cousin of this drink, mixed with cola in red plastic cups, she couldn't possibly be immune to the shock.

'She won't even answer my calls.' The phone those calls reached was probably languishing at the bottom of whichever stretch of water the ferry had crossed. Mia sipped again, face impassive. 'She doesn't really talk about boys. She sometimes mentions Seth in Year 12.' She held her glass with both hands, like an infant with a Tommee Tippee full of milk. 'But I don't know if he even knows who she is.'

Rachel needed more. 'How do you know she likes him? What does she say about him?'

'She thinks he's cute.'

'Does she use the word "cute"? What does that even mean? Does that mean he seems young? Do you want to squeeze someone who's cute, or kiss them?'

Mia rolled the glass on its base, forming a wide arc across the table. 'I don't know. Both.'

'*Does* she kiss him?'

'No. They don't really speak. She just mentions him. She just nudges us if he walks by.'

'Does she kiss other boys?'

'I don't know, I suppose so, at parties and stuff.'

'Do you see her kiss them?'

Mia picked at the wood of the table, digging her thumbnails in and forcing splinters out from the grain. Rachel didn't take the bait. 'Mum, that's really weird. It's not like we watch.'

'So, you've never seen her kiss any boys?'

'That's a totally creepy question.'

'The rest of you must. Is she the odd one out?'

Mia didn't answer.

'Does she talk about kissing them? Does she talk about having sex with them?'

'That's gross. That's really gross.'

'Do you talk to her about you and Aaron?'

A pause. 'It's really not any of your business.'

Rachel pushed harder. 'Does she talk about other boys, older ones?'

Mia sighed. 'She likes Ross, in your play, I think. But I don't know if she likes him like that. She just tells us funny things he's said.'

'But she doesn't confide in you? She doesn't tell you who she likes, or what she's done with them?'

'Sometimes.'

'I thought you were friends.'

Mia still stared at the table. 'We are friends.'

'Mia. You have to tell me absolutely anything else you know.'

Mia didn't look up. 'I already told the police everything.'

When Rachel spoke again, she could hear that her voice was harder. 'Mia, look at me. Look at me.'

Mia moved her head as if it weighed too much. Rachel waited until she sat straight, until she pushed the hair back from her face. She met her daughter's eyes, brown where her own were blue. Mia didn't look away, but she still couldn't get to her, couldn't unpick what was hiding there.

'Mum. Don't. Please'

The crease between Mia's eyes deepened. Rachel could see where it would one day etch itself permanently. She saw a flash of her daughter's grown-up face. Eyes tense, mouth firm. 'Mia, I have to. Do you have any idea how serious this is?'

'Of course I do.'

'Then act like it. Act like you give a shit. This is real. Do you understand that? And if you just sit there and keep quiet, you are part of it. You are responsible.' Rachel was standing now and, as she spoke, she slammed her mug down on the wooden table. The sharp rap resounded around the kitchen; liquid sloshed over the edge of the mug, soaking her hands. Rachel's breath wouldn't settle as she heard the words she was speaking, felt their impact on herself as well as on her daughter. 'This is serious. This is as serious as it gets, Mia.'

Mia didn't look away. Rachel could see the alarm in her eyes.

The thud of the fairground's beat had hit her bones with every step. The impossibly loud blare of dance music had made every other sense blur. He'd taken her hand and led her through the crowd at speed, pushing past shoulders and backpacks and tripping over toddlers in the dark. The mud beneath their feet had been hard and dusty, the grass rubbed away. They hadn't looked back once. She'd felt nothing but his grip on her wrist, his fingers on her skin. He'd bought candyfloss without queuing and fed it to her, holding the clouds of pink so high she'd had to tilt her head right back to catch it on her tongue.

Everything had smelled sweet and her mouth had crackled with sugar. They'd driven to the cusp of another county, so no face in that crowd would light when it saw them.

With her head tilted, she could see the strings of bulbs draped between the stalls, the flags, the letters painted in varying shades of the same colour so they became three-dimensional, so they leapt from their wood. From that angle, the movement of every ride was terrifying. Machines were spinning and diving all at the same time, all in different directions. Limbs were flying outwards, flailing, so near to smashing together. So few seconds from disaster. Mouths were yelping with the glee of it, the horror. Everything reached higher than it should, incredible in the face of gravity. The thud, thud, thud of the bassline held together the clashing melodies coming from every ride. Looming from each hoarding were the faces of celebrities created from spray cans. She couldn't take it all in. His hand on the back of her neck. His fingers, sticky with pink, in her mouth.

He'd bought tickets for the waltzers, little old-fashioned paper stubs they had to show before they could sit in a carriage. The metal railing pushed against their middles. As the machine jolted to life, Mark leaned over, right into her ear. 'Scream.'

They spun slowly, gaining momentum with every cycle.

'Scream now. Like you're never allowed to. I want you to.' He had to raise his voice to be heard. 'Scream as loud as you can.' They were picking up speed, being hurtled backwards with each loop. She felt the strain on her arms and cheeks, desperate to stay sitting, to stay solid and not be pushed so hard they morphed into the wood and metal behind them. The man who ran the waltzers was suddenly above them, wolfish, giving them the attention he'd usually reserve for groups of girls. Ponytail and earrings. He spun them recklessly, so hard it should have shaken them, should have been hideous. But Mark's gaze was locked on hers. He couldn't lean into her, but his eyes did the work his mouth couldn't. *Scream.*

So, she screamed. It was a shriek at first, a high wail, wavering and fragile. Then she pushed it deeper. The noise came from her stomach, not her throat. She screamed as loudly and as fully as she could. It was the sort of noise that would make people come running. Mark's hand gripping hers. The grin of the waltzer man over her head. She was all scream. Mark's eyes firmly on hers, his fingers laced through her fingers. He was seeing the wild creature he so wanted her to be. She screamed and screamed until tears sat on the tops of her cheeks, until the ride stopped and the man disappeared, and they stumbled together, inner ears scrambled, tripping into the neon dark in any direction at all.

Rachel slid the phone from its jack. Taking Mia's phone no longer seemed transgressive. It was no longer frantic, but stoical. She kissed her sleeping daughter goodnight, then took the device. It was the one place she could hope to see her, to untangle what she knew. The bricolage of their teenage lives – the pictures, the messages, the timelines of social media sites –

was easy to navigate now. She'd already pored over every photograph posted that year, pinching outwards to stretch them bigger, scrutinising every detail, but there was surely more to see.

Rachel knew about the terror teenagers could inflict upon each other; the bullying that a virtual world made permissible. Words that flowed from fingers could be harsher than anything tongues could bear to utter. She knew about the American kids who'd been blithely goaded to suicide. She was braced for it, prepared to read those words – *skank, slut, ho, thot* – and shudder at how girls could treat each other. She'd tried the words out, felt the shape and taste of them in her mouth, but never found any. With each new site she explored, each month she scrolled backwards, Rachel feared she'd hit the mother lode of horror, but their online universe was odddly sycophantic. They praised each other, bleating superlatives at every selfie – *Love you, Queen. You are so unreal. Idk who I fancy more. Tu es séduisante. Ur amaze* – and putting themselves down in every group shot. *You're the hottest of them all. What is wrong with my legs? Why does my face always impersonate a fish? No way! I'm nothing on you.* They were encouraging, cheerleading each other through every image, every choice – Keira's new dance leotards, Abby's Spotify playlist. Rachel knew there were other sites she couldn't reach. Snapchat had self-destruction built in, gobbling images and words as soon as they'd been glimpsed. There was a slew of messages she could never conjure back, but she could interrogate what she had.

If she looked closely enough, if she analysed their comments like poetry, unpacking their meaning beat by beat, she could see more. She could argue that Lily came off worse. She lacked the nous of the others, the detached irony. She showed the things she loved, not those that would increase her social standing. The others were harsher with her. Their comments were less gushing. *#Fail. Awkward.* The slights were hidden amongst grinning compliments, but Rachel could imagine the reaction they'd provoke. Lily garnered fewer likes, by fifty or sixty clicks. The judgement now seemed glaring.

It was often near Rachel's midnight by the time Tim could talk. They'd discovered in the early months of him being away that the phone was not enough. Engaging only one sense was too isolating. So, they relied on Skype. Rachel wanted to linger that night, finding out about his day, how the project was progressing. She wanted to hear his voice, to see his body moving, as if he was there with her, not alone in a hotel room. But the connection was fragile. However the information scrambled itself to travel, it struggled to land. Their faces didn't remain whole, but fragmented into monstrous, jawless fuzzes. Every second sentence turned robotic. *Snowed under. Diary like a barcode.* In the first weeks of his six-month secondment, they'd talked for hours, but their nightly catch-ups had become more bulletin than communion.

It wasn't Tim's face Rachel could see. It was a digital rendering that looked near enough to fool a stranger. The hair colour was right, the shape of his forehead. But she couldn't meet his eyes. To look at the screen eyes meant missing his real gaze by inches. They were never able to make full contact. The nearest approximation was to focus on the laptop's camera, but eyeballing the computer felt hollow, and the stare it created was uncanny. Rachel found it easier to watch her own face move through the conversation from the small box in the corner. The call lasted only twelve minutes.

When Rachel pressed the button to break the connection, the silence in the bedroom buzzed. It felt like her room now, not theirs. It was where she lay without him. The stroke of the sheets against her skin was the nearest she came to physical contact. The weight of the duvet when she could bear it. Her body ached to be manipulated the way it once was, his hands on her flesh, moving her limbs where he wanted, teaching her how best to touch his body. The rasp of male cheeks against her own, the grazes they left behind. The bruises in places no one else could see.

Rachel couldn't ask. She couldn't request anything more than the information that flowed her way through the standard channels: school updates, television bulletins, internet news. But she could look. She'd set up Google Alerts for Lily's name, for Mark's name, streaming the results as soon as they arose. Nothing of Mark had shown. She needed to see beyond the mainstream articles and newspaper headlines to blogs and comments; she needed to dig into the gossip and conjecture.

Someone else must know what she knew. She sat in bed until the early hours, her light off so as not to alert Mia, her face lit to ghoulish green by the phone's screen, deep into tweets and comments on tweets, mired in Reddit threads. She rummaged through the hashtags she knew were rich seams: #LilyDixon, #whereisLily. She checked their flows, learned the imagined situations they explored. None of them were close to the truth. Screen after screen of speculation scrolled past, and there was no sign of Mark in any of them.

Rachel knew for certain that they were together. The bone-deep thud of recognition hadn't left her. She knew. And she knew she couldn't sit on that knowledge. She was part of it. She was culpable. She couldn't rest. One call, and Mia would be a step closer to having her friend back. She had to make the call. She had to, she had to, she had to. Only a monster would keep it to herself. It had already been too long. It was Thursday morning now, after another night of almost no sleep. She had already lied to the police.

Rachel could feel the phone's faint pulse ringing down her arm. She breathed in time with it, let her weight slump against the cushions on her bed, dreading the moment a human voice would spring from the receiver. As it clicked and the person on the other end began to speak, she slapped the phone into submission. It was the eighth time she'd tried that morning. Saying those words would shatter everything. She hadn't even practised how they would flow, just tried to trick herself into blurting it out. She knew what would happen when Mark was caught; what they would say about him, think about him. It would all be her doing.

She could have stopped it. She should have known. She could see Lily's vulnerability; she'd heard those longing comments about being flattered by an impressive man. She should have listened to her words fully, pushed behind them, unpicked her expressions. She was trained in how to do this. It could have been prevented so easily.

The phone knew the number, so only a tap was needed to call it again. The purrs started up immediately. Rachel tried to focus on nothing but that mechanical trill. She wondered if the rings at the other end came at the same moment or were perfectly syncopated. She wondered if . . . the phone clicked, and a voice greeted her. The words she needed to speak were suddenly too heavy. Someone else must know; someone else would tell. Rachel closed her eyes and swiped the call away.

It had been a corner shop. The type of shop that sold basics – tea, milk, bread – then an extraordinary mix of lurid alcohol and fizzy sweets. She hardly ever went into one. She had assumed he'd popped in to pick up another bottle of the sugary drink he loved. She'd expected him to select a vial of pink or red liquid, pay with cash and then they'd be gone. But he'd walked up behind her, careful not to touch her, not to be seen, and whispered. 'Take something.'

She had laughed.

'I'm serious. Take something. Steal something. I want to see you do it.' He spoke almost without moving his lips, turning his head away from the man at the counter.

'I'm not going to *steal* something.' She mouthed the words back to him, eyebrows high.

'Do it. Please. I want you to. I want you to do it.' His eyes were so close to hers that she couldn't focus. His two eyes merged into one, one enormous eye with lashes that tickled the bridge of her nose. He walked out of the shop. She was left in the middle aisle, alone amongst the dry pasta and jarred sauce. She turned to follow him out, but stopped. There were no CCTV cameras in the corners of the room, just one of those bulbous, fish-eye mirrors. The man at the till was reading a paperback, folded over on itself. He was hardly aware of her, not concerned, not watching. It would be the easiest thing in the world.

She could already feel the blood thrum with more force. It was ridiculous. She couldn't possibly consider it. She put her jacket on for something to do. The air-conditioning made it viable. She forced herself to inhale slowly, then walked down the aisle in casual curiosity, her head scanning the products. *No, no that is not what I'm looking for.* She reached the end of the row, blithely turned, and headed down the next. *Maybe down here.* She bent down to the fabric conditioners, plucked a bottle out and pretended to read the copy on the back. *Suitable for delicates. Dermatologically tested.* She nodded to herself, and replaced the bottle neatly on the shelf.

The bell above the door dinged as a group of kids stumbled in. They were no older than ten, not yet in secondary school, and no one she recognised. They were miles from home. The man placed his book down, splayed open, bending the spine, and watched as they squabbled over which bottle of fizzy drink they were going to share.

At the far end of the aisle, nearest to the door but blocked from his view, were loose sweets – packets of gummy animals, single servings of chocolate, strawberry laces. She leaned over as if to examine them more closely, picked up a thin, flat bar of toffee and pushed it up her jacket sleeve. Its plastic wrapper was cold against the skin of her wrist. With a glance around the room, as if checking in case she'd forgotten anything, she left the shop, closing the door firmly behind her. As it clicked shut, she ran. She ran like crazy. It felt pure. As her legs pounded and she dodged sluggish pedestrians, she had one straightforward fear. Getting into trouble. Her bag thumped against her side; her hair blew over her face. The fear was overwhelming in its simplicity. She just ran.

She ran around the corner to where she knew he'd be. She pulled the toffee from her sleeve and held it to him like an offering. As he took it from her, eyes wide with delight, she started to laugh, laugh until she bent double, gripping onto him for support. In a small alley between the shops they couldn't be seen. His arms were around her, his mouth on her hair, her neck. Her veins fizzed with the thrill of it all. The waves of laughter kept coming, uncontrollable and racking.

He was proud of her. He lifted her shaking body upright and pushed her backwards against the rough wall, his mouth on her mouth.

Either no one had thought to take the posters down, or they'd feared it might upset some delicate balance. It meant that Lily's face, in near-perfect profile, loomed out from every notice-board in the school. Rachel stood in front of the main-entrance board and touched the A3 picture. The paper was glossy. They'd paid substantially more for it. They'd used the camera from the art department, borrowed their complicated lights and a white reflector board to hold under Lily's chin, just out of the frame. They'd spent hours on eBay, eventually finding a little plastic unicorn that looked like it could be made from glass.

Behind the words – the name of the play, the dates and times it was showing, the school's address, the ticket prices – Lily's face was blurred. The unicorn in her hand was in sharp focus. Despite the blur, she glowed. She glowed the golden glow that is entirely made of youth, that is the preserve of those who can't possibly appreciate it. Rachel knew the only chance of emitting anything like it over thirty was to be exceptionally well loved, or exceptionally well rested.

When the posters had arrived from the printers in a heavy cardboard box, when they'd run an open scissor blade down the tape and her face had jumped out, Lily had been horrified. 'You can't! Ms Collins, please. No.' Her printed face was marginally bigger than life-size. Its colours were marginally brighter. Her words protested, but the set of her lips let Rachel know she was thrilled. Her face was about to be broadcast down every corridor. People who had never spoken to her would know who she was. 'The unicorn looks lovely, though.'

Rachel could remember the day they'd taken the picture. She'd expected an afternoon of stemming giggles, of trying to capture the one moment when Lily wasn't in the grip of embarrassed hilarity, but the girl had been determined. She became grave when the lights were on her. Shot after shot, her face was still, her eyes fixed. She wanted to try out a range of different expressions. She knew the faces the old Hollywood stars made. She had evidently practised them in the mirror, altering the tiniest angle, the slightest muscle to change the geometry of her face. Lily transformed over and over. When they checked the miniature images in the camera's display, she didn't settle. She saw ways to make it better, insisted upon trying again, improving it, aiming for perfection.

The toilets were empty. Their location – at the juncture of the canteen and the science block – was out of the way. They were rarely used. A new block in the main building had endless mirrors and light, but Rachel wanted to be alone. She had a free period after lunch, and could hear the corridors fading to quiet. She ran the taps. The hot water was scalding, so she ran the cold until the force of the flow half-filled the sink. She plunged her arms in, scooping handfuls into her armpits, unconcerned if her vest or bra got wet, sluicing the day away.

In the heat, just having a human body was a chore. Just keeping it suitable for public approval was a job, and school was always public. When that teenage stink smacked the air of her classroom, Rachel made certain that her own body emitted almost nothing.

She unclipped the buckle of her sandal and leveraged her right foot into the running water. It was a feat of flexibility gifted from adolescent ballet. She rubbed the grime from between her toes. In the heat, her body was just meat, a lump of flesh always at risk of turning. The constant vigilance was exhausting.

Returning her feet to her shoes, Rachel rested her forehead against the mirror. She didn't want to catch her own eyes. The guilt of her inaction made her face look unfamiliar. It was the face of a woman too aware of what she had to lose. Rachel couldn't remember a time when she hadn't felt tired. Her head had felt woozy and untethered for so many days, as if she was always on the brink of a swoon. The ache at her core never stopped nagging.

'I thought you might need to chat.' Marianne. Calm amidst everything. 'School must be a nightmare.'

Rachel felt her eyes twitch as she nodded. They were ringed with red.

Marianne sipped a flat white, somehow finding the capacity for a hot drink despite the temperature. Rachel pressed the iced glass of her mineral water against her wrist, willing the coolness to enter her bloodstream and chill her entire body. Marianne sipped, but asked no other questions. Rachel had half-feared the offer of a coffee was a pretence to get information from a source inside the school, but Marianne left it there.

'It's horrible. School. It feels like everything we once took as read is upturned. We know something's happened, but no one is quite sure what.'

'It's so unpleasant, but none of you should feel responsible in the slightest. We all know what teenagers are like.' Marianne rubbed her hands over her face, across her cheeks and eyes as if she was wiping away tears. 'None of us can control them.' She had no fear of smudging make-up. Her face was the face she had woken up with. Rachel envied it. The ease. The embrace of her skin, her uncoated eyelashes, the hair that sprung out into a tight natural Afro. Rachel lamented every new crease that formed. The ghosts of her smiles were beginning to stay. The skin beneath her eyes was starting to puff out, to be bagged by the glee and tears of her past. It was like a penalty for feeling too much, for showing too much.

Marianne didn't wait for Rachel to reply, granting her the right to stay silent. 'The girls must feel even worse than we do. Lily must have hinted at something. They can't keep anything quiet, you've heard them. She must have dropped something out, if only they'd been paying attention.'

Rachel wanted Marianne to keep talking. She wanted those comforting words to be the soundtrack to her whole day. And if Marianne stopped, Rachel might talk. She was so tired of not talking; so exhausted from hiding what she knew. She could tell Marianne. It would be simple; it would flow out. She just had to open her mouth.

'The thing is . . .' Rachel began. If she told her, they'd both know. The onus would no longer lie with Rachel alone. If she told Marianne, Marianne would take over; she would call on Rachel's behalf. Marianne would know exactly what to do. There, in that wood-panelled chain coffee shop, her hands around a sweating glass of fizzy water, Rachel could tell.

'I'm almost definitely sure . . .' Rachel's throat closed. It clenched so firmly she could feel the sides pressing together. She could only croak. She could only squeeze out easier words: '. . . that Mia doesn't know.'

Telling Marianne would have been such cool relief, but Rachel's body wouldn't allow it.

Mia had torn one of the posters down. It lay, ripped at one corner, on the kitchen table when Rachel got home. It was sticky with fingerprints, creased as if it had been crushed into a ball, then smoothed back out. Mia must have been sitting at the table alone, staring at the image of her still-missing friend. The friend who had withheld the biggest secret of their lives, who'd overtaken all of them and not even looked back to say goodbye. Rachel could hardly bear to glimpse it. Those eyes, gazing unblinking from underneath their lashes, from behind her Lady Di tilt, were no longer clear, no longer simply blue.

There had been a moment that changed them; charged minutes in an empty classroom that were the only way this could have all begun. Lily must have gone back to his physics lab to retrieve some abandoned cardigan after school had ended for the day. He'd still be in there for another hour, silently marking. She'd know that. She'd have learned his routine, watching him for weeks, months. She must have waited until after the buses had left and the corridors had emptied. She'd have lingered in the cloakroom, in the ground-floor toilets, until her friends had gone. Did she tell them anything of her plans? Her steps would have echoed as she walked towards the science block. The air would have felt heavy with anticipation. The school looked so strange when it was empty. Had it surprised him, when the door opened – would she knock? – when she was there with no one else? Just the two of them in his impossibly tidy classroom, with his *System of Colours* print on the wall, his phases-of-the-moon poster, his Nikola Tesla quotes. It looked more like the office of a tech start-up than a comprehensive-school room.

Did she seem different to him as she stood in the doorway? Had she found some reason to lean across him as he sat, to reach for something – some paper or ruler – to brush his bare skin with her own? Did their eyes meet? How many seconds had to click by before they moved towards each other? Did he murmur some protest? Did she stop his lips with hers? They must have kissed. Nothing ever starts without a kiss.

*

'Mum!' The yelp came from downstairs, horrifying in its shrill-ness. 'Mum!'

Rachel dropped the hanger she was holding, let the skirt fall to the floor. She could decipher Mia's cries as clearly now as when she was an infant. This wasn't hunger or frustration. It was distress. She took the whole staircase in two leaps. Before she could swing her body into the living room, Mia called out again.

'It's Mr Webb.'

Mark's face filled the screen. It was twice its real size on their enormous television, twice as big as she'd ever seen it, as anyone ever had.

'Mum. It's Mr Webb.'

The photograph was a Facebook profile picture. He was at a wedding. Grey suit, grey waistcoat, pale shiny tie.

'They're saying Lily's with Mr Webb. Mr Webb from physics.'

It must have been taken years ago. He looked nothing like himself.

'They're saying he took Lily. They're saying Mr Webb took her.'

He looked blank. Staring dumbly with that tense smile. The photographer would have lined them up, made them pose for so long their muscles would have frozen. The groom's close family and friends, the wedding party alone. Dozens of photographs of the same people in the same positions, before they'd even had a glass of wine. No one ever looked natural at weddings.

'Mum, they know he took her.'

They knew. They knew it was him. Everything she knew was known by everyone. It was over. There was nothing she could add.

'It's Mr Webb. He's taught us since Year 7. And they're together.'

Mia's eyes were enormous. She looked stuck somewhere between disgust and wonder.

'What will happen to them now?'

Every element of her seemed alert, but she barely moved. Nothing so thrilling could ever have happened to anyone she'd ever known.

'Mum, will they bring Lily home? Will he be in trouble?' Her hand was now clamped permanently over her mouth. She talked through it, straight into her palm. Rachel wasn't sure why. It could be to stop herself saying something irretrievable, to keep her thoughts firmly in her head. Or it could be to stop anyone getting to her lips. Lips might suddenly seem more perilous than before.

'I don't know, darling. I don't know what will happen.' Rachel wasn't lying.

'Fuck.' Mia said the word more as incredulity than cursing. Rachel made no move to reprimand her. It seemed an entirely reasonable response. She had come up with little better herself.

'Yeah.' She exhaled slowly. 'Fuck.'

'Does this mean Lily's okay?'

Rachel could only shrug.

'Does this mean they know where they are? Where he's taken her?'

She gripped her hands together to stop them from visibly shaking.

'Will it all be okay now? Is she safe? Will she . . . will he . . .?' Mia trailed off. She seemed to run out of ways to ask. She seemed to have reached the end of her ability to comprehend it all. Rachel realised she was watching the moment it dawned on Mia what adults could do. The process was inevitable, but it was meant to take years, decades even. It was happening to Mia over the space of one ten o'clock news bulletin. They both stood still in the centre of the living room, the television blaring.

Rachel couldn't offer herself as a better grown-up. She'd missed her chance, missed the moment to absolve herself. She'd done nothing. She'd hugged the knowledge close, kept it only for herself. She'd abandoned Lily. Someone else had done it. Or technology had beaten her to it. They'd surely scoured the CCTV, and finally found a clear shot of his face. From then it would only have taken minutes to trace those tiny calibrations of eyebrow and nostril width to his NI number, his postcode. It didn't register in Rachel as relief. There was no flood of calm, just a different form of tension. She was indicted by her silence. She could have done the right thing. She hadn't imagined that this would feel worse.

4

His face in the paper didn't look handsome. They'd dug further into his social media accounts now, gone beyond the public profile images. Of course, they'd landed upon a picture where he looked cruellest: his stubble patchy and his hair hanging in sullen strands, his eyes dark and blank, his lips reduced to a thin line. The headlines blazed. *PERVERT TEACHER GROOMED MISSING GIRL. PHYSICS CREEP KIDNAP SHOCK.* Lily's picture had been hidden pages into the newspapers, but Mark's was smeared across every front page. It took no flicking, no print-stained fingers to find him. He was public property now. The papers remained uniformly po-faced about Lily. A decade or so before, they may have salivated over her, practically peering up her skirt, but it was different now. Things had happened, high-profile horrors that made any kind of titillation too repulsive. Puritanical dismay was all they could get away with. There were no pictures of Lily on blurred nights out, no underwear peeking above or below her dress. She was all innocence. It was Mark they could lick their lips over.

Rachel ran her hand across the printed picture of him, the way Mia had traced Lily's image. *Pervert teacher groomed missing girl*. Mark was eyeballing the camera, staring right down the lens like he was furious. Rachel searched the image for a face she recognised. This was a different man. This man was made up of dots, thousands of tiny dots that merged to form a whole. If she moved her face closer to the paper, he disintegrated, fractured to nothing. When she pulled her head back, the image made perfect eye contact.

'He looks rough.' Mia was looking over her shoulder. 'He doesn't look like Mr Webb . . .' She trailed off, staring at the pictures for a moment before seeming to decide something. 'It's disgusting.' Her voice was firmer now. 'He's so old.' She corrected herself. 'He's so much older than Lily. Think about it, his hands all over her.'

Rachel was thinking about it.

'Do you think he looked at all of us?' Mia's fingers were on the image, smudging the ink as if she was trying to get to him, to understand him. 'Was he just a creep?' She was already using the words from the headlines. 'It makes me feel gross.' Her hands now stroked her own arms in a gesture somewhere between cleansing and comfort. 'To think about what Lily's doing with him.'

*

Mark hadn't asked for her order; he'd just swung off the round-about into the drive-through and gone for the classic option. Big Macs, strawberry milkshakes, fries to share. There'd been no question that she'd take what he bought her. They'd eaten it from the ripped paper packaging, in his car parked near the woodlands. That rush of saliva the second before the first bite, the way the salt and sugar spliced together, each needing the other, the smack of gherkin. There was no better bite in the world.

She'd become suddenly ravenous. It had only been hours since lunch, but she'd taken another bite, far too big for her mouth, filling her from tooth to tongue, jamming her with bread and meat and cheese. The force of it was undeniable. Her synapses had fizzed at the mustard, the ketchup, the onion; no thought of the five hundred and sixty-three cal-ories she knew lay within.

Mark held one of the fries out to her, at the height of her mouth. She twisted her lips, tilted her chin to manoeuvre it in, then ate it right down until she was licking his salty fingers. The heavy scent of fried food filled the car. Without speaking, they clambered into the back. He unbuttoned her jeans one metal stud at a time. She could see blue denim, the flick of blonde hair, the faint blur of her own cheek.

He pushed her down against the full length of the back seat. The windows were wound low to let the breeze flow and, as they moved together, the sudden hot sound of siren burst in, insistent and terrible. They both froze, cramped in position, and not even the muscles of their faces moved. She could feel his heart race through the light jersey of his T-shirt, through his skin. He kept low, hiding her, keeping their heads beneath the level of the windows. The siren came closer, unrelentingly louder, and she half-expected it to slow, to wail right up to them, but it dashed by, past the entrance to the car park and down the road beyond. It didn't sound like a police car close up, but an ambulance, lumbering to someone's rescue. Mark didn't move, even when the car grew silent again, but stayed frozen in the moment, a grin spreading its way across his mouth.

'Alright, Miss. Miss! Do you have any comment?'

Having grown men call her 'Miss' felt humiliating. Rachel just walked.

'How well do you know Mark Webb?'

One television crew had felt intrusive only a few days before, but that Friday morning there were scores. The school was surrounded; the car park was so overtaken that staff members had to vie for spaces in the leafy side streets off the main road. The lanyards were no longer exclusively around the necks of young, stubbled men. The whole gamut was represented now: dozens of men charging around, an occasional impeccable female newscaster.

Rachel found herself speed-walking from her car to the door. The weather felt more aggressive than ever. The heat wasn't the main perpetrator; it was the glare of the sun. Even so many hours before midday, it had the power to redden her bare arms. It was working to physically harm her, to wreak permanent, deadly damage upon her skin. It was a hostile force she needed to protect herself from.

As soon as she entered the gates, cameras sprung up from every angle. Bug-eyed monsters that loomed towards her, seemingly of their own volition. And voices, insistent, coming from within them.

'Did you know Mr Webb well?'

'Did you suspect him at all?'

'Did he seem weird to you?'

'Was he a creep?'

Repeating voices with no logic. Rachel walked faster, her eyes fixed on the door. If she could get there she would be inside, away from the voices, the cameras, the questions, the violence of the sun.

There was still a clear hour before the pupils would start to arrive, if their parents allowed them to arrive that day. An email in the early hours had told the teachers to go straight to the staffroom. As vociferously as he liked to be called Graham, the head liked them to call the staffroom *The Hub*. He'd arranged for that name to be embossed onto a metal door sign. He intended for the room to become *a sort of open-forum, hot-desking space, to convene and collaborate*. He'd bought a gleaming chrome coffee machine and seemed to take it as a personal slight if they stirred Nescafé into their mugs. Rachel saw how he frowned at anything that retained the whiff of the municipal. He visibly cringed at the clank of the ancient photocopier, at the shirt buttons that strained across the paunch of Mr Donnelly from the music department.

There was nothing slick about The Hub when Rachel entered that morning. Everyone in it looked crumpled. No one was sitting down, as if it wasn't possible to relax that far. They just paced or leaned, or slumped against the furniture. It was no longer just the heat that made the place uncomfortable. The room was almost silent. Mouths kept opening to speak, but few sounds emerged. They all seemed too scared to articulate anything, unsure what their words might indicate. There was only the odd muttered outburst.

'It's just disgusting. Disgusting.' The tears over Lily's disappearance were now dry eyes of horror, disbelief. Hands covered mouths or raked through unbrushed hair.

'I just can't fathom that something like this could happen. Not here.'

Smatters of conversation started up around Rachel, as people tried to pick their way through the new information.

'Can you believe he's done it?'

'I don't know, he was always a slimy bastard.' Any closeness to Mark was denied, dismissed, as they wriggled themselves as far from association with him as possible. They were already beginning to turn on each other.

'You were in his department, didn't you see anything weird?'

'Did she hang around his room?'

'Of course not. Of course we didn't see anything.'

'You were her form tutor.' They were already using the past tense.

'What the hell's he gone and done?'

'How could he let it go that far?'

Mr Donnelly spoke under his breath. 'You know what the Year 10 girls can be like, though? They find make-up and short skirts all at the same time.'

Rachel could practically hear the room start, the heads jerk. The comment was given no more than a second of oxygen.

'No way.'

'Come on, that's not on.'

'Absolutely not, John.'

Rachel knew that back in the early years of John Donnelly's teaching career, comments like that would have been prolific. They may have prompted the odd tut, but nothing more. He'd have been met with sniggers, even a back slap. But the world had changed. Not a single teacher let themselves be seen to assent. Every head shook. Every voice made sure it clearly articulated disgust.

A gritty silence fell again. Cressida's voice was the one that broke it, thick with emotion. 'Not Lily. Lily's not like that. She's not. She's sweet. She's so innocent.'

Cressida looked at Rachel, as if urging her to agree. Instead, Rachel made tea. She made tea in every mug she could find, remembering as many people's preferences as possible, and inventing the rest. She filled her hands, gave herself an endeavour. Mug after chipped mug of builders' with milk and one, made from stale water that had bubbled for too long in the urn. Teabags pressed against the side, then piled up in sad heaps. The clink of teaspoon against ceramic. She handed them out, insisting that no one so much as walk across the room to get theirs. The minutes they'd all been in there seemed to have stretched out already into hours.

Rachel barely looked at anyone else, but then Gail was walking towards her, her neat grey bob as firm as ever. Gail, her fellow English teacher, suddenly rubbing Rachel's upper arm, as if to warm her.

'God, Rachel, this must be so wretched for you.'

Rachel's heart thudded, one single beat, nothing more. She could only stammer. 'Sorry . . . ?'

'Being so close to it all.'

'No. No. I mean, we're all close to it, I'm not . . .' Her throat closed to the air; no breath could eke in. Gail couldn't know. She'd have no glimpse of what Rachel had done, of what she hadn't done. Rachel gripped the mug in her fist so tightly it felt like the handle could rip from its roots.

'I mean with Mia being such friends with Lily.'

The mug slipped to the floor. Rachel couldn't move to clear it up, just watched as Gail rushed for napkins, dabbed the tea stain from the new blue carpet. No one knew what she had known. They didn't know how she'd sat silently, with the knowledge stewing inside her. They didn't know how she'd carried it around with her, feeling its heft in every moment.

Graham strode in at eight exactly. Rachel noticed he was straight-backed as ever, but there were creases in his suit. He must have been up since very early, or not slept at all. He didn't need to say anything for the room to turn to him. In the fluorescent lights, he looked ashen.

'Thank you for coming in. You've all heard the news. There is no point in going over it again.' He was brusquer than usual; he'd lost the matey pauses and hand steeples. Rachel preferred it.

'First of all, nothing is to be said to the press. Not a word. Not even if you think you are helping. We will issue a formal statement, but nothing more is to be said. I will deal with all press interaction.'

He stopped, swallowed, breathed, moved onto his next topic. There were no Blair hesitations now, no exhalations in the middle of phrases.

'We will hold an assembly for all students at nine am. It is mandatory. Make sure all your forms attend. No exceptions.'

He seemed to speak in bullet points.

'We're obviously in an incredibly difficult and unpleasant situation.'

No one even nodded.

'The school is already being watched very closely, and that isn't going to stop anytime soon. We are of course going to work with the police in any way that will help to return Lily safely home, but we're going to face intense scrutiny.'

It was so quiet that Rachel could hear the swallow of other throats.

'Parents send their children to us for six hours a day, most days of most weeks, and we have a duty of care over each and every one of them. This is going to be very challenging indeed. People will make judgements, terrible things will be said and written, we will be accused of every oversight, every folly in the book. But we must be seen to stay calm and professional. We must be honest, to acknowledge if we could have done more, and make changes accordingly. We must rise above it. We must carry on teaching. We have no option. The parents need to feel like they can absolutely trust us. The students need to feel safe.'

Mutters of approval came from the group, even the odd clap. He sounded like a leader for the first time Rachel could recall. He turned as if to leave, then swung back around.

'Also, I'm going to assume that none of you had any idea this was going on, but I advise you now – if you have anything to share, go to the police immediately. We will not be lenient if anyone has been protecting Mr Webb.'

No one was calling him Mark any more.

Rachel felt the blood flush her cheeks, felt the small of her back turn liquid. No one knew. No one would be examining her with particular interest. She didn't have to calibrate every feature. As Graham left, the room sparked to life. Their comments reduced to squawks in Rachel's head, a cacophony. Noise with no meaning. She closed her eyes against it.

A calm face came easily to Rachel, far more easily than to express what she was really thinking. There was no way to communicate that. There was no one she could possibly tell.

The mood in the room had become brave; Graham's speech had roused them to a consistent level of stoicism that enraged Rachel. She knew it was the only way to get through the next few days and weeks, but no one seemed furious enough. They should be inflamed; they should be calling Mark every name, every slur they knew; they should be screaming for some brutal form of rough justice; they should be hollering to lynch him, to string him up. What he'd done, what he was doing, was unforgivable, repulsive, it was against everything they stood for as educators. It blackened the reputation of all of them. Their fury was too tempered.

But they also seemed too harsh. Too quick to judge. No one had proved loyal enough to show empathy. He was their colleague, their comrade. They'd stood side by side with him as he faced the same stresses and tensions they all did, the same absurdly increased workload, the same eternally raised expectations, the same graphs and charts, the same bureaucracy, the same flaming hoops. And Mark stepped up more than anyone. Mark ran after-school science clubs two nights a week, sending water bottles flying through the air to demonstrate trajectory, determined to get the kids to grasp it, to master it, to seize that C grade at GCSE. Mark Webb was more dedicated than any of them. But no one would utter a word in his defence.

Rachel sat behind her concerned face, livid with every emotion that should be tearing around the room.

*

Rachel's phone rang seconds after the lunch bell. It never rang at school, and seemed so much louder than necessary. The trills screamed through the classroom, as feet still scuffled out of the door.

Tim already knew the developments. They'd talked briefly the night before. She'd updated him on the news, explained who Mark Webb was. But here was his name in digital letters on her flashing screen.

'Bloody hell, Rach, your school is all over the internet.'

He'd already known the facts, but they didn't appear to have registered until he'd seen them on Twitter. His concern had suddenly triggered.

'What a fucking creep! Totally unbelievable. Are you guys all okay?'

'Tim, we spoke about this. It's awful, but we're as okay as possible.' Rachel's words echoed around the empty classroom. Transatlantic calls seemed to demand a volume, a clarity that felt absurd as she paced around the desks.

'What a creep.'

That word, parroted from tabloids, was becoming sticky, unshakeable.

'What was he like, this Mark Webb?'

'I don't know him well. He's quiet. He seemed okay.'

'It's always the quiet ones, though, isn't it? That's what they say. Hiding all their twisted thoughts behind crap conversation.'

Tim was talking loudly too, not the corridor greetings he

usually kept to, not the stilted words from that Cincinnati business hotel. That hotel room twelve hours away, half a day of flight. So many months had gone by. He worked every weekend, trying to cut the time down, but it always expanded. Six months had turned to eight, and his return date was now stuck deep into autumn, those cold months Rachel could barely imagine.

'It's bloody horrible, though. Is Mi going to be safe in school?'

'Tim!' The note she hit on the exclamation was familiar. She'd reached it so many times throughout their marriage. 'Tim, it's not a conspiracy. There aren't packs of middle-aged men prowling the corridors, waiting to look up their skirts. We're not pimping them out. Everyone is horrified. *Horrified*. It's school. She's totally safe.'

Tim laughed; a big yelp of a laugh that jabbed Rachel's ear down the phone line. 'I'm sorry, I'm sorry. It's not funny. It's not. You just paint a vivid picture, Rach.'

Tim had always been swift to find the wit in every situation. His reactions were so animated, they could lighten anything, but the playful edge in his voice grated on Rachel. It wasn't over. It wasn't so distant that a joke was appropriate.

His voice changed. 'I'm sorry, love, that was really insensitive. It's just so hard to get my head around. This sort of thing doesn't happen. It must feel totally surreal.'

'It does. It's like a weird dream.'

'I can imagine, sweetheart.'

But Tim wasn't there; he couldn't possibly understand.

★

Mark could have used a grey Formica desk, like all the other teachers, but he'd chosen one with history. She'd felt the varnished grooves of its wood and wondered what else it had known. How many other hands had spread flat upon its surface? So many exercise books, salmon and slippery, equations scratched in biro, had piled on it, hundreds and hundreds of sheets of paper. Had anyone else been lifted onto it like they weighed nothing? Had anyone else looked at the ceiling lights from this angle, worried their legs were dangling foolishly? Was hers the first spine to run its full length?

The world had narrowed that afternoon. Just his breath and her breath, just the sound of no footsteps in the corridor, the click of his dry mouth. His whisper. 'I've imagined this so many times.' The tightness of his eyes was a challenge. The door might not be locked.

Sat at this desk, he had imagined her. Whilst his classes stumbled to calculate force by blending mass with acceleration, grappling with Newton's thoughts, his mind had been on her. The feel of her, the smell of her. She couldn't walk away, no matter who might knock on that door; she had to embody his thoughts. She took the lead, the way she imagined he'd have imagined, tugging at his tie, biting on her own lower lip, tilting her head to look up at him through her hair. Every noise made her tense, but his eyes were on her. She couldn't let the light in them snuff out, couldn't let the moment turn to ashes. She had to be his longing made flesh. Thighs bare on his wooden chair, shoulder blades pushed backwards, making her body into a parabola, a problem for him to solve. Her arms stretched to the full extent of the desk. Then, the realisation that she could accept sensations, that her body was a receptor as well as a transmitter. Her hair pooled on that thick varnish. Sensation after sensation, with no resistance. She'd let her head fall back against the grained wood.

As she walked down the corridor to her classroom, Rachel had to summon the swagger that usually came so easily. She forced her back to hold straight, her shoulders to sit low. She made the heels of her sandals click evenly as she strode. She managed to clear a gaggle of squawking Year 7 girls with no more than the raise of an eyebrow. She usually felt invincible in school. That day she had to force it, to mimic herself.

Three boys from the year above Mia were in the corridor ahead, blocking the way. Rachel had to consider how she would usually deal with the situation. She wasn't a young teacher, but she was the only one to wear a leather jacket all spring, a fur-hooded parka all winter; the only one who could comment on their taste in music. She channelled archness in school, a brittle humour that could put even the cockiest little upstart in his place. She rounded on the tallest boy in the group. He held a half-eaten doughnut from the canteen in his hand. It wasn't until he turned around that she saw who he was. He must have been in school for his final exam.

'Aaron.'

The other boys turned to her, nudging one another in the ribs, snickering. Aaron seemed taken aback that she knew his name, but only stared.

Rachel prepared her voice. 'Aaron Mitchell, could you kindly refrain from such public mastication?'

When Mark had pulled in and parked facing the water, it was the first time she'd seen the river properly. She was only faintly aware of it, lying on the edge of the town. He hadn't waited, but got out of the car, instantly tugging his socks and shoes off. She'd thought he'd wanted to paddle. The cold water would have lapped against their toes, licked up their ankles. The bottoms of their jeans would get damp – they'd have feet that were white under their socks on the journey home – but it would feel incredible. She untied her trainers, pushed her socks into them, then rolled up her skinny jeans, padding down the grass to the water's edge. She reached for his hand, but his hands were busy. He hadn't stopped at his socks, but had pulled his T-shirt off, his trousers, until he stood in the gloom wearing nothing but snug black jockey shorts. He'd looked to her to follow suit, nodding towards her in encouragement. She shook her head.

'Come on.'

'No way!'

It was dusk, nearing full darkness with every minute. It was ridiculous. They couldn't walk around naked so close to the main road. But he didn't look away. She couldn't say no to him, not when his eyes were on her. He didn't look away until she'd peeled off her jeans, her top. The cool air hit her flesh. It was still weeks before the real heat would come. She wanted to jiggle on the spot, keep her blood moving, rub her arms, warm herself, but she stayed still for him. He walked towards her, now entirely naked, black and white in the half-light, like a film, like a still from long ago. He grabbed her hand and walked them towards the edge of the water. The river widened at that patch, splayed out into a pool. It was pretty for picnics. Children watched for fishes and frogs. The edges were shallow, but the centre – only metres out – grew rapidly deep. Signs all around warned of it. *DANGER. STRONG CURRENTS. DEEP WATER.* Together, they took one step in. The water was so cold, she felt it as pain rather than wetness. They gasped at the sensation. It was early May, and the air was beginning to warm with each day that passed, but the water still held the memory of winter.

They inched their way in, torturing themselves. There was no quick dunk, no reckless splash; instead they savoured the feeling. She couldn't decide if she liked it or hated every second. She kept her arms high as they walked. Their eyes locked. His were wide – too wide, the whites bright in the dark. They stepped again, again, until the water was up to their knees. A stray wave flashed across the water, the wake from a lively fish or duck, and it lapped higher, into the soft, warm scoop at the back of her knees.

'Oh, God!'

'Isn't it incredible?' His hands clutched her fingers too hard. 'When have you ever felt like this? When has your body ever felt so alive?'

Mark strode forwards, taking long steps as if he didn't feel it at all. With her hand firmly in his grip, she had to keep pace. He wrenched her forwards. Every step seared, until their thighs were in the water, their waists. Her mouth gaped at the outrageous shock of the temperature on her groin. He didn't stop, so she didn't stop. The water crept up their torsos, covering her breasts. The water pooled into her bra, making it heavy and abrasive. She wished she'd left it on the grass with the rest of her things. The ground beneath their feet changed from solid earth to silt, grainy and shifting, and the water buoyed them up, so every step felt less firm. She forced her shoulders under the water, her eyes on Mark the whole time. They were together. It was their water. Once they were submerged, the sensation altered from one of temperature to something more textured. It wasn't painful, exactly, but a constant pressure. She tried to submit to it, to embrace the wildness, to let herself get drunk on the glorious intensity, and not think about her clothes on the grass verge or how they would ever get out safely.

'Rachel. I'm sorry. Can you talk for a bit?' Cressida was in the doorway before Rachel reached her classroom. Rachel wanted to be alone, with the door closed.

'Of course. Of course I can, is everything okay?'

Cressida tucked a wisp of hair behind her ear, seemed to bite her lips together from the inside. 'I just wanted to talk outside of the staffroom, you know?' Her expensive education was present in every word. She took every syllable right to its very end, letting the final sound trip off her tongue before starting the next.

They sat on adjacent desks. Sitting on the chairs meant for pupils always felt odd – too low, too cluttered – so they sat on top of the tables instead. Rachel's classroom was a sacred space. She spent a whole Sunday every holiday, and troubling amounts of her own money, to transform it. She'd wash away every foot scuff, every slump mark on the walls. She'd put pads on the metal chair legs so they wouldn't screech. She'd decorate the walls. Not with the Blu-tack other teachers used, not by spacing out some foolscap A4; Rachel hung frames and replaced the contents every term. This summer it was a poster of Sam West as Hamlet in 2001, troubled and stubbled and soulful, and a letterpress version of Anne Sexton's 'The Black Art'. She'd burned candles every morning until she was found out and forbidden to use matches in school. She liked the room to smell like sandalwood or amber. It should be a chapel of learning, and in those few minutes before every term began, those shimmering moments, it felt perfect – a place where literature could be set free from the dusty shelves of GCSE anthologies.

Rachel tucked one leg underneath her in a mime of relaxation; Cressida crossed hers at the ankle and let them swing. Up close, her eyes seemed paler and her ears glowed pink through her hair. Rachel had long feared Cressida wasn't tough enough even for their suburban comprehensive. Despite their healthy Ofsted report and limited discipline issues, her glassy consonants seemed too fragile.

'Is there anything wrong, Cress?' The nickname sounded foolish, but Rachel had the urge to calm her. Cressida still chewed on her own lips.

'I just . . . I wanted to ask you about Lily.'

Rachel stared at her. Cressida was surely too gauche to wield any weapon. This meek creature – who Rachel could scarcely imagine commanding a class to conjugate a single French verb – couldn't possibly have the knowledge to damage her.

'I worry that we – as a school, you know – could have done more.'

Rachel's reply was swift. 'What more could have possibly been done?'

Cressida suddenly crushed all her fingers into her eye sockets, as if trying to stop herself from crying. 'I just don't understand, Rachel. She is such a sweet girl, but he was always so lovely as well. I don't understand how this can have happened.'

Rachel could move again. She unhooked her legs and crossed to the desk Cressida sat on, placing a hand on her shoulder. 'Hey there, I know. I know it doesn't make any sense.'

'He was always so caring, so supportive. I can't bear the way they're portraying him on the news, but also around here. I can't stand the way people talk about him in school. They make him sound like a monster, and he's not. He's just not. He's kind.' Her mouth made sticky noises, gluey with the beginnings of tears. 'They just don't know him like I do.'

Rachel stiffened again. 'Don't they?'

'No, they don't. He was wonderful to me. He took me out for coffee when he could see I was struggling. He gave me such good advice about how to get the kids onside. He really opened up about how hard he'd found it at first, how tough he found his classes. I'm not sure I'd have got through last term without him.' She was practically blushing, confiding a treasured secret. 'We even went to the ballet together, in London. *The Nutcracker*. It was beautiful, Rachel. He knew I needed a treat, something to pick me up.'

Despite the heat, Rachel flashed cold.

'He's not the man they're making him out to be. He's not. He's truly lovely.'

Rachel inhaled. 'I'm sorry, Cressida, but to be honest, I just didn't know him that well.'

'Ms Collins, can we watch the rest of *P and P* today?'

'Please, Ms C, you know it's perfect revision.'

'And it's practically the end of term . . .'

Rachel gladly slid the DVD in, then settled at the back of the room whilst her Year 12 class watched the adaptation she'd seen so many times. She sat silently, facing in the direction of the television. The screen flickered, the images registering as stills rather than coherent scenes. Flashes of a few seconds each. *Girls flitting through the house, tying bonnets at their throats.* Cressida had come to her to confide. *Five girls trotting through the streets of Meryton.* Mark had sought Cressida out. They'd sat together, their bodies only inches apart in a darkened theatre. *Arch jibes being traded across a beautiful room.* Cressida, pale, insipid Cressida, with her soft cardigans and wispy hair. There were so many echoes of Lily. *A white muslin dress getting smattered with mud.* Mark had surely pursued others. There may be a string of seductions, a parade of vulnerable young women. There may be other stories, just waiting to emerge. Rachel's teeth were clenched.

She stood up, nearly knocking her chair to the ground. The nineteen students who made up her lower-sixth class were gripped by the screen, hopelessly in love with actors who were twice their age when the series was filmed nearly two decades ago. Their eyes were on the women in silk and men in uniform stepping through complex dance sequences. Their thoughts weren't on Rachel. They didn't notice her stand up, walk to the window. She needed to breathe, needed to feel cold against her skin. Rachel pressed her flaming cheek against the window's glass, exhaling, her breath making clouds that vanished instantly.

With the water up to her neck, with her shoulders fully submerged, she'd tried to enjoy it, tried to abandon herself to the sensations. She'd gripped her insides tighter, pushed her feet up from the silty ground and tilted onto her back. She'd let herself float. The water, so cold it felt almost solid, had shocked her scalp, searing the final patch of virgin skin. The last part of her was no longer dry. The top of her skull was at once wet and cold. The stab of pain down her spine felt glorious because he was watching her.

After searing seconds, she pushed her hands down, using the weight of the water to get back to standing. She was almost out of her depth, perching on tiptoes to keep her chin above the surface. It became alarmingly apparent that the water was not still, not a stagnant pool, but a living, flowing river. The current tugged at her legs as she stood, pushing her metres further down. It had grown so dark that she couldn't discern the edges of the water. Mark was further downstream now, fuzzy in the dim light. The current flung itself against her legs again, knocking her off balance. She kicked, feeling desperately for the silty bottom, unable to find it, her head under the surface for a second as she tried to stand. The water lapped into her mouth, her eyes; reeds brushed against her bare calves and she wanted to scream. Her whole body was covered in dirty, freezing water. There was no way out except through the silt and the mud, and it might not be possible to heave herself up the banks.

Then the water buffeted her again, and she was suddenly standing, firmly, in safe depth. He was taking in every reaction. She threw her arms up and out, letting the water buoy her weight so she floated to him, tethering herself to him with her legs, stroking the water from his cheeks, his eyebrows, kissing his filthy mouth. The cold stopped being the primary sensation in her body. With his skin against hers and his approval granted, she could nearly be carefree, nearly find the grime liberating and the dark only a thrill.

Rachel nibbled on a triangle of warmed pitta bread. She didn't dip. The homemade hummus sat in a ring of bright yellow oil and smelled thick with garlic. She'd hardly emptied a plate in over a week. The idea of eating had become repulsive. She felt lighter, less encumbered, as if her body was readying itself to flee at any moment.

The book group was scheduled for every fourth Friday night of the month, and Rachel had waited for the cancellation message to light her WhatsApp notifications, but it never arrived. So they gathered at Tina's house as the rota dictated. They took turns to host, providing the wine and nibbles that accompanied their conversation, shouldering the responsibility of selecting the next novel.

'I absolutely love this, Rach.' Samantha reached over and rubbed the material of Rachel's sequined shrug between her thumb and forefinger, grazing the skin of her shoulder. Rachel winced at her name's one abrasive syllable.

'Thanks. I wasn't sure. It's just impossible to know what to wear in this heat.' Rachel pulled the top away from her body to let a waft of cool air in.

'Your top is . . .' She struggled for the word, taking in the aquamarine halter, digging a little into Sam's neck: '. . . gorgeous.'

They treated it like a night out; dressing up and indulging in both food and drink in a way that would seem reckless otherwise. Tina was hosting, but it was Sam who carried the plates of antipasti in from the kitchen, who poured every glass of Pinot Noir. It was Sam who tapped the iPad to trigger Spotify, Sam who selected the young male singer-songwriter to croon along in the background. Rachel held her red wine in both hands, unable to sip without imagining the splash, the pooling carnage on Tina's silver-grey sofa, her dove-grey carpet.

Rachel had been part of the circle of mums for well over a decade, but never at the centre. Debbie, Sam and Tina had known each other far longer; since they were at school themselves. They had a lifetime in common. They'd never left their hometown. They'd joined the same NCT group when they fell pregnant – posing for pictures with distended bellies and wide grins – and it was inevitable their daughters would grow up together. They still knew the mothers who'd borne sons, but the connection was weaker.

Rachel had moved nearby just after Mia's first birthday. When Mia started playgroup, she'd immediately marched over to Ella and Lily, comparing the bored eyes and puffed lips of their plastic Bratz dolls, leaving Rachel no choice but to chat to their mothers. Mia's instant attachment to that gaggle of little girls meant that Rachel and Tim became automatic invitees to dinners, parties, barbecues. The other women couldn't have been more welcoming, but Rachel never fully relaxed. If they'd met under any other circumstances, they simply wouldn't have mixed. Their groups at school would have been dichotomous. They'd have seen Rachel's hair, her nails, her clothes, and baulked. But time had dissolved their differences, or Rachel had actively erased them with her marriage, her suburban home, a child at twenty-five. They were bound now by motherhood, and Rachel had been drafted into their gang. She so often found herself deferring to their tastes, their views, grateful to be included even when she didn't want to be there. Marianne was the only one she sought out.

The group was usually made up of five, but Debbie was absent as expected. With only four, the balance was thrown.

'So, what did we all think?' Sam held up her copy of the novel, a film tie-in edition with an actress festooned in purple lace on the cover. Last month had been Rachel's turn to host and she'd selected *Madame Bovary*. Their taste as a group usually sat in a pacier, modern space, but she remembered the book as a favourite from her youth and wanted to see how it landed now.

Tina spoke up first. 'Well, I quite liked it.'

'Yeah?' Sam prompted her to elaborate.

'I thought it was very interesting.' Tina shifted in her seat, sipped her wine, evidently had no more she wished to say.

Marianne took up the mantle. 'I found it almost unbearably

sad. This poor deluded woman who just seemed to make every decision the wrong way. I wanted to march into that book and shake some sense into her.' Marianne was older than the others, nearer fifty than forty. She'd clocked up over a decade in London before having Dominic.

Sam nodded, swallowing a mouthful of prosciutto, licking the fingers she'd held it in. 'Yep. Totally. I just wanted to tell her to appreciate what she had, and not get all stupid about some bloke. She throws away everything for nothing.' Sam bent the book back and forth as she spoke, taking her disgust out on the paper itself.

'I suppose she was just destroyed by her daydreams.' Marianne sat back.

Rachel waited for the silence to fall. She tried, in these gatherings, not to play the English teacher, not to correct them or lead the conversation, not to point out that they'd all read from different translations. She made sure she was the last to speak.

'I loved it. And, more specifically, I loved her. We all have an Emma Bovary inside us, don't we? I think the incredibly gruesome physicality of her demise shows so clearly how women are treated, especially women who try to—'

Sam cut her off. 'But she treats her husband like dirt. She only seems to like shopping and parties. Do you not think she's a bit of a bitch?'

Rachel smiled. 'Of course, but don't we all have that in us? The part of you that gets bored and just wants to experience something exciting?' Maybe they didn't. Maybe these women were not straining at the seams of their circumstances. Maybe their lives fitted them.

Sam pressed her lips together. 'Well, quite. But look where that gets people.'

It was almost a relief. They'd tried, but the pretence could end. The news had hung in the air like a fog. They had tried: they'd talked about the book and anything from that moment couldn't be called gossip.

'Debs must be feeling awful.' Tina spoke up again.

'Oh, God, she must.' Sam shook her head slowly. 'It makes you wonder, though, doesn't it, if they'd discussed this sort of thing enough?'

'I know what you mean. I talk to Abby all the time. You've got to keep your guard up around boys, I tell her. She has to come to me first, before anything goes too far. You can't trust them.' Tina sat up straighter as she talked.

'I mean, how on earth did she miss it?'

'She must have picked something up. Lily must have been behaving differently. She must have been.'

'I'd definitely know if something was up with Ella. Definitely.'

Rachel's glass of wine had vanished in easy mouthfuls. She enjoyed the feeling of it seeping through the flesh of her mouth, numbing her from the lips down. She closed her eyes. Would she know if Mia was plotting something; if it was her and not Lily? Did she know the inside of her daughter's head with such confidence? Before she opened her eyes, the glass was full and red again.

Sam was the first to mention the school.

'I still can't believe that something like this could happen at St Joe's, can you?' Sam glowed in her concern, her oblique involvement. Her Facebook updates had become hourly, uploading pictures of Lily and Ella together, snapshots where they were unambiguously close, the best of friends.

'Rachel. What has it been like? Is everyone shocked?'

Rachel had known it was coming. She felt the eyes of the group light upon her. They hadn't yet grilled her for staffroom gossip. She knew what she had to do. 'Of course! Of course they're shocked. It's been awful, to be honest. Really awful. No one knows what to do with themselves. The kids are freaked out, we're just doing what we can to keep things as normal as possible for them.'

Sam wasn't satisfied. 'But was it a shock that it was him? That it was Mark Webb. Did you have any suspicions?'

There was the meat of it. She had to stay steady. Rachel sipped from her glass, buying a few seconds as she swallowed, as she licked the residue from her lips. 'A total shock.'

'Really? There was nothing weird about him? Nothing that gave it away?' Tina was chiming in now. They weren't giving up.

'Not really, no. I didn't know him well. He was pretty quiet, always seemed very pleasant.' Rachel kept her voice firm.

Sam leaned forwards slightly. 'Well, there must have been *something* odd about him. We know now what he was doing.'

'We know he was grooming poor Lily the whole time, planning this all along.' Tina's eyes were wide. 'He's a monster.'

Sam agreed. 'Totally. It's disgusting. It's pathetic that he couldn't get someone his own age.'

Rachel had no more breath to exhale. Sam was louder now. 'What I don't understand is what on earth she saw in him.'

Tina leapt to agree. 'I know. It's not like he's even that good-looking. I don't get it. We met him on parents' evening, and he's just not the sort of man you really remember. He looked like a bit of a wimp to me. A bit wet.'

Sam was nodding. 'A bit of a creep.'

That word again. Rachel nodded slowly, biting down on her lower lip, hard enough to send a pulse through her whole body. She set her face, determined to look committed to the sentiment. She reached forward to spear a green olive from the platter on the coffee table, and lifted it to her mouth. Marianne caught her eye, but her features didn't move.

Sam spoke again, bold and clear. 'There must have been boys her age she fancied, or even boys in the sixth form. I have no idea why she'd go for him when there are younger lads around her who are far more attractive.'

Rachel put her cocktail stick down and used the silence to ask a question. 'Don't you remember, though? What it's like to fancy a boy?'

They turned to look at her, but no one spoke.

'Maybe it's not all that complicated. It's not about how good-looking he is, or how clever or how funny, or even how cool. There's always someone who can beat them on any of those grounds. He's amazing just because he's the boy you fancy. He's the one you chose. He's *your* boy.'

Sam interrupted. 'Isn't that exactly the point, Rachel? He isn't a boy, he's a grown man.'

'Exactly. It's inappropriate.' Tina's voice was lower.

'It's not like fancying someone your age at all.'

Rachel knew she had to stop, had to let them talk around her, but allowed herself one quiet comment. 'It is to her.'

Had they forgotten it, or never felt it in the first place? That energy might never have coursed through their veins. The Robs and Jasons and Simons they kept at home may never have sparked that feeling. Twenty-five years ago, Rachel would have dismissed the women sitting around that table as plain and dull, but they had grown into a solid web of support. It was their numbers she called to ask not only about the logistics of bowling parties and shopping trips, but to seek advice about fussy eating, sickness bugs, how to handle three teary nights in a row. They were invaluable. Her teenage self would never have understood, and Rachel sometimes mourned that clarity. The status she would have granted herself over them had all but dissolved, but she was still different. At least Rachel had some sense of what Lily was feeling.

'It's not really about attraction, though, is it?' Marianne spoke softly from her corner of the room. 'It's about power.'

Ethanol in her blood usually fortified Rachel for these occasions, gave her the strength to get through to ten o'clock, but now it was doing nothing but depleting her resources. It felt like slow poison. Rachel wished she could press her fingers against the tangled blue and green at her wrists and stop its progress through her body.

'He had power over her, and he abused it. It's as simple as that.'

Sam nodded, 'Yep. He abused it.'

'Lily is too young to give her consent. He's the perpetrator here. This is no love story.' Marianne's face was firm.

Suddenly, Tina emitted a strange noise. 'I'm sorry.' It was close to a sob. 'I just can't stop thinking about what might be happening to her.' The thought seemed to force her head backwards. 'I can't help worrying that she's frightened. That even if she wanted to go with him, she might not want to be there any more. She might have changed her mind.' Her chin pushed into her neck and concertinaed the flesh there into a series of folds that added years in seconds.

Sam was next to her by then, arms around her.

Tina sighed. 'Sorry. I don't want to bring us all down. It just upsets me.'

Rachel stood up. She wanted to get to the downstairs toilet, to be alone for a moment, to close her eyes and gather herself together. She wanted to be alone with the pearl-coloured tiles and the handwash that smelled of lemons or lavender. As soon as she started to walk, she felt her legs wobble. She felt suddenly untethered. She was aware of her shins hitting the coffee table, the sofa, of being moved against her will, but it wasn't until she was sitting back down that she realised she'd been caught. Caught in their capable mothers' arms, well trained for this sort of situation.

'Come here, Rach, love. Drink some of this. Come on now.' A glass of water was pressed into her grip, and warm hands wrapped around hers to lift it to her mouth. It was cool. If she kept her eyes closed, and it was just her and the water, she'd be okay. Then the glass was gone. She was pushed forward, and her arms were removed from her sequined shrug.

'You're better with this off now, darling, you must be over-heating.' Marianne's voice near her ear.

Rachel had enjoyed how she'd looked as she left the house. The sequins looked dressy enough for the occasion, but still edgy over her jeans, her faded T-shirt. Without it, she looked too casual next to these women in their satin tops. All she could smell was perfume; three different perfumes mingling together to form a floral fug.

Someone else leaned over, pressed the back of their hand against her forehead to see if she was burning up.

'I'm fine. Really, I'm absolutely fine, just got a bit dizzy. It's the heat.'

Their flesh was still pushed against hers. 'You poor thing. It really is too much for any of us to cope with.'

'I said to Jase, this is too much for us all; too much for the kids and too much for us.' Tina's voice was still wobbling.

'And you're right at the coalface, having to be in school every day.'

'I don't know how you do it, darling.'

Now Rachel was cooler, now she was sitting down, the arms around her felt genuinely comforting. It was days until arms would be around her again.

'And having known him, having worked with him, it must be awful.'

'I can't imagine how you must feel.'

Rachel swallowed. 'Thank you. Thank you so much.'

If they knew. If they knew that she'd failed to speak, that she'd abdicated her responsibility to Lily, to their daughters, their faces would hagger and harden. Over a decade of friendship would vanish in a heartbeat.

'Sweetheart, you just rest.'

'We'll look after you.'

They'd kissed in the freezing water, their blue lips locked onto each other. Their goose-fleshed bodies had tangled together, half desire, half necessity. The current felt stronger, more urgent, and she'd felt herself being tugged from him, the river urging her to come downstream, always downstream. It wouldn't be discouraged. She clung to Mark: he was taller; his feet had a better grounding in the silt; he'd be able to keep her safe. They were too far from the shallows where they'd paddled in, but he could get her to the far bank without panicking, without swallowing too much of the grimy water.

They could climb out and walk from there. It would be fine. It would be over. But the river kept on tugging and when Mark released his grip, she felt herself being torn away, out of his arms, out of her depth, at the mercy of the current. A shot of pure panic coursed through her.

She called to him. 'Please, I want to get out.'

He looked over to her. The cold was growing unbearable; it was weighing on her limbs, pressing on her lungs. She couldn't fake it any longer. The fear was urgent.

'Help, please, help me get out. I don't like it.' She was treading water as fast as she could, too scared to put her feet down in case she realised how far from the bottom they were. 'Please, I want to go back to the car.'

He stared right at her and smiled. She held her arms out to him, expecting him to catch them, to pull her towards him, to guide her to the edge with a firm grip. He didn't move.

They were dropped home in Marianne's people carrier. Rachel clambered out of the back seat, stood in her porchway, and waved them goodbye. She watched the sevenseater amble around the corner, but she didn't enter the house. She didn't go in to where Mia waited for her, watching television, or maybe lying in bed, bathed in her phone's glow until sleep took over. Instead, she bent down, unlaced her silver leather trainers and left them on the front step. It was finally dark, properly dark, not just the tail of endless dusk.

Rachel padded barefoot across her own garden to the lawn of the house next door. The grass felt luxurious between her toes. The gardens of the cul-de-sac were patchworked, sometimes separated by painted fences or neat hedges, sometimes flowing into each other, guarded by invisible borders. The grass in all of them was rich with nutrients, fed like a pet every weekend, mowed in contrasting stripes. Rachel walked across the garden of number six and cleared the hedge to number eight in one leap. It was as oppressively warm as in the daytime. She wished the sky would cloud over and rain so the dust would wash away.

It was after eleven, and downstairs lights were beginning to be flicked off; the lower halves of houses were being put to bed, and the upstairs were stuttering to life. Rachel knew all the people in all the houses: their names, their occupations, how many children they'd managed to have. She knew where they went on holiday, and when they got their houses valued. She'd seen inside so many of those rooms, seen the furniture and the wallpaper they'd chosen, how they'd transformed their kitchens and exactly how much it had cost. In the light of nothing but streetlamps, the red-brick exteriors were indistinguishable from each other. Without numbers, it would be impossible to recognise one as your own. Hundreds of neat boxes, all the same, each connected to pure, perfect broadband, so no one ever need be bored for a second ever again. She knew that in those upstairs there would be cursory kisses, and nighties despite the heat. Rachel found herself suppressing the desire to scream. She wanted to shout, just one great bark of sound that would wake the place up, just to see what would happen.

Rachel walked out of the cul-de-sac and onto the main road. Grit from the warm asphalt prickled her bare feet in a way that wasn't quite painful. At that time of night, there was hardly any traffic. Rachel stepped off the pavement and walked along the middle of the road. She kept her feet carefully within the boundaries of the central white lines, like a gymnast on a balance beam, taking step after step towards nothing clear. Pools of light gathered underneath each street-lamp she passed, fading to near-darkness at the furthest points between them. She walked that way for minutes, down the straight road – passing cul-de-sac after cul-de-sac – before a car's lights were suddenly on her, appearing without warning, abruptly close and sharp and real. Rachel leapt – two steps, three – to the kerb. She turned her face away, into the bushes that grew along the pavement. Her heart jittered. She held her breath until the car had driven by, until it was out of sight, out of earshot, and she could be sure the driver hadn't recognised her barefoot and alone in the night. A few more steps and she'd be there.

His mouth had been curled into a grin, but his words were flat. He'd grabbed both of her arms, securing her to him, so the river's current didn't tug her away. She didn't feel any safer.

'Don't be so fucking boring, Rachel.'

When she didn't respond, when she didn't throw her arms into the air and whoop with glee, or match his smile and laugh it off, when she froze in position and stared at him, the grin dropped.

'What are you doing?'

She couldn't read his face. The cold was gnawing, and her heart wouldn't calm. The dark was treacherous and, in that black river, the look on his face when he turned to her had seemed like nothing but disappointment.

'I thought I knew you.' His grip didn't lessen.

She knew she was supposed to be special, magical, not like any other woman of his age. She was supposed to have stayed wild. His expression was blurred. Ripples on the surface were lit by faraway streetlamps, but everything else fuzzed. They'd been wet for less than ten minutes, but it felt crushing. Everything was a shade of blue, as if every other colour had drained from the world. His face was so close she could feel his breath. She couldn't speak.

'I thought I knew what you were like.'

She wasn't supposed to see the danger. He moved them a few feet, dextrous in the water, able to shift it at his will. Nothing so fleeting as a wave could knock him off balance. His hands were on her arms, her neck, holding her face. They gave no warmth. He was looking right at her. His eyes reflected the moon, the streetlamps. His pupils flickered, back and forth, up and down, as if he was trying to locate her within her own head.

'Rachel. I thought we wanted the same things.' The drama in his voice neared despair.

Her face was between his hands, closed in his grip. In that dark, he looked betrayed. She'd reneged on a promise she hadn't realised she'd made. She was supposed to have behaved a certain way, made him feel a certain way. Their limbs were tangling in the water, grappling with each other to stay afloat. They were only metres from the bank, from the parked car, only minutes from her house, but it felt like wilderness, utterly remote from anywhere safe. She needed him to get her out. She tried to smile, tried to acquiesce to him, but there was more in his voice than disappointment.

'Why are you being like this?' He stood still. His hands too hard on her side, anchoring her in the freezing water.

She was always going to fail him. Forty years of existing made it inevitable. She couldn't erase them. He wanted real youth, not some middle-aged mimic. Not someone who had calcified into conformity. He wanted the real thing, and was furious with her for being false. He knew the risk of the real. He must have hoped he'd never have to seek it, hoped that Rachel would be enough. But she was terrified; she was pulling away; she was challenging him. It was more than disappointment.

'You're boring me, Rachel.' It had been a threat.

Mark's flat. That's where the road had led. It was no more than twenty minutes from her house, but she'd never walked there before. She'd only been inside a handful of times, but knew what sat behind the dark of that window. It was a one-bedroom flat in a converted industrial building that had kept the exposed brick, the wrought-iron window frames of its previous life. It was as urban as it was possible to be in that town. He wasn't in there. He hadn't been in there for well over a week, but other people had. There would be police footprints and fingerprints on everything. Everything he had gathered and collected in his forty-one years would have been ransacked to prove what a terrible person he was. They'd have been looking for the worst. They would have found almost nothing of Rachel. Her prints, her DNA, fibres from her jacket and shoes would be present, but nothing bigger, nothing visible to the naked eye.

Rachel reached down and, in the small patch of garden underneath Mark's window, found a pebble. It was smooth and perfect, nearly round, the sort of pretty thing a child might squirrel away. It felt cool in the soft of her palm. Rachel drew her hand back and threw the stone. In the fraction of time before it hit the window, a spasm of panic ripped through her as she realised that the window could shatter, and if it did the hours that followed would be excruciating; the conversations, the explanations. All because of a stone no bigger than an acorn. She could practically hear the smash, the clatter. But the window didn't break; the pebble just rebounded onto the shrubbery beneath.

The stone lay pointless and Rachel felt it as an anti-climax.

Despite the fear, she wanted to cause destruction, something that proved she'd been there. Something that proved she could have an impact. The stone she'd thrown now sat at the feet of a cerise rhododendron bush; lurid and flimsy. Rachel grabbed a handful of the bright petals and pulled them. Everything that had simmered in her, pulsed under the surface for so many hours, so many days, began to shift. Whole clusters came away easily, and she threw them into the dark air. They fell like confetti over her head. She ripped off more and more, flinging them behind her, carpeting the ground with pink. She tore at the shrub until it was naked of flowers, until only its thick leaves remained. She tugged at those. They came away, but it took far more effort. She opened her mouth as if to scream but didn't allow herself the noise. She mouthed obscenities into the air. *You fucking bastard. You fucking creep.* Nothing but ghosts of words to articulate her rage. *You bastard.* The words, even if screamed, would seem pathetic in the face of her fury. Her hands were red, sore with the strain; she had to push her feet against the shrub's trunk to gain enough traction. It wasn't enough. She wanted the whole bush to suffer. Kneeling in the dry mud, Rachel used her hands as shovels to dig into the soil, scooping clods of earth away, smashing her fingers against the meaty, fibrous roots, trying to get around them, beneath them, so she could leverage the whole beast. Memories of him flashed through her. The sweet hit of candyfloss in a far-flung fairground. The smooth wrapper of a stolen slab of toffee. The varnished wood of his desk. She gripped the branches and tugged with all her might, grunting with the effort, the frustration. The cold fear in that river. She yanked until her nails split and her fingers stubbed and her arms screamed. She was doing herself damage. But it was futile. The bush was anchored firmly, and all her raving hardly dented it. She flopped, filthy with soil, smeared with sap, to the ground, fully aware that if anyone saw her, if any resident of a ground-floor flat just happened to look out to investigate the noise, she'd seem nothing but a deranged middle-aged woman.

5

Rachel had kept a picture of Debbie Harry in the pocket of her coat for nearly five months. It only left when she transferred it to her handbag on days it was too warm for a jacket. White lines slashed through the image from where it had been folded and refolded. It had become floppy and curled from the damp of her grip. It was of Debbie Harry in the seventies, wearing almost nothing but a tight slogan T-shirt and a studded belt, her fingers stretched out towards the camera.

He'd handed it to her in the corridor. *She looks like you.* Pupils had bumped into them. Rachel had palmed the picture and kept on walking. There was something in the rise of Debbie Harry's chin, something in the slant of her eyes, that did recall Rachel's face. They did have the same lemon-blonde hair. Rachel's had once been messily natural, but now cost £120 and nearly two hours every eight weeks. Her vainest thoughts would have taken her to the comparison, but she'd never have voiced it. When she later protested, he was emphatic. *She looks like what I see when I look at you.*

There were so few mementos, so few fragments she'd managed to store from Mark. He sent almost no messages to her phone. He rarely dialled her number. He liked everything to be transient. He wrote notes that couldn't be traced back to his pen; he'd never given her a single gift. But he'd cut this picture from a magazine. She'd hoarded it like treasure.

Rachel had barely spoken to Mia since Wednesday. The house felt empty, even with them both in it. It seemed to goad her, flaunting its spare rooms, space for the children she didn't have, the husband who was so far away. The third bedroom had been reconfigured to form a study that none of them used.

Rachel paused in Mia's room before she came home, breathing it in. She needed to see inside Mia's physical world. Written in two-foot characters over Mia's bed were the three letters of her name, created by fabric stretched over thick cardboard and stapled into place. They'd made it together when she was twelve, taking a trip to Liberty to select the fabric, splashing out on dense prints. Rachel had been grateful for the brevity of the word. It hadn't been her first choice. Tim had pulled her back from more bohemian impulses, tracking away from Persephone and Foxglove to something good and solid. They'd found common ground in pop culture. In their mid-twenties, they'd both deemed Tarantino's Mia Wallace suitable inspiration. Rachel had encouraged her daughter to seek out the root of her name, but she'd never seemed the slightest bit intrigued.

Mia's desk was right-angled, every object on it placed carefully. Her homework diary, a copper Anglepoise lamp, a stapler, a ruler, three packs of chewing gum, a Moscow Mule cup full of black biros, a potted succulent. She was taking the first year of her GCSEs very seriously. She had always been a disciplined child. It made Rachel smile. Her daughter could seem so far away, and the moments when their characters aligned were joyful; the moments when Mia seemed to be made of fragments of Rachel, collected up and recast. She was proud of it. Proud and scared. Part of her willed Mia to shrug that trait off like an unwanted hand-me-down, the trait that left nothing unplanned, that nagged at the edges of everything. The trait that made so little *good enough*, that drove her to want control over things that should be left wild.

On the shelf above Mia's desk, there was a framed photograph. Her parents' wedding day. Rachel froze. It hadn't been there before. It was a photograph Mia couldn't possibly decipher. She couldn't know how significant it was to prop that framed 8" x 12" print against those books now. She couldn't know. Rachel steeled herself to look at it. It had been taken only months before the end of the century, when everything was Ray-Bans and grins. The day had been determinedly laid-back: sausages in rolls, bridesmaids in wellies, loose hair, mud and flowers, a live band. Tim was so tall and gentle, his arms around Rachel's waist, over the place where Mia would start to grow only weeks later. Rachel remembered dark lipstick, tumblers of bourbon and a dress that showed her clavicle. She never knew if the memories would have faded without those photographs. It sometimes felt as if she only recalled the moments when a camera had flashed. The minutes and hours between them had blurred. It was those stills that had stopped her hand, silenced her voice. Despite her concern for Lily, it was those pictures that meant she could do nothing to save her.

The heavy silver frame didn't suit the picture, totally misread its dishevelled charm. But Mia had curated it. She'd found the picture, bought the frame and placed it there deliberately.

One week after her last gathering, Mia had guests again. This time there were only two, Keira and Dominic, but Mia always took hosting seriously. She'd filled bowls with pretzels, with M&Ms, with blueberries, and strewn them casually on the floor of her bedroom. They had no plans but to loll there, picking at the snacks with lazy hands. Rachel occasionally refreshed their glasses with the sparkling elderflower Mia had insisted upon. She savoured those minutes in the room with them. She wanted to see Mia relaxed, to decode her actions. Each time she poured from the bottle, the girls nodded their approval, but Dominic voiced his.

'You spoil us, Ms Collins, but you know we love it.' There was always a twinkle of the wicked in his grin.

Mia lay across the bed with her ankles resting on Dominic's thighs. The three were intimate in a way Rachel could never quite fathom. With only an eighteen-month age gap, Keira and Dominic were close. Dominic was in Year 12, two school years above, but acted like their peer. He seemed to dote on the girls, fitting into the space in Mia's life where a sibling might be. Rachel often felt a pang that she and Tim hadn't managed a second child, that they'd left Mia stranded in a generation of her own, with no playmate, no ally. Rachel was grateful for Dominic. But she was curious about his willingness to spend his time with a younger group. She wondered if his devotion to Mia ran deeper, or if his preferences lay elsewhere, and the girls served as a safe space. She left the door ajar, so snatches of their conversation reached her own room.

Keira's voice was as loud as ever, but she relaxed around the other two. The enforced japery faded when the group was smaller. 'I know what Abby's message said, but even if we're allowed, I'm not really sure. It's only been a week since she went.'

Dominic seemed to agree. 'I know what you mean. It's crazy, but it feels sort of wrong. Does that even make sense?'

'Yeah. And I know Ella will be pissed off if we don't go tomorrow, and she's right, it's not like there's some predator out there, it's not like anyone's watching us, but it feels kind of weird.' Keira was softer now. 'Are you guys worried?'

There was a shuffling, as if they were changing position, moving around the room, maybe just reaching for the snack bowls. Dominic's voice was muffled. 'What do you mean?'

'I don't know. I think about whether Lily's having an okay time, whether she's alright.'

Rachel's breaths became shallow, her body rigid.

Dominic's response was swift. 'Lily wouldn't do anything she didn't want to.'

There was silence, then a snort, a sound that Rachel knew to be distinctly Mia. 'Why do we even care, though? It's ridiculous. I mean, she chose to go.'

There was a strain to her voice. Even across the hallway, Rachel could sense it. There was something she hadn't heard there before. Even in the days they'd feared the most for Lily, there wasn't that tension, that pitch that felt forced. Rachel sat, straight-backed, desperate to catch every sound, but could hear only the click of the door shutting.

Rachel lay on her bed. She tried to claw back some of the sleep she'd missed over the last week, but her eyelids wouldn't seal themselves shut. Whatever she thought of, however deliberately she breathed, she found herself staring at the wall. It had been weeks since she'd last shared a bed with Mark. Since she'd fought sleep rather than longed for it, since she'd abandoned herself to the exhaustion of the next day. She'd almost looked forward to the mid-afternoon slump that would remind her of what she'd been doing instead of resting.

Her skin had been cooler then; the warmth of his hands had been welcome. He'd lain her on her front, and traced the spaces between her moles, finding the fleshly constellations and whispering the names of each one as he drew it with his fingers. A messily sketched W. *Cassiopeia*. A jagged diamond. *Cepheus*. A curved swoop that took up the whole of her shoulder blades. *Draco*.

He'd leaned down and planted a series of kisses on the inked image that lived on the small of her back. That nook almost no one else ever saw, that never met the sun. The stubble from his chin had grazed the pale skin there, the series of jagged black lines. He'd smiled when he'd first seen her tattoo. Those radio pulses, transmissions from a distant spinning star. Joy Division's *Unknown Pleasures*. Rachel hated how famous it had become, hated anyone who wore the T-shirt. They were hers, those tortured wave forms that looked like a ragged heartbeat, a mythical mountain range. They'd meant the world to her when she was eighteen, years before tattoos in that spot were given derogatory connotations, years before jeans were worn so low the world could see the curve of a spine.

The thought of that night was both a balm and an irritant. It was tainted. Mark had memorised the names of the constellations and the shapes they formed. He had deliberately learned the dozens of ancient gods and creatures that shifted every day, entirely different from summer to winter. He'd learned them for a purpose. His fingers might have traced scores of backs, sketching the stars onto every one. Rachel's eyes wouldn't close.

★

When Rachel woke that Sunday morning, her WhatsApp icon bore a red circle. Her messages never came overnight. She clicked with barely woken fingers. It was from Tim – no words but a picture – a selfie of his face, smiling. He'd missed her calls the night before, the trills ringing into nowhere, four or five times before she gave up. This grinning snap was an apology.

Looking at him was always a jolt. The blond of his hair was growing redder with age, moving through auburn on its way to grey. In the weeks since he'd last been home, his stubble had grizzled to a near-beard. When they'd been young, he'd been known for his outdoorsy looks; white-tipped hair and sunburned cheekbones. His skin was sallow now, from too many hours at a screen. At every first glimpse, she registered him as old. Her eyes took seconds to accustom. Every three or four weeks, when he returned for the weekend, she'd be stunned, for a moment, at this middle-aged intruder. She wondered if his eyes went through the same shock.

The girls got ready in Mia's room. Mia, Keira, Ella and Abby. Lily remained tangible in her absence. They left the door open, letting their voices fill the whole house. Rachel couldn't face the farce of motherly pottering, so lay on the cool sheets of her bed. She could see them flit past the gap in her door; she could grasp the gist of what they were saying.

Ella had evidently convinced the others that a night out was far from inappropriate. Sam had corralled the parents. The request initially sent shockwaves. The mothers had messaged incessantly, debating whether cosseting them was the right approach. Sam made the case for the teenagers. It wasn't reasonable to punish them for Lily's choices. They deserved some fun; it had been a gruelling week for them all. Curfew had to be agreed upon. It only worked if they were all aligned. Ten was settled on for school nights and Sundays, eleven for Friday and Saturday. They were being fair. Rachel would rather have kept Mia at home, behind a locked door, all summer.

The girls turned iTunes up high, singing along with every trill of Taylor Swift. Keira's misgivings appeared to have been put to one side.

Ella's shouts rang through the house. 'You look amazing!'

'Shut up! I look like a thumb. You're the gorgeous one.'

'You're idiotic. But at least you can dance.'

'*Tu es la Reine dansante!*' Keira deepened her voice to parody, making the others laugh.

Rachel couldn't hear Mia's voice. She didn't join in with the others in their shrieks. Rachel couldn't decipher her silence; it could be a spasm of distress, or mute horror at what she knew about her mother. Rachel had tracked every possible route by which Mia could have uncovered her secrets. She played them over in her mind, feeling for the cracks where the truth could have seeped out. Mia couldn't know. The girls chimed together on the chorus, and surely Mia was singing too. It's impossible to sing if you're not happy. She couldn't sing if she knew. They were still fifteen, and it was still summer. Sam was right about that.

To Rachel, their music was as sugar-coated as their perfume; peppy girls rhyming about heartbreak or friendship or the sort of empowerment that's used to sell trainers. It seemed so tinny. Rachel closed her eyes against it. These girls were nudging sixteen but didn't adore a single man with a guitar. At their age, Rachel's whole firmament had been filled with heroes holding Gibson Les Pauls, Fenders. She used to pocket plectrums from the stage after gigs.

The process of getting ready took over an hour. The destination wasn't even a club or party, but a park where they were meeting some boys. Despite the venue, the girls worked to create their faces from scratch. New eyelashes were glued on. *Keep your mouth open, it stops you from blinking.* Nails were put under heat until their colours were permanent. They brushed on sharper cheekbones, finer noses. They teased hair that had already been dyed using techniques Rachel had only heard of. *Vernissage, balayage.* When she was that age, hair hung in whatever frizz or lank sheet nature had cursed you with; now they could all have armloads of tousled waves. They had the means to look however they wanted, but they all chose to look the same. Only the colours of their hair differed. Rachel thought back to the clumped mascara and Heather Shimmer lipstick she'd glopped on in her teens, and felt a wave of gratitude that her aim then had been to look cool rather than beautiful.

When they were done, it was hard to tell one from another. Mia no longer looked like Rachel's daughter; she no longer bore the stroppy pout her genes had gifted, or the eyes that always looked sleepy. Her face had been recarved to match that of her friends, any aberrant features contoured out with precise shadows and highlighter. Rachel wanted to grab a flannel and scrub it off, to get underneath and see her daughter's real skin, her real bone structure, the tiny movements of her face that might give away what she was thinking.

With the girls gone, the house echoed. Rachel paced the full length of the building, from kitchen to living room, upstairs and to the corners of every bedroom. She felt caged. She tried to work instead of rest, laying books and papers on the kitchen table. Every evening was vital. Restrictions on set texts were grasping harder, and demands for lesson plans would weigh on her all summer. She should be making a dent in the stack of marking that had built up, but she couldn't focus on those biroed words. After no more than fifteen minutes, she gave up. She needed to see where Mia was, how she was acting. She needed to see her daughter.

She packed supplies as if she was going on a road trip: a Tupperware container of fruit, a bottle of water that could sit in the cup holder. She practically tiptoed to the car, even though the girls would already have reached the park. She knew which stretch of green they had gone to. The roads were quiet, and Rachel killed her lights full minutes before she reached the destination. She knew where she could park the car to be able to see them. A thicket of trees hid the vehicle from sight. The dark was seeping in. It was the kind of summer dark that made you wait, but was all the lusher when it finally descended. If she was silent, if she turned the light of her phone face down, they would never know she was there.

They were exactly where she had expected. They were shrieking so loudly it was impossible to miss them, reaching the exact pitch that jabs the spine and makes eyes clench. They were gathered around a bench, facing the other direction. Rachel could see their hair glinting in the streetlamp above. The boys were apparently playing it cooler, leaving the girls to linger.

Rachel could see their mouths moving, but even with the window rolled down, the nuance of sound was lost in the air. Without words, it was easier to read them. Ella took her place at the front of every picture, made sure her laugh rose the highest. Keira contorted her body to emphasise her jokes. Abby rigged up her phone to play music and – as the boys emerged at the far side of the park – the girls danced.

They danced as if it was practised. They stood on the park bench and wove their bodies together. Their arms moved languidly, raised above their heads, undulating slowly as if they were in a dream or a memory, not a patch of scrub three hundred yards from a main road. Their hair looked as if the wind had styled it, not twenty minutes with a BaByliss. Maybe teenage girls always seem lyrical in the dusk, but Rachel couldn't look away. Mia glowed.

Her bodycon dress ended halfway down her thighs. Rachel

couldn't fathom where those legs could have come from. No logical combination of her and Tim could have produced those limbs. It made her smug. Whatever decisions she'd made along the way must have been the right ones. Those little capsules of folic acid she'd swallowed so religiously during pregnancy must be packed full of whatever pixie dust makes legs gleam. She must have breastfed so magnificently, her milk so sweet and creamy, that when Mia had suckled, she'd gained a gloss that would never fade. She must have spooned just the right quantity of pureed butternut squash into her infant's mouth for her to grow rich and golden. Through the tint of the windscreen glass, Mia looked to have the sort of insouciant beauty that usually indicates enormous wealth. She seemed to be in no distress. As she dropped to a sudden deep crouch, then slowly curled back up, Rachel felt outrageously proud.

In the dark of the car, hidden from their sight, Rachel allowed herself to relax. She eased each set of muscles. Yoga had given her the routine – feet then ankles then calves then thighs. She consciously softened each gripped tendon until her body slumped against the car's seat. Her mind wouldn't comply so readily, but cleared enough to let in a chink of light. She had spent so long not thinking of him. She'd blocked him out as best she could, but now he was all she could imagine. When she closed her eyes, Mark was all she could see. But his eyes were far away, and looking at someone else.

Suddenly, every muscle was tight again. The ferry they'd

caught had gone to Dunkirk. It had been all over the news. But she knew him. He wouldn't have gone north and settled over the border in some safe, unknown nook of Belgium. It wouldn't suit him at all. She knew he was in France. She knew how his mind worked. He'd have wanted Paris. All his treasured cultural references took him there. The girl with brutally short hair and the *Herald Tribune* T-shirt, the students in the spring of '68 with books in their back pockets and Molotov cocktails in their fists. Only Paris or New York would do. If New York had been nothing but a ferry ride away, he would have holed them up in Greenwich Village, eaten Chinese noodles from white cardboard cartons, and played Dylan on vinyl. But Paris was too crowded, too prominent. He'd need somewhere safer. Rachel knew exactly where they were.

In the months they'd spent together, they'd only gone away once. Mia had been invited to spend the weekend with Keira's family, and Rachel persuaded Mark to take a trip. She'd booked the tickets and insisted. One weekend in the first French town she could get flights to. Rouen. They'd indulged in every cliché over those two days, revelling in the fact that no one knew their faces.

He would have gone back there. He needed to play safe, to hide, and he would choose somewhere he already knew, whose lines of sight were familiar, whose geography he wouldn't have to pick up from scratch. His scientist's mind could be deeply pragmatic. He'd select the same apartment; the same building, the same rooms. He'd want to control every variable. He'd have remembered the name and the number.

Rachel's hands clutched the faux-leather of the car seat so tightly it hurt her fingers. Mark was in that town, just a few hours' drive from the ferry port, with its cobbled streets and beautiful buildings. He was there with Lily. Rachel watched Mia dancing, watched her golden thighs flowing from side to side. She watched her daughter, who seemed unaware of her mother's behaviour, of the danger that had crept so close to her. Mia knew nothing of the secret that could sever her family, that could rip away the security she'd been raised in. Mia flipped her hair, a darker blonde than her mother's, over one shoulder. Rachel knew where Lily and Mark were, but she also knew there wasn't a chance she'd tell.

Mark would have lifted her phone from her hands as soon as the ferry began to move. Lily's impulse would have been to grip it so hard he couldn't wrench it free, but Rachel knew she'd have let it slip to him. Then she'd have watched, stunned, at the arc from his hand into the black water. He'd have kept his own turned on for a few more days.

A false wind would have whipped at her hair. The movement of the boat would have made it trail behind her, streaming into his face, as bright as a ribbon. He'd have wanted to stand on the deck, to watch the shore recede behind them. The throb of the engine would have trembled Lily's legs from the feet up as the ferry moved away from the dock. Every second that passed would have moved her further away from anyone who knew her. She'd have felt a jolt, a flash, been seized by something close to panic. She'd have been primed to run inside, to clatter through those plastic chairs on that patterned carpet until she found a kind woman whose phone she could beg to borrow. She'd know her home phone number, her mum's mobile, by heart, but it would take a few attempts before she'd be able to dial it, be able to sob down the line when it connected. But then, his arm around her, close and firm despite the heat. She'd have softened against him. With every sway of the boat she'd have known he was becoming hers.

The sun's reflection on the water would have been startling. They'd have squinted to see, until the shore was just a line. Lily would have breathed it in, taking great gulps of air. There was no way back. The sea would have been the exact shade as the sky, and his lips would already taste of salt.

The message came on a slip of paper. An eager Year 7 with a thick fringe had trotted in during Monday-morning registration with the paper neatly folded, held in both of her hands. It was only one line, typed by Graham's assistant and printed out. No greeting, just a demand. It jumped out to Rachel in jolts. Ten-thirty. Deputy head's office. Police interview.

Rachel could hear her heels click as she walked down the corridor. Period-two lessons were underway, and it felt as if hers was the only body moving through the school. The dread of every student ever sent on that journey filled each one of her steps. The endless lengthening of the corridor, the weight of her legs, the lack of air. The numbness. At the end of that corridor were people who had the power to shatter every delicate thing she'd so diligently gathered. The relationships she'd nurtured. Both Tim and Mia could be lost. The knowledge that sat in the deputy head's office could rip it all away. A handful of words from their mouths is all it would take. And it was Mia's world they'd smash. The world Rachel had built for her. The world she'd never intended to put in peril. She couldn't rob her daughter of that stability, couldn't expose her to that pain. She couldn't change the blueprint of Mia's future relationships, hardwiring her for loss, teaching her that things end. She needed to preserve the purity. She needed to keep Mia close. She would do anything.

Rachel kept walking. Step after step. With hands that felt unattached to her wrists, she knocked on the door.

'Thank you for joining us, Ms Collins.' That name, in the mouth of an adult, always sounded strange. It was the name of the woman who did her job. The three syllables of her real surname were now lost for ever. Rachel smiled with closed lips. It wasn't the name she was born with, but it was the name she shared with Tim and Mia. It bound them together through the matching swirls of their signatures.

'Can you tell us your relationship to Mark Webb?'

'Colleagues. We were colleagues.'

'Yes. Of course. Did you get on well?' DC Redpath was back,

introducing herself as Moira, as if Rachel couldn't remember her; as if they hadn't drunk tea in her living room just over a week before, as if that afternoon might have faded from Rachel's mind. The young man with his notebook and questions was gone. It was serious now.

'He was always pleasant enough, I suppose.'

'Would you say you were friends?' Moira Redpath had rid her voice of the sing-song that had irritated Mia on Sunday afternoon. The Sunday afternoon that felt like another life. By that Monday morning, her tone was flat, official.

'We were acquaintances. We'd sometimes chat in the staffroom.'

'Did you ever see each other out of work?'

Rachel swallowed, kept her face still. 'Once or twice.'

'Just the two of you?'

'Yes, I think so.'

DC Scott sat silently, just like before. This time neither of them took notes, just listened. Rachel's voice was being captured by a black box in the middle of the desk. The room had been brightened for the occasion. There were flowers now, in a vase, as if the cameras outside could see in, as if the police would take it into consideration, gain a more positive impression of the school. The colours jarred Rachel's eyes.

'What would you do together, Rachel?' Her first name now. The affricate at the heart of the word clashed in Moira Redpath's mouth. It sounded like an accusation. Rachel's saliva was suddenly viscous.

'We attended a few school events. He drove me home once.'

What would they do together? She'd never find the right phrases to describe it.

Moira tucked her already-neat hair behind her ears, leaned forward a fraction more. 'Did you talk much?'

'He played music in the car, mainly.'

They'd been in the same school year. Their memories were perfectly aligned. They'd sat their A-levels in the same weeks of 1993, and she'd headed to Bristol as he'd driven to Manchester. The collections of CDs, vinyls, endless mixtapes they'd packed into the back of those different cars would have been almost identical. He made playlists for when she drove, and strung the songs together with impressive deftness; Sonic Youth album tracks nestling up against PJ Harvey, The Pixies, Pulp before they became popular, a smattering of Riot Grrrl. He loved those songs more than anyone she'd ever known. They would have dressed the same way as teenagers: clunky boots and faded T-shirts. They would have hated the same things. They would have faced the same darkness.

They'd spent so little time together. Stolen afternoons and evenings. Less than four months between their first and last kisses. Little more than one hundred days. Rachel could feel her heartbeat in her throat, her eardrums.

'Did you ever go to his house?'

'His flat? I waited outside in the car, and popped up with his bag once, but not really.' No hairs of hers would have been found in the fabric of his sofa, no skin cells would be picked up in his bathroom, in his bed. The place would be nearly clean of her intimate debris. She'd hardly spent any time there, but had clocked every detail. Every inch of that flat was curated. A whole bookshelf with only the spines that defined him. Penguin Modern Classics. Professionally framed film posters. *A Clockwork Orange*. *Pulp Fiction* in German. *Drei schwere Jungs und ein Flittchen*. Warhol prints. His beloved vinyl albums propped up by his record player. They'd never chopped vegetables in his kitchen, never drunk tea in his bed, or napped away a hangover on the sofa. That wasn't what it was like. They'd never gone out to a local café for brunch, never walked hand in hand down a nearby street. They'd never woken up together in his bed. Nothing adult, nothing ordinary. This tidy woman wouldn't understand.

'Did you ever notice anything unusual about his behaviour?' Everything. Everything about his behaviour was unusual. Moira wouldn't understand; she'd misread every moment, too bland to grasp the nuance, the beauty. Rachel drank from the flimsy plastic cup of water she'd been given.

'No, nothing unusual.'

'Did he ever talk to you about his pupils?'

Rachel swallowed the water, but her mouth remained arid. 'He was very passionate about his subject, about physics – he thought it had bad PR – and he worked very hard with the kids, especially the ones who were struggling. But he never mentioned particular pupils.'

'What about women, did he talk about girlfriends?'

Rachel forced her eyes to stay open, focused, steady. No spasm of thought could show. His hand on her thigh, his hands in her hair, his tongue down her spine. She made her face a mask, forced it to twist in disgust. 'No, never, we really weren't that close.'

There would be no trace. Mark would rarely talk on the phone. He hated to text, although Rachel wheedled him. He preferred the methods of spies, or lovers from old books: notes passed in corridors, indecipherable messages hidden in plain sight on the staff noticeboard, times and places scribbled on scraps left between pages fifty-six and fifty-seven of Pat Barker's *Regeneration* in the sixth-form library. There would be no way to connect them.

'And how did he behave around women?'

Rachel's back was stiff against the wooden chair. Their eyes on her seemed intrusive. They had been inside her home. Their lips had touched her mugs. She was pleased she'd given them the ones they never used.

'To be honest, I never saw him that way.' Rachel felt her vowels become more clipped, the words pushing to the front of her mouth, up against her teeth. She sat as straight as she could, her legs crossed at the ankles. She was a schoolteacher, an upstanding member of the community; she was beyond reproach. She could not be implicated. No one could ever know about her and Mark. No one could know how she was drawn to him, this man they all loathed, this man who had done something so terrible.

'Did Mr Webb ever confide in you about his feelings for Lily Dixon?'

'What on earth are you implying? Absolutely not. I knew nothing, nothing about any of this.' Her voice was painfully high, even to her own ears, and the chair screeched as she rose to her feet.

DC Scott spoke for the first time, crouching out of his seat, hands spread wide, physically calming the air. 'Sorry, Ms Collins. We are sorry. We have to ask, we're asking all of your colleagues the same thing. I know it is unpleasant, but it needs to be done.'

Rachel sat back down, face firm. 'Well, for the record, I think he is a monster, preying on that young girl, grooming her the whole time. It disgusts me that we were ever associated with each other. I think he is repulsive. He's a hideous man, running off with that child. I mean, it's pathetic he couldn't get someone his own age.'

Lunch was fish and chips. Rachel knew she needed substance, so went for the heavy offering despite the temperature. She carried her food to the table, the contents of her tray precarious, sliding dramatically to one side in her bloodless hands. She headed for the empty chair next to Graham. Since his inauguration, staff were encouraged to sit together in the school dining hall. It was an open replica of the high table from Graham's Cambridge college. Hiding away in The Hub was frowned upon now, and they were instead urged to sit side by side and be part of the school community as they ate.

'Rachel.' Graham smiled as she twisted into the seat next to him and leaned over to fill her Picardie glass with water from the metal jug. He didn't break from scanning the rows of pupils. They were all bolting down their chips so they could get outside, visibly uncomfortable in their uniforms. 'How's your day been? Have you spoken to the police again today? I know they are going department by department, starting with science, of course.' Graham didn't so much as incline his head towards hers. She had to assume the question was addressed to her.

'Yes. Earlier today. Pretty standard stuff.' A smile felt inappropriate.

There was a pause whilst Graham swallowed his mouthful of fish, his fork circling in the air to imply the action, and that she should wait. He speared each morsel with precision, but loaded his fork so heavily that every bite jammed his mouth.

'He's a fool if he doesn't know how this ends. There's only one conclusion. Only one. It's just a matter of time. Of where and of when. There is no ending to this that doesn't see him behind bars. We just need to tell them everything we can to hasten that.'

Rachel nodded.

The clang of cutlery against crockery hundreds of times over meant talking took effort. Rachel peeled the batter from her fish and ate only the flakes of white that lay inside. She could feel sweat beading in the crooks of her knees, the liquid squirm exacerbated by the plastic of her chair. Graham hadn't even loosened his tie.

'Rachel. I've been meaning to ask you.' He stopped as if the sentence was complete. Rachel had no choice but to ask. 'Yes?'

'I've been meaning to ask if . . .' He stood up without warning, his chair screeching backwards. 'Could whoever is whistling please desist immediately?' His voice cut through the canteen's tumult, freezing it in time. He waited for a few seconds in silence, then sat back down. 'Sorry, I just won't stand for low-level disruption. Not during all of this. So, I was wondering if you and your husband would like to come round for a spot of dinner.' Somehow the sentiment sounded old-fashioned. He didn't pause long enough for her to form a response.

'We'd – we being Mandy and I – we would love you to join us. Are you free on Friday?' He stopped to sip from his water glass, to lift another laden fork to his mouth, all the time facing directly forwards.

It was a night in late February, just as spring was beginning to take hold. That night they'd been the last two people in the staffroom and conversation had sparked. They'd barely spoken before. They'd never discovered the rich frequency they shared, never littered the room with curses that turned the air electric. His eyes had lit with the delight of having found her. Before that night, they'd meant nothing to each other. Before he strode across the room, held her arms without asking, pushed her backwards against the wall by the notice-board. Before he tugged the buttons of her shirt loose, and tossed the material on the floor, flicked the clasp of her bra with stunning dexterity. Before he crashed into her life and made everything, from the coffee machine to the stained carpet, sparkle. Before he'd greeted her the next morning with a detailed story about his weekend plans, in a voice only a smudge too loud. Before he'd let the pinkie of his right hand brush her arm as he reached over for a teaspoon and, in that brief touch, let her know it had all been real.

Mark would have bought the dye in advance. Rachel could picture him standing in Boots. He'd have compared the lids of the boxes at length, taking in the names – Mocha, Sienna, Brasilia – before selecting the one he could most imagine staining her blonde hair dark. He'd have put the thought in, sensitive to how she'd look, how she'd feel. The passage time of the ferry would be too short, and the detritus of the pro-cess too messy. So, he'd have stopped the hire car at a service station just outside Dunkirk. She'd have perched on the seat of a disabled toilet cubicle, waiting for him to knock three times on the door when it reached half past. Without her phone, time would be slippery.

The smell would have overwhelmed her, chemical fruitiness covering something dark and eggy. In the cubicle's mirror, Lily would have stared at her own face in dismay, smudges of inky dye around her ears and forehead. She'd have done a sloppy job, underestimating the skill needed to apply it evenly. She wouldn't be blonde any more. The second she'd squeezed the applicator and watched the claggy liquid hit her hair, she'd have been changed. The molecules of her hair would have been forever rejigged.

With no distractions, thirty minutes would drag. Rinsing would be near-impossible in the tiny sink, drying it under the electronic air would burn her scalp. Then, her hair would be dark. A flat, even raven with no nuance. It would have recalibrated her features, changing their dimensions, making her skin pinker, her eyes a paler blue. She'd worry that the process had taken something from her, robbed her of that golden glow. She'd fear opening the door, and seeing on his face that he hated the change he'd mandated.

Rachel watched the three-minute clip over and over on the tiny screen of her phone, parked outside the school. The car had become her sanctuary. It was the one place she could be alone, shut away from everything and everyone. She wished the windows were blackened. She watched the clip until she knew every word, every sigh, every slight movement. It had juddered and stuttered at first, the circle endlessly chasing its own tail whilst it buffered. Then it became smooth. She had to lean her head close to the screen to make out the details. Their faces were no bigger than fifty-pence pieces.

It felt shameful to watch it anywhere else, in front of anyone else, on a screen bigger than her hand. The car kept it private. At the beginning, after the police constable introduced them, there was the smash and clatter of cameras, so loud that nothing could be heard over it. They had to wait before they spoke. Their names were printed on signs that sat in front of them. Rachel had never asked their names. Rebecca and Eric Webb.

The idea of Mark having parents was absurd. He was surely born fully formed, born of the earth, self-sufficient and cynical. But here they were. They sat with their chairs close together, holding hands, faces firm as they spoke. His father held a piece of paper in his other hand, and read from it slowly.

'Mark. Wherever you are, we hope this reaches you and we hope you are well. So many people here are very eager to hear from you.' His mother nodded. They kept their heads straight, their chins up. Unlike Debbie and Gary, there was no crying, no pleading, no slump of sheer anguish. They were dignified. His mother was the sort of woman who would never allow herself to be referred to as Becky; always the three full syllables of Rebecca.

Rachel had never imagined meeting his parents. That was never the plan. There was no world in which she'd have wrapped expensive hand lotions and bottles of port to take up the M40 towards Congleton for Christmas. She'd never pictured kissing them on both cheeks when they met, had

177

never envisioned his mother finding a quiet moment in the kitchen to say how delighted they were, how he seemed so much happier than before, how they'd stopped worrying about him. That wasn't the sort of relationship they had. It was ridiculous that Mark even had a family.

Now they were in a room with Lily's parents, an awkward clutch of in-laws with neither of their children present. They all sat along one side of a table, but only Mark's father spoke. It had been almost a week since Rachel had seen Debbie, since she'd been lost to the police process. Rachel had sent short, supportive statements on a group WhatsApp. Debbie looked several pounds heavier, several years older.

They wouldn't have even said Rachel's name. Not one of them would know how close she was to the centre of their story. Not one of the conversations they were having with the police, with each other, would even have referred to her. His parents would have no idea who she was.

His father's voice was sonorous. 'Mark, Lily. We're not angry with you. We are here for you. We just need you to get in touch.' He was addressing Lily too. He was speaking to them both, as if they were a proper couple, as if Lily was a legitimate part of their family. It made sense. Mark seemed like less of a monster if it was real, if they were in love. That way, he wasn't a predator, just a man swept away by his feelings.

'You know that you need to make contact. Please do so by any means you wish.' Mark's mother said nothing, just sat, hands now carefully positioned in her lap, face stern, as though she was only disappointed. They both sat upright, both wore jackets, like they were attending a wedding. They couldn't have contrasted more with Debbie and Gary's crumpled jeans and jumpers.

At two minutes and forty-three seconds the camera zoomed in on their faces. Rachel paused it every time. Mark had his mother's colouring; black hair against pale skin, dark eyes. He had his father's straight nose. She pressed the arrowed circle to make the video play again.

The girls' routine didn't alter that Monday night. They got ready in Ella's bedroom, still taking a clear hour to replace their school faces. Rachel waited for them at the park. The boys rocked up around twenty minutes after the girls had settled around the same bench, the same streetlamp. That night, they pulled bottles from their bags; alcohol lifted from the back of parents' cabinets. Rachel didn't want to see it. It was a school night, and Mia was fifteen. She'd rather have looked away, but kept watching. Someone had to keep an eye on them, check they weren't going too far. She was their guardian now.

It was like a dumb show of teenage interaction. Rachel watched Mia drink from a bottle of vodka, rapid swigs that can barely have wet her lips. The music still blared, and the girls still danced when the mood took them. Bottles sat empty at their feet. A few of the boys lay down on the grass, sprawled as if it was far later, as if they'd drunk far more. Rachel sipped on her bottle of water in the dark, picking slimy wedges of mango between two fingers, wishing she'd thought to bring a fork. She had to lick her sticky fingers clean after every mouthful. Her eyes hardly left the dozen teenagers.

Even through the pane of glass, Rachel knew them well. She could see Ella making sure she was in the centre of which-ever cluster seemed most active. She could see the way Abby hung back, plaiting sections of her own hair, dyed a shade of red that nature could never create. The girls touched each other constantly; little pats as they walked by, arms around waists. Did they think of Lily? Did it sting that she'd chosen somewhere different, that she'd already outgrown this patch of grass?

As the others drifted away, Rachel saw Keira stand on the bench alone. She was the shortest, her body tight and hard like a gymnast. The others formed a huddle under the lamppost. Keira climbed, arms outstretched, onto the thin wood at the top of the bench. She got one foot on, then wobbled wildly before the other found its place. She stood there for a second, with the wind catching her curls enough to lift them. Rachel could imagine her eyes narrowing, her brown skin burnished in the light. For a moment, she wasn't quite real. Rachel willed Mia to look up, to clock her friend's feat, willed Dominic to see his sister. For a moment, Keira was silhouetted in the hazy twilight. She lifted her arms above her head in a mime of freedom. Then she fell.

There was barely a wobble; she just disappeared. She was

standing in her full glory, then was nowhere. She must have been on the ground – the gritty, grimy ground. She could have fallen straight onto the glass of their empty bottles; it could have torn right through her legs. Rachel gripped the steering wheel to stop herself slamming out of the car and running to help. She watched as the teenagers froze.

'Come on!' Rachel whispered to herself. 'Move. Do something.' Surely Dominic would rush to help his sister.

Ella got there first, screaming. The others leapt to action at her siren call, picking Keira up, sitting her on the bench. Rachel leaned forward in her seat. The darkness on Keira's bare calf could be shadow, or a thick trickle of blood. She should run over there and swab any wounds with antiseptic. But she could do nothing. Any action would reveal her. She was rooted to her car seat, unable to move, as she watched them stumble through a situation too adult for any of them to cope with.

They'd gone to a club in London. Not Central London, not Soho, but an alcove of Zone 2 that had felt far enough away from home to be safe. It was the sort of club that brands the back of your hand with an ink impression of its logo. It had been early, and they were the first people on a dance floor already fogged with artificial smoke. It was the sort of club they'd never have gone to when they were young. Groups of teenagers, scarcely old enough to be there, had clung to the edges of the room.

Mark had been aware of his audience. He danced like the music was following him, and that night it didn't miss a beat. The drum snapped just as his head turned, the bass guitar thwacked with every step he took. Rachel could see nothing but him. The club's theme was intended to be ironic; archly playing songs that were released when they were teenagers, but nothing could have felt less like a joke. They filled the floor with just their two bodies.

For the first songs, Rachel struggled. She tried to move her body the way she would have back then, the way Mark could, but every cell seemed to carry two decades of heaviness. Rachel could feel it drain her. It could have weighed her feet down altogether, but she couldn't let it. That was not who he wanted her to be. Locking eyes with him, forcing everything around them into a blur, she shed twenty years. She made the loose ease of her limbs return, the blithe freedom that let her jerk every joint without thought of how it could ache in the morning. She let her neck fall slack, as her core jolted, her hair whipping around her face. That was what he wanted, what he expected. Disappointing him wasn't an option.

Rachel focused on the twist and snap of Mark's feet, the flow of his arms that knew exactly where to go, that anticipated the crux of every lyric. He told every story through his limbs, he knew every word, and his eyes were narrowed and only on her. She tiptoed up against the warmth of him, and whispered right into his ear. *You are so cool.* She needed to keep him looking at her. In that crowded room of people young enough to be their children, she needed him to stay focused. The effort took every muscle of her body.

He kissed her the way they would have kissed when they were young. *You are so cool.* Back when their lives were too fierce to be captured by telephones, when they would never have interrupted a moment to upload, when there were too many sunsets for Instagram to possibly fathom. When she had stood on that stage in ripped tights and sung; when everyone's eyes had followed her. When she could make them scream by throwing one hand into the air. When she'd leaned so far back, microphone in her grip, that any mortal would have toppled. When people she'd never met had shouted her name. He hadn't known her then, but he looked at her like he could see it. Like he could remember. She'd had it in her to be magnificent. He was the only one who could see it glow through her suburban disguise.

It couldn't last. Ten songs in, twenty songs, the darkness began to make her tense. They couldn't see the faces that lined the room, not clearly. It would only take one pupil from their school to have ventured into London for the night, buoyed along by an older cousin, ID scratched from the internet, a thirty-five-minute train journey with pilfered alcohol. It would only take one pair of eyes to light on them and it could all unravel.

The following night, Tuesday, Dominic arrived before the other boys. When he was there, the girls danced freely, for once not seeming to think about what they looked like. They became a mass; Rachel couldn't quite see where each ended and began. Above them, there was a flock of starlings in their final frenzy of the night, swooping and diving in unison, turning the sky black. The streetlamp made halos of the stray hairs their styling couldn't tame. The sky streaked blue and purple, mottled and beautiful, and for a second those popular suburban girls were maenads.

Rachel could sense the change before she saw the boys. She loathed that moment. The weight of the air became apparent. The magic vanished and each girl became herself again. Their moves changed; their limbs stopped being free, and every action was now designed for impact. They slowed down; their backs arched dramatically; they writhed in unsubtle mimics of sex, their hands caressing their own hips, their fingers trailing down their own throats. Ella's shorts barely covered her underwear, riding up her rump as she bent over. Rachel sweated in the stifling heat of the car. She'd opened the window only a crack. The heat made having a body more than an afterthought. The mechanics of the flesh were so much more apparent. Her thighs stuck together beneath her dress, and she remembered the days when they'd held such power, when they'd been as tight and firm as shark's skin, when she'd wielded them like a weapon.

Mia and Aaron were the only distinct couple in the group. The other girls sometimes sat on boys' laps, but perched rather than leaned back, hopping off after only minutes. Mia and Aaron stood together all night. As he came into sight, she directed her dance at him. When he reached the bench, she stepped down. When he kissed Mia's forehead, his arms stayed around her waist. Rachel was shocked by the intimacy, the tenderness. Her daughter was in a grown-up hold with a man. She hadn't seen her parents interact that way in so long. She'd learned it elsewhere. His fingers were in her hair. There must be something gentle in those brutish fingers, because when Aaron was there, Mia picked him over her friends. She was closer to him than anyone. She was closer to him than to her own mother.

Dominic reached down to lift something from the ground. Daisies. He was weaving them together. It was too far to see, but Rachel knew he must be pushing his thumbnail into the flesh of each stalk, coaxing another through the fissure. He stood on the bench and placed the circle of flowers onto Mia's head, crowning her. She spun around, seemingly in delight, and the other girls raised their hands as if in joy. Through the dusk, Rachel could see that Aaron hadn't moved, hadn't reacted to the impromptu coronation. He turned his back on Dominic and kissed Mia so fully that she leaned back, and the daisy chain fell to the ground.

They'd have eaten out on that first night. Everyone would still be snug in the belief that Lily was safe elsewhere. As soon as they realised she was missing, restaurants would become unthinkably dangerous, but for that one night they could celebrate. There was a restaurant just below the apartment. Rachel knew Lily would apply her make-up carefully. Dark hair would make her face seem washed-out, so she'd pile on more pigment to pick out her features. Her cosmetic bag was one of the things they knew she'd packed. She'd powder her cheeks, darken her eyelids. She'd want to look sophisticated, so would employ parts of the palette she'd never dipped a brush into before. She'd want to look French. But she'd stroke on too many layers, making her eyes sooty and her lips jammy. She was too young to understand exactly how much less was more.

Mark would order wine, and when the waiter poured an inch into his glass he'd swirl it around, then sip, letting the liquid rest on his tongue, closing his eyes before nodding his approval. There would be no sugary drinks now. He would be all adult. Lily would see that his lips were already marked by the wine, a tinge of red where they met. It would be the first time Lily had held a whole, deep glass to herself. It would dry her throat rather than quench it, and she'd leave a greasy pout on the rim, not knowing about the surreptitious lick that was needed first.

He'd order for them both, trilling the rs and blurring the ts of each word so expertly, she'd think he was a god. *Confit de canard. Moules marinière. Terrine de campagne.* He'd linger his hand on hers across the table, and she wouldn't be able to breathe. In daylight, he could seem unremarkable, but in any kind of dark, he shone. The candlelight made him flicker; he was there, then lost to the dark, then back again.

He'd have grown the beginnings of facial hair in a bid to disguise his features. The candles wouldn't let anything stay still; their plates, glasses, both of their faces would constantly be in motion, bobbing and weaving as they spoke. She'd be holding her heavy cutlery, the linen napkin folded in her lap, trying to remember the things her mother had chastised her for at the table.

Pudding would be crème brûlée because she'd never tried it. He'd let her crack the sugar on top, then feed her creamy spoonfuls. Lust would announce itself to Lily as nausea. A feeling of her stomach being too full. A desire so intense she needed it outside her body, an unbearable twitch across her nose and mouth, the tightening of her throat, a flood of unwanted saliva. When he reached the pale mound over the table on his spoon she would focus on her own lips as they covered it. She'd close her eyes the way he had tasted the wine. With the spoon still in her mouth, she'd look at him, chin tilted down, eyes widening. The candle would gutter. In the blinking shadows, she wouldn't be able to see his face.

6

'So, I'd like to meet this Aaron.' Rachel immediately cursed her phrasing. The awkwardness didn't escape Mia. She was concocting her breakfast that Wednesday morning: a fashionable blend of yoghurt, overnight-soaked oats and the almond butter she'd made Rachel add to the shopping list. Her friends were dedicated to a young Instagram health star, and were refusing toast or cereal. They had to think about their slow-release proteins. Mia stopped mid-stir.

'What? "*This* Aaron." What even is that? No. No way.'

Rachel pulled her feet onto the chair, sipped from the mug she held with both hands. She made her voice rise, innocent. 'Why on earth not, Mia? You obviously like him, and I'm sure I'll like him too. I'm sure he's an incredibly charming young man.'

'No way. It's weird. We're just seeing each other. You don't need to meet him. It's not serious.'

'That's not what I've heard.'

Mia thudded her bowl on the kitchen table and sat down in one slumped movement. 'Oh my God. I hate that you're a teacher. I get no privacy whatsoever. It's a violation. Why can't you teach at a different school? What have you heard?'

'I've heard enough that I want to meet him.'

'You don't need to. You literally spend all day in the same building as him. This is ridiculous.'

Her voice was high now, nearly a whine.

Rachel didn't give up. 'I want to meet him properly. Here. For dinner.'

'Please, no. He won't want to come. It will be awful.'

'It will be perfectly lovely. We'll eat dinner, we'll talk. He'll be delighted to join us, I'm sure. His exams are over now, and I'm sure he has no plans for tomorrow night.'

'Dinner? That is hideous. No one has dinner.'

'We all have to eat, darling. Even Aaron. He can just eat here. With you and me.' Rachel watched as Mia bowed her head over the bowl of brown and white swirls. Her hair fell in a sheet, hiding her face. She pushed the conversation no further, just swallowed her hearty mush in stolid resignation.

The drama studio remained a cool sanctuary from the blazing days. Briony, Ross and Dominic still turned up twice a week at lunchtime, eager to hone scenes, to nail their lines. The show was not scheduled until the very end of term and, with over a fortnight to go, they seemed convinced that if Lily came back it could all go ahead, just as planned. She didn't have many lines: Laura Wingfield was rarely in scenes four and five; she was more talked about than talking. They could rehearse around her, and she could slot back in on her return. Rachel knew it was impossible, but let herself be buoyed by their conviction. It was foolish, but it would have been so much worse to recast, to cancel.

As the others moved through the scenes, Rachel held her highlighted copy of the play and read the lines Lily had memorised. It was unexpectedly humiliating. Dominic had dedicated himself to perfecting the walk, the timbre of a full-grown man. The rock back on his heels, the latticing of fingers, the frown. Briony was working hard to add several decades to her stature to play an already-faded belle. Rachel had to do the opposite. She had to shape her face, her voice, to become a convincing ingénue. She couldn't just say the lines; it wouldn't be fair. They were working so hard; she had to commit just as fully. But she couldn't capture the cadence. Lily could do it so well; when she spoke Laura's lines, she was all fragility. Every note Rachel struck felt false. She whispered so softly it became a lisp.

'I – don't suppose – you remember me – at all?' The lines sounded unbearably flirtatious. She was standing where Lily would stand, saying the words Lily had committed to memory, tilting her head the way Lily had tilted hers. But her eyes would never again feel untired. The skin would never hang more lightly from her bones; it would never tighten, no matter what unction she might massage into it before bed. She could never be Lily.

'Blue Roses!' Dominic usually touched Lily's hand on that line. It was the first time their characters made contact, a landmark for timid Laura. Lily's Laura had lit up every time. Dominic didn't touch this new, stand-in Laura, just hovered his hand over her wrist. Rachel imagined how the skin of his fingers would feel, hot and damp on her own dry hands. His awkwardness pushed the humiliation further. Rachel couldn't face the rest of the scene. She broke character.

'Okay. Okay. I think we're good from here. Why don't you guys go back over scene six? From when you go out onto the fire escape to the end. Try to get that dialogue really popping.'

She left them to work without her. As they began the scene, she walked across the studio, towards her own image in the dark of the door's glass. At first, she was just a fuzz: blonde hair, pale skin, black vest – she could have been almost anyone – but she watched herself growing smaller and sharper with every step.

He'd seem younger when he slept; the details of him would jump out to Lily. The lines around his eyes, between his eyebrows, would seem to melt, and his skin would become smooth, almost waxy. He'd look gentle. She'd want to count his eyelashes, his ribs. His skin would look paler than usual in the half-light, and she'd be able to see what he might have looked like ten years previously, twenty, when he was the same age as her, when she could have matched him month for month. She wouldn't touch him, wouldn't want to wake him, because the moment his eyes opened the years would race forward, and he'd be grown again. Instead, she'd sit awake and watch the roll of his eyeballs under his lids, the slow bulge as they lolled in their sockets. Mark's sleep was never broken.

Wednesday was the fourth night Rachel had followed the girls. They sat in the same place; she parked behind the same trees. Her concerns were beginning to fade. Mia didn't seem to be troubled. They were just kids making the most of the late sunset to pack in as much summer as possible. The music they listened to over these few months would ingrain itself into their souls for ever. Rachel didn't need to watch it happen. It wasn't her responsibility. But just one more night. One more night where she could watch them rather than the television, where she wasn't alone. When she watched the girls, she didn't have to think about anything else.

They followed their usual rituals. It was so predictable that Rachel let her eyes wander, picked a slice of apple from her Tupperware, sipped from her bottle. When she looked back, everything was askew.

The whole group were crowded together. They were usually draped around their little domain as if it was someone's bedroom. Rachel had never seen them in such a tight cluster. She sat up straighter in her seat, waiting to see what was in the centre of the huddle. A plume of smoke spiralled towards the streetlight. The boys occasionally posed with a Marlboro, but that wouldn't capture the attention of the others. This was not a cigarette. Rachel felt her heart thud. This was something new.

It was a moment she'd dreaded. All parents must. She knew it was naïve to hope that Mia would skate around the edges of that danger, but she had never expected to witness it. They remained bent over. Rachel knew it was hypocritical; if they really were smoking something other than tobacco in those Rizlas, she had no right to judge them. But there was a difference – the slivers of marijuana they'd acquired in her own youth were just tiny shards of pure nature. The stuff the kids got hold of now was nasty; tarry synthetics that could tie their brains in knots. She could see the orange-red tip burning in the dark as they sucked it one by one, the occasional flash of the Zippo as they had to relight.

Then came the water. One by one they swigged from a two-litre Evian bottle. Rachel felt her throat tighten. After their gulp of water, they walked away, thinning the huddle until Rachel could see more clearly. They were picking something up, swallowing it, then drinking from the ceremonial bottle. She was a teacher. She'd seen the pamphlets, watched the educational videos. She knew the pretty little drops they were sharing were not sweets. They'd be in pastel shades, like macarons, with tiny pictures miraculously carved into them: seahorses or the CND logo or Harry Potter's lightning bolt. She knew the names – *doves, molly, thizz*. She'd cringed during the inset day when the trainer had pronounced the words as if he'd cracked some eternal code. She was sure that teenagers would never use those terms, but is that what was sitting on their tongues, swooshing down their gullets, whirring their brains?

The distance made the movements blurred. Ella was, of course, the first of the girls. The boys had stayed low, but she tilted the bottle right back, making it dramatic, sending her dark hair halfway to the ground. Only Abby stood back, suddenly eager to search through her bag, away from the others. Rachel wanted to drive away, to unsee it. But if she turned the engine on, they'd see where she was sitting, watching them, stalking them from the bushes. She had to stay there. Mia would swallow a pill. If that was what was in the outstretched palm at the centre of the circle, she would swallow one. Rachel knew it as a fact. It wasn't just the pressure of the crowd. She'd have to prove to herself that she was whole. The slogans on Instagram never spoke of living a careful life, a life that avoided danger. They were all about taking risks. Mia would fight her natural caution. Lily wasn't there, but the gauntlet she'd thrown was. The others had to be every bit as wild. Rachel still knew Mia. She could still predict how her daughter would react, still understood how her mind worked.

Rachel knew she should march over, grab their arms, throw the pills to the ground, tell their parents. But she froze. She felt the tears growing heavier behind her eyes. She was trapped by her own machinations. She was stuck being their silent guardian. She knew it wasn't enough. It was outrageously irresponsible not to act. The other mothers, other teachers, would be horrified. They'd be over there now, calling everyone's parents, dashing to the hospital. Rachel just sat in her car and sipped from her own plastic bottle, staring at the same patch of scrubland she'd watched for so many days.

The girls were shrieking now – Ella, Keira, Mia – throwing their heads back as they laughed. They were stumbling, gripping each other in amplified hilarity. Rachel's heart hammered so loudly it had to be audible. They could be caught in the frenzy of a reckless stimulant. It could be smothering them, snuffing them from inside. Or they could just be laughing. That's what girls did. They might have swallowed pellets of gum, Tic Tacs, Smarties. It was too dark to see in the dusk. The girls danced around much like they had before, fingers in peace signs covering their faces, the dandelions of summer still catching in the breeze. Rachel wanted to see inside Mia's head and understand what was happening there.

Rachel was rigid behind the glass. She hit the steering wheel with the heel of her hand, letting out a guttural shout. She bucked like a toddler in a pushchair, desperate for any release. The seat belt she hadn't unclipped choked her neck. She was stuck in her response, harnessed in the airless cocoon of her car as the tumult of youth danced in front of her.

Rachel scooped the guts from a butternut squash, and slammed the masher into them. It always felt like a compromise. She'd rather have been pulping fluffy masses of potato than this sweeter, glossier, less satisfying mound, but she knew about fibre and calories and made her decisions accordingly. It could be a fight to keep her flesh compact. She played by the rules. She counted tablespoons and made willing sacrifices. The only time it became easy was when everything else was hard. Anxiety always went for her throat. She knew she was tense when swallowing became a trial; she could shed ten pounds over an Ofsted visit, and Tim's first month away had whittled her down to something fragile.

Rachel mashed hard, pounding the bottom of the bowl. Aaron was the first boy Mia had ever brought home, even if it was under sufferance. He was the first man to eat at their table in weeks. Mia was supposed to help – they were supposed to have driven to the supermarket that Thursday night, picked out the right ingredients and then cooked it together – but she'd pleaded homework, hunkered down in her room and left Rachel to sort the food alone. Rachel had stared at Mia, trying to discern a change, to see the impact of a drug on her daughter's face, her actions. Mia looked the same as ever. Rachel had spent considerably more than she'd intended to. She filled the fridge with covered plates, and readied the salmon to grill once Aaron arrived.

The food they'd be eating would be packed, bulging, into a string shopper, so French it almost seemed sarcastic. Mark would go to buy it alone. It would be too much of a risk for

Lily to be outside. Rachel knew the boulangerie he liked. He'd keep his head down, barely speaking, paying from the wads of euros in his pocket, aware all the time of people looking too hard at his face, of the CCTV cameras that leered down from every lamppost.

The bread he chose would be so fresh and warm that yeast would seem to rise from it in clouds. Rachel could imagine the smell. It would be a different substance altogether from the sliced white Lily was used to; that bread would seem dead compared to these breathing cobs. They wouldn't cut it, just rip great handfuls from the loaf, smearing each ragged chunk with butter. They would fill little glass beakers with red wine. They'd eat chocolate with seventy percent cocoa.

They'd drink fresh ground coffee in the morning, so rich it was nearly sweet, and eat meat sliced so thinly it was transparent on Lily's plate. These would be nothing like the meals she'd eat at home, nothing like that bland, sodium-saturated food, piled too high by her mother, laced with disappointment if she didn't finish it all. This was the food of adults. The little morsels would be an assault on Lily's virgin taste buds. The new flavours would jar her tongue, these deeper, darker notes stimulating parts of flesh that had lain dormant. *Do you like it?* He'd watch her, not looking away, waiting for the moment she swallowed.

When the plate was in front of him, Aaron turned his fork around and used it like a shovel, scooping up fish and mash and wilted spinach. It somehow looked butch rather than childish. The food seemed too small for him. Butternut squash had been the wrong call; Rachel realised she should have gone traditional, meat-heavy, substantial. He seemed too big for their table, taking up half the room with his bulk. Without Tim there for balance, he felt too male for their feminine home.

Mia had hurtled down the stairs when the doorbell rang, greeting Aaron like she hadn't seen him an hour previously at school. She clung to him, tended to him, showing him where to sit, hanging his coat up. Rachel pursed her lips into a smile. She played the role she'd rehearsed so well; calm, polite, curious. Every time she ventured a comment or question, Mia glared, but Rachel persisted, gaining the outline of where he lived and with whom. It became clear that Aaron had the kind of divorced parents who battled for his affection. He'd been indulged. Rachel clocked up the visible spend on his body. The Nike Flyknit trainers, so clearly outside of the school's regulations but worn along corridors every day. Two hundred pounds. The G-Star RAW jeans. Sixty, seventy pounds. The Diesel watch with three dials on the screen. Two hundred and fifty at least. He was impeccable, and it reeked of testosterone. Rachel tightened the grip on her knife, letting the urge to interrupt, to bark the question she most wanted to ask, abate.

Despite how flimsy it looked on his fork, Aaron ate Rachel's food with enthusiasm, loading his plate with more mash from the white bowl in the middle of the table. He wasn't the monosyllabic grunter she'd expected. Instead, he dominated the conversation, keeping up a steady commentary about finishing his exams, about the outrageous loss the school football team had suffered against St Christopher's, and his plans to apply to Loughborough next year. Rachel's mouth ached with the tightness of her grin. It was Mia who sat silently. She ran her fork through her mash as if she was grooming it, but rarely lifted a scrap to her mouth. She kept her gaze determinedly on Aaron, never acknowledging her mother.

So, this was Aaron. Rachel searched his face for the charm, the specific quality that had beguiled Mia. His hair was still nothing but stubbles with a flourish, but at this proximity, his eyes were startling. Rachel couldn't understand why she hadn't noticed them before. They were so blue they were nearly navy, against a spray of ink-black lashes. Could so much power reside in a space so small? Could those balls of aqueous fluid, that would take up no more than the very centre of a palm, really hold such sway?

When Aaron left the kitchen to use the downstairs toilet, Rachel raised her eyebrows at Mia; a query, a check-in. Mia looked away, then stood up and started to clear the plates. She clattered each one heavily into the sink. Rachel bit back the instinctive criticism. The plates should be rinsed, then stacked correctly in the dishwasher. They could chip in the sink. She sat still as Mia thumped them down one by one, raining cutlery onto the pile. Rachel closed her eyes to cool the simmering just under her skin. The tension was broken by Aaron's voice in the hallway.

'Is that you, Mrs Collins?' He was standing in the door of the toilet, pointing at a framed photograph.

Rachel flinched at the Mrs; at school she was firmly Ms. She'd allowed herself to hang the picture as an indulgence. It was of her on stage in the mid-nineties. She wore ripped tights and her skirt was riding high up her thighs. Her mouth was parted as she sang. The band – *Hurricane Gloria* – had never taken off, not properly, but they'd released an EP on an indie label, had played the major venues in London, even had a fanzine briefly created in their honour.

'Is that really you?' There was no doubt that it was. Her face hadn't changed so considerably. The face in the picture looked somewhere between her current self and Mia's. The question was a provocation.

'Yes, Aaron, it is. A long time ago. When I was very young.' Rachel stepped into the doorway to see it more closely, to remind herself of its contours.

Aaron reached his thick finger out and jabbed, his skin on the glass above the image of her waist, her stomach. It left a smudge. 'How young?'

Rachel was now fully in the tiny room with him. 'Nineteen, I suppose.' Over half her life ago. 'It was 1994. A hell of a year.'

He pushed the corners of his mouth down and nodded his approval. 'Hot.'

Rachel ground her molars together. Her pictured self was

not considerably older than he was now – a few years, nothing that couldn't be overlooked. She was suddenly on his level. He was assessing her as a peer, and casting his judgement. He was deciding if she was someone he would pursue. She'd framed the picture only months before as an act of wilful vanity; now it felt exposing.

Mia pushed past her mother to get to Aaron. She gripped his shoulder, pressed herself against him. All three of them were now crammed into a few feet of space – all four of them: Aaron, Mia and both Rachel's past and present selves. Her adult self and her teenage self. Mia leaned in towards the picture, mouth distorted.

'That? I hate that pathetic old picture. It just looks weird.'

He'd have occupied every gap in her mind for so many months. Every advert break, every quiet classroom moment would have been filled to bursting with thoughts of him, all the more solid because they couldn't be voiced. They had to be held inside her head. She couldn't doodle his name in the back of her folder, couldn't dissect their conversations with her friends. She couldn't talk to him without revealing her gaucheness. She wouldn't know how to prepare for him, and had no one to ask. The black underwear she had taken from her mother, that leotard made of lace, would feel tacky and foolish now they were together.

She'd be feeling blank in that bare French room, with nothing to say to him. There would be so little she knew that he didn't also know. The only pockets of information she'd be able to clutch at were banal; Kardashians, make-up, her friends. She'd wish she could scrub her brain of it all, and fill it instead with nourishing facts, stories he'd find fascinating. She hadn't even sat her GCSEs yet. She'd wish she could tell him something, explain something new to him. But there was nothing. Everything she'd accumulated would feel like dirty pennies. She'd hate how little she'd managed to lodge in her skull over fifteen years.

With no phone, she couldn't even google the references she missed, the names that went over her head. He'd have signed her into the apartment as Kim Gordon. Rachel knew how he thought. He wouldn't have risked Thurston Moore for himself, but would have opted for Steve Shelley, the drummer. Lily would have no idea. She'd only have the small bag of clothes she'd packed, only the knowledge she'd carried with her. She might never have heard a single Sonic Youth song.

They sat around the table in the garden, sipping on a non-alcoholic fruit punch that had seemed a good idea to Rachel in the supermarket. She'd thrown a handful of pomegranate seeds into each of the glasses of garish orange fizz and watched now as they lazily drifted to the surface when they'd garnered enough bubbles, then slid back down once they'd shed them. The sun was low in the sky, and it was still warm. It should have been relaxing, but Rachel couldn't ungrit her teeth. Tim would be home the following day. She wished she'd waited for him.

Aaron's hand sat now on Mia's leg, far too high up her thigh. He was taunting Rachel, pushing her, seeing when she'd crack. She'd watched every gesture between them. Aaron had been nothing but tender, his fingers on the back of Mia's hand, lightly at her waist, but it still seemed brutal.

'So, Rachel, what do you think about all the Lily stuff?'

Rachel breathed in, then out. He was in their back garden. She had invited him to dinner. It was reasonable for him to use her first name. 'I'm not sure what you mean, Aaron.'

'I mean, don't you think it's all a bit much?' He was leaning back in the wooden garden chair, taking up every inch of it and spreading beyond its confines. His voice had deepened, mimicking the modulation of adult conversation.

'A bit much? What, the reaction?'

'Yeah. I think it's all a bit ridiculous. I mean, she's nearly sixteen. In a few months, no one would care. She can make her own decisions.'

Mia, leaning towards Aaron, pushed right against the edge of her own chair, nodded. 'She's going to be sixteen in October. October the third. She's a Libra.'

Rachel sighed. A bird landed on the fence behind them, stood with its legs apart and squawked with gusto. The noise was alarmingly loud. Rachel turned to see it; small, brown and speckled, with its throat open and its beak wide. 'But it's only June.'

Mia seemed immediately riled. 'So, it's just about a couple of months, is that what all of this is? Three or four months?'

'To an extent, yes. She is a child. She can't legally give her consent, even if she'd very much like to. That isn't her choice, I'm afraid.'

'That's so stupid. What's meant to happen in that time? What's going to change so much about Lily that it would be okay then?'

Rachel paused. What magic did those months hold? What seismic alterations were set to take place across those ninety days? What in Lily's body or soul could grow so much? The law assumed some gift of learning would make her suddenly robust enough for the new experience, resiliant in a way that was previously impossible. Rachel felt her words blur. The bird squawked again. 'It's far more complicated than that.'

'Is it?'

'Yes, it is. Even if she had already turned sixteen, it wouldn't make a difference. Mr Webb is her teacher and he has abused that power.' Rachel's tongue felt clumsy in her mouth. 'He'd be in trouble either way.'

Aaron leaned forwards, placing his empty glass on the table. 'She's old enough to know what she wants, though. Shouldn't we respect that?'

'I don't think it's really about respect . . .'

Mia leapt in. 'I do. I think that's exactly what it's about.

Respect. And how adults constantly demand it, but aren't willing to give it to us.'

Rachel inhaled slowly. 'People are trying to protect Lily, to do what is best for her.'

Aaron's hands were on his knees, his elbows forming a cage. 'Doesn't she know what's best for her, though? Maybe they're really in love.'

Mia snorted.

Aaron turned to her. 'What? They might be. People do fall in love. It might be real. They might stay together.'

Mia looked stricken. 'Mum? Do you think that's true? Do you think they're in love?'

Rachel could barely lift her voice to be heard. 'I think they might think they are.'

Aaron didn't miss a beat. 'What's the difference?'

This boy, this man, this blue-eyed marauder who was more than likely fucking her daughter, more than likely feeding her poisonous hallucinogens, who would more than likely break her heart with one callous swipe, was sitting on her chair, drinking from her glasses, and lecturing her on love, lecturing her on Mark. He was filling all the space available to him and playing the role of the great romantic.

He didn't stop. 'If they think they're in love, isn't that exactly what love is? Shouldn't we respect that?'

Rachel wanted to leap from her seat and grab him by the meat of the back of his neck, then thud his dense head over and over against the red-brick wall of the kitchen, letting the bird's squawks disguise his shouts. 'No, Aaron. People are trying to protect Lily because she might be in danger. She is a child. She doesn't know her own mind. She's far out of her depth and she might not be safe.'

Mia's hand covered her mouth. 'What do you mean?' Her words were muffled. 'Could he be hurting her?'

Rachel couldn't hold back. 'It's a possibility we have to consider. She has been abducted.'

Aaron opened his mouth, but Rachel cut him off before the words formed. 'Legally, that's what this is, like it or not. She's been abducted, taken far away and we have no idea if she's being treated well.'

Mia's eyes were full, 'You don't think he'd hurt her, you don't think Mr Webb would do that?'

Rachel could see the distress contorting Mia's face, but couldn't calm herself. 'I very much hope not, but we can't rule it out.'

Then Tim was there, in their porch, less than an hour after Aaron had left. They hadn't expected him until Friday morning. He always messaged from the airport. The aeroplane emoji, then a house with a sloped roof, a chimney, a single window, to show he was on his way home. This time it was a surprise. He filled their doorway, all six foot one of him; his forearms, his shoulders, his grin. Mia squealed and kissed her father's whiskery cheeks, her hands around his neck, his arms tight on her waist, lifting her off the ground.

'You're here!'

'I wanted to see you.' It was his apology, for not being there before.

Rachel hung back. She let Mia think their real greeting would be private. She wanted to hold Tim, but the weight of space between them was too great. The surprise felt like a secret he'd kept from her. She didn't know how to hug him, didn't know where her kisses should be aimed. She felt like a different person from when they'd last touched.

'What did you get us?'

Tim had formed a habit of picking gifts from duty free. Expensive tokens grabbed from under bright airport lights. Treats they could never have afforded without his secondment. Rachel saw the amounts taken from their joint account. It was the material bonus of their situation. He bought make-up in black plastic cases that shut with a snap. Rachel had never owned those brands before. He'd buy them both the same products in the same colours, as if their lips, their eyes, the shades of their skin were interchangeable. The gifts were barely used. They suited neither of them. The carve of the lipsticks remained pristine, the palettes almost unsmudged. But Mia would clap her hands as she opened the white card-board bags and boxes, clutching the tissue-papered loot to her chest.

Graham's doorbell was resonant. It was a dong that belonged in a grand double-fronted Georgian, a noise that should be followed by a butler, a coat being taken, a drawing room, but his house was sweet rather than grand. A red-brick terrace, built for workers but now reserved for those who could take on the heft of the mortgage. A hanging basket to the right of the door was hectic with purple lobelia.

Tim hadn't flinched. Despite the flight, the time difference, the cruel sting of jet lag, he was eager to attend. Rachel was grateful. She'd longed for just a few hours of pleasant, adult conversation, of being a woman with her husband at her side and her life held firmly together. A few hours of a Friday night where she could forget. As they stood waiting, Tim's hand felt too warm on the small of her back, making it already damp with sweat. Rachel wanted to wriggle away, but didn't move.

Rachel had imagined Graham's house to be slick; minimal and high tech. He ran the school like a business, and she'd assumed his home life was every bit as pared-back. But when he opened the door, tea towel over his shoulder, the room behind him was cluttered. There were air kisses between them, handshakes, introductions. Graham settled Rachel and Tim on the sofa, and handed them both a glass of Moscato.

'It's our favourite. I hope you like it. It's a bit sweet for some people.'

Tim widened his eyes at Rachel after one sip. Rachel grimaced back, grateful for the moment of camaraderie.

Their living room was more like a study, with paper piled in stacks on every surface, *Guardian*s from weeks ago, folded the wrong way, with articles circled, or stuck with Post-it Notes.

Rachel tensed. Mark's face would be tucked in there, staring out into nothing. Books lined every wall, shelves bulging with novels, historical tomes, works that explored the art of pedagogy. Tim pulled out a hardback and flicked through it. Rachel leaned back on the sofa, as if she was relaxing. One wall was papered with a William Morris print: swirling leaves and flower fronds, speckled with tiny birds. Four or five unhung paintings were resting against the wall.

The room couldn't have been further from the sleekness she'd expected. Graham had launched his career at KPMG – and had flown high, according to staffroom gossip – but he'd left. He'd left that world and that salary to work in a school. He'd been fast-tracked from the history classroom to senior management, and had brought the spreadsheets, implemen-tation systems and efficiency with him, but he was still a man who had left the cold commerce of the city to work with teenagers. On the back of the sofa was a delicately woven antimacassar. Rachel hadn't seen one since she used to visit her grandparents' house. She sipped the cold, fruity wine and took in the smell of the books. She could breathe there.

Graham came back in, after a few minutes, holding his own glass. 'Sorry about that. Risotto's nearly done. Should be ready soon. Mandy's on her way down.' He opened a cabinet and pulled out a CD. He still used hard copies. Tim had linked all their speakers to Spotify. As he placed it in the player, Graham held it like it was fragile. Piano music Rachel didn't recognise tinkled out.

'Sorry, sorry. I'm Amanda, lovely to meet you both. Rachel, isn't it? And . . . ?'

'Tim.' They shook hands. Amanda's trousers and short-sleeved shirt made Rachel's dress feel frivolous. She smoothed it down as they spoke. Amanda introduced herself by describing her job. Finance director for a children's charity. Tim responded by outlining his current project.

'It's the creative side of IT, you know, where it gets strategic.'

'And you're in Ohio?'

Tim nodded, 'Cincinnati.' Rachel rested a hand on his arm, supportive.

'How are you finding it?'

Tim ran his fingers through his hair in mock-exasperation, then exhaled. 'Do you know, it's shameful, but I've not really seen the place. There's an Arby's I'm pretty well acquainted with, but that's about the best I can offer. It's an amazing city, though, so they tell me. It's the hometown of Steven Spielberg, as Cincinnatians brag at every opportunity. They're very proud of that. It is, of course, also the hometown of Charles Manson, but that gets mentioned a great deal less often.'

Amanda laughed in one single shout.

'Speaking of work, did you always want to be a teacher?' Graham's voice was soft. He leaned forward towards Rachel from his side of the sofa, his glass resting on his knee. He seemed genuinely curious.

'Gosh. No. No, not really. I've always loved books, loved

literature, but I thought I'd be something quite different, I think. Didn't we all?'

'Not me. I always wanted to do this. I got fairly substantially side-tracked, but a big part of me always knew. What did you imagine instead?'

Rachel paused.

'Don't play it down, Rach.' Tim reached over to take her hand in his. 'Rachel was going to be a rock star, she was in a pretty successful band.'

Amanda raised her eyebrows. 'Wow.'

It felt like betrayal. There was a time Tim would have known what not to say. There was a time he would have been on her side. All Rachel could think to do was nod.

They took their places at the wooden table by the kitchen window. Graham spooned great heaps of risotto onto earthenware plates. None of them had mentioned the situation at school. The topic was carefully avoided in the spirit of sophistication, of tact. Every time someone spoke, Rachel wondered if they would break the embargo.

Graham addressed Rachel again. 'Okay, if you had to pick one, which book would be your favourite?'

'Impossible.'

'You've got to.' He smiled at her. 'And just one.'

It had been so long since someone had asked her that question, Rachel had no ready-formed answer. *Jane Eyre* nearly tripped off her tongue for the sake of ease, but she stopped herself.

'Okay. Okay. Gun to my head, I'd have to say *Rebecca*.' As soon as she said it, she remembered it was Mark's mother's name.

'Ah! Fantastic. I haven't read that in years. I must do. And what a film! I always think of Olivier looming over Olivia de Havilland, no Joan Fontaine. Joan Fontaine. Wonderful stuff. Excellent choice. Anyone else?'

Amanda sighed. 'Graham, you know there's no point in asking me.' She placed her cutlery down. 'I know what you're going to say, but it's just who I am.' She looked at Tim. 'I just can't get along with fiction. I try, I really do, but it doesn't work for me. I read something like, I don't know, "Kevin walked up the stairs", and I just want to shout, "No he didn't!" There are no stairs. There is no Kevin.' She threw her hands in the air. 'It's all a ruse.' Her small body took up so much room.

Tim shook his head. 'To be honest, I've read almost nothing since my teenage Terry Pratchett phase.'

Amanda laughed. 'Who has time, you know, when you've been at work all day?'

Graham put his hand on her arm and rubbed slightly. 'I think you just have to make time.'

Rachel felt her mouth form a grin. It was an act that both men required of her. The room demanded it. She wondered what Mark's eyes would see if he looked at her now, if he'd recognise her. If that's why he was so far away.

'And what about you?' Rachel turned to Graham. 'You have to pick too. That's only fair.'

'Gosh.' Graham latticed his fingers and stretched his arms in thought. The action caught the top of Rachel's glass and sent pools of the perfumed wine fizzing over the table, spilling into the food, the wood. Rachel leapt up to stop it from dripping onto her, but wasn't fast enough. The wine poured onto the skirt of her dress, turning it from green to black, from silk to Lycra, making it cling to her thighs. Graham grabbed a stack of paper napkins to stem its course, then they all tried to dab the table dry, loading the napkins into a sodden heap.

'Oh, God. Sorry. I'm so sorry. Your dress! Will it be okay? I can be so clumsy.'

'It's fine. I'm fine.' Rachel held the material away from her skin.

Amanda stared at her, eyes moving up and down the dress. 'It's hot tonight, it'll dry. You'll live.'

'I'm so sorry.'

There was something sweet about Graham's panic. He seemed to be in constant battle with himself. It appeared to take enormous endeavour to conceal his natural ungainliness. His taste could be erudite, his words could be elegant, but he was ultimately betrayed by that lumbering body.

He carved out glops of homemade tiramisu, and Rachel was thankful for the hit of sugar. She filled herself with sticky mouthfuls, around that wooden table with her husband and her boss. The Moscato didn't seem to do what alcohol is supposed to. It barely made a dent. Rachel could feel her energy flagging, and accepted the offer of coffee. She knew from school there was no chance it would be from a jar. Graham went to the freezer and pulled out a folded foil bag, then scooped three servings of it into a gleaming cafetière, using a knife to even out each measure. There were flickers of precision, but in his crowded home, surrounded by the things he loved, there was also something gentler. He plunged the cafetière with such care, inching it down, never shocking the coffee. Rachel felt the caffeine begin to revive her.

Mark would sometimes come back with more than food. He'd have bought her a new nightgown, white cotton like a French girl would wear. Her pink Primark pyjamas just wouldn't fit the scene. Rachel knew that room. The bed was made up with white sheets, blankets and no duvet, there were wooden shutters at the window. The furniture was ramshackle: café chairs with frayed lattice work, a table with well-worn wood. It was basic, almost scruffy, but Lily would feel like she was on a film set. She'd let the nightie ride up her thighs as she sprawled across the sheets with her dark-dyed hair. Her skin would be featureless from sleep, her hair tangled from the pillow. She'd bite down on her lower lip. He'd look at her with his eyes slightly watery, like it upset him.

When she'd strip to her underwear and lie on the gritty slats of their tiny balcony to catch the sun, he'd become tense at first, edgy at the clatter of the white-painted wood. Other windows could see into their room. It was too dangerous. But he wouldn't wrench her back into the shadows, he'd watch in wonder. She'd turn over every half hour, wanting her skin to flush evenly, suddenly aware of her new power, learning how to wield it. She'd let him, eventually, join her out there, kissing the parts of her the sun didn't touch. He'd emit something guttural, half desire, half self-censure at the corniness of it all. He'd be infuriated with his inability to resist.

He'd come back with a red dress. It would be a size too small, and she'd be mortified by her own flesh, but he'd paint lipstick onto her mouth, right from the bullet, turning her face this way and that, smudging the red with his thumb. He'd play songs from the radio in the kitchen, and they'd drink whisky and dance on the balcony, where anyone could see them. The risk would become all thrill. He'd be in full view, kissing his teenage baby in the heat of the sun, the whip of the wind, above every downtrodden concern, miles high, elevated from everyday bleakness. That room would be no domestic sanctuary. They were no longer in suburbia. They were in the heart of a busy tourist city, dancing in the sky as everyone scurried beneath them. Her lips, her eyelashes, the hemline of her dress. He couldn't do it without her. Without her he'd be a sad single man, drinking alone in a town he didn't know. With her, he was all protagonist.

She'd be miming his steps as they danced to his songs. It wouldn't be the sort of dancing she'd done with her friends; the red dress was too tight for the writhing they favoured. She'd wonder what they'd make of this dance. With no phone, there'd be no way to gauge their jealousy, their condemnation.

There'd be no way for them to snipe their throwaway criticism. *Fail. Awkward*. This would be hers and hers alone. It was something they would never understand.

Washing her hands, Rachel examined her face in Graham and Amanda's mirrored bathroom cabinet, her cheeks pink from the heat or the wine, or the brandy they'd moved onto after pudding. She opened the cabinet. It was full – boxes, blister packs, jars – abundantly full. A single bottle of aftershave sat at the front, an old-fashioned bottle with a round glass stopper and a grey ribbon at its neck. Rachel opened it and touched it to her wrist. It smelled like leather, trees, spices. It smelled like a grown-up man. The sort of man who desired a woman. The sort of man who sat with his arm draped around his wife's shoulders. A man who indulged his benign desires: bagels thick with cream cheese, steaks that oozed to the cut, goblets brim-full with Barolo. Rachel pressed the stopper to her neck, letting a little of the liquid drop into the dip at the bottom of her throat.

She'd been away for nearly too long to be polite. She needed to get back. Back to those pleasant adults with their light conversation. Rachel opened the door and hurried down the stairs too quickly. She could hear Tim's laugh echo from the living room. As she turned the corner, Graham was on his way from the kitchen, and they bumped into each other. Rachel reached out to stop herself from stumbling. Her hands against his chest, his arms instinctively catching her. They were suddenly so close they could breathe each other in. He'd be able to smell his own scent on her skin. They smiled at the mishap. His chest was solid, and Rachel felt grateful for the substance. It seemed, for a second, to anchor her to the world.

Tim smelled unfamiliar. Back in their bed, she inhaled the sharp scent of stranger. The shower gel from that Midwest business hotel lingered on his skin, holding some mix of citrus and sandalwood her nose didn't know. She could remember when they'd sprayed from the same opaque glass bottle, when their pulse points had matched.

Rachel felt her chin tilt, as if trying to seduce this man. His eyes were easier to catch in person. She leaned in and kissed the mouth that looked so much like Mia's. She did it for Mia. For her marriage. This man was her husband, the flesh of her flesh. It was an act of devotion. She traced his face with her fingers. The crags were all new. She only knew the soft-skinned man who made her laugh. She closed her eyes to conjure him, but all she could summon was Mark. Tim's body was nothing like Mark's. He had none of Mark's slinky angularity. Mark's stomach muscles had been tight, he'd borne scooped hollows at his collar. He was the kind of lean that took effort; that flaunted the discomfort he'd withstood.

Rachel wasn't supposed to think of him. It was meant to be no more than a fun distraction, a boost that made it easier to meet her own eyes in the mirror. It was wild, fleeting, reckless. It was a teenage dream. It wasn't her, but the adolescent in her. But he was still there. The ghost of him flickering in the edges of the room, luminous even in the dark; the smell of him, the warmth of him hovering above her. He infected everything. Her blood might never be clean of him. It took seven years, they said, for a body's cells to regenerate entirely, but he would surely cling longer.

As she moved with Tim, Mark's shadow darkened the room. As she kissed her husband's neck, as her hands gripped his shoulders, tugged at his hair, his was always a body she had betrayed. Her body had been his for so long. Her kisses were sticky with guilt; every caress covered a lie. Her body was taut with secrets, with everything she'd locked up so tight it could never squeeze out.

It was surely the smell that was new to Lily. The deepness of male scent, when it is not hidden. Teenage boys smelled of so many things – layers of synthetic scent, sprayed on to avoid the shameful smell of themselves. Mark smelled of man. It might be too much for her. The salt of him, the rich umami Rachel knew so well on the back of her tongue. Her mouth dry, then the gush of saliva when she most needed it. He must be able to hear the blood sluicing through each chamber of her heart.

Lily would curse herself for not racking up more experience when she'd had the chance, wishing back those nights at parties when she'd faced advances, but demurred. She could have been more prepared for when it mattered. She'd try to dredge back memories from films, the man looming, all shoulders and sinews, the woman's mouth open, her jaw slack then tight, but would only have smudgy recollections to go on. She couldn't have been ready for his visceral, grown-up maleness. The hair that smattered across his chest, the height of him.

It could be the first time she'd seen him in his entirety. Their previous fumbles would have been hurried, partially clothed, elementary. This would be real. She'd have to take in the man who stood in front of her. It might be the first time not a stitch had come between them. Would it be lingering? Would she have time to let the moment settle, or only seconds to get up to speed? The surprising warmth of his neck. The gap behind his ears that neither his hair nor stubble quite stretched to fill. The weight of him on her.

The light from the blinds would zebra-stripe her skin, painting her in contrasts. He would be harming her. He would be doing something destructive. Even if he was gentle, the act itself was savage. Her consent was not hers to give. Her appetite was irrelevant. Her pleasure was forbidden.

She could only be passive for so long, but she wouldn't know the tricks. She'd be aware of her clueless fingers, her chapped lips. He'd stroke the tendons of her neck and she'd consider it elegant for the first time. She'd struggle to navigate him, to chart his tides. She wouldn't know what each noise meant. She'd feel different even whilst it was happening. It would feel as if the act had visibly stained her, tattooed her skin for all to see. Ink forced beneath the layers where it could never be scratched away. She'd worry that he'd notice. She'd struggle to enjoy his breath on her cheek, the wonderful rasp of his face.

The preparation had taken Rachel days. She'd needed it to look like she didn't care. She'd shunned anything that reeked of the suburban. It had proved a challenge. She'd essentially had to redecorate. The books she'd stacked by her bed were books she hadn't read for years, savagely bent so the spines showed wear. The objects on the dressing table were carefully scattered, the bracelets dropped from a great enough height that they splayed casually. She was braced for his judgement. She found a black dress she hadn't worn since she was twenty-three and squeezed it on, sat down in it to crease the middle, then pulled it off and draped it deftly over her chair. The bedroom still depressed her, so she shopped. She bought a black sheepskin rug she could lose her hand in entirely, an outrageously expensive candle, matching underwear in deli-cate leopard print. Mark might not notice the room, if he only looked at her. The room no longer held Tim. His presence was erased by her seductive flourishes. He had been there so little, it no longer felt like his domain.

Rachel didn't believe Mark would arrive until he was there in the room. Several times they'd sketched a potential date, only for him to be suddenly detained. He was impossible to grasp. She had to wait for a day Mia was out, then pin him to a time. But he was there. In her space. He'd wanted to sneak.

Stealth came naturally to him; his voice kept to a breath, slinking up the stairs, mouse-light on his feet. Although the house was empty, they stifled their voices to nothing, their movements to whispers. She was happy to do whatever made him eager. He held his hand over her mouth, so she didn't so much as moan; she bit down on the juicy flesh of his finger buds, willing him to shout out. Then, suddenly, a key in the door and Mia's greeting called up the stairs.

'It's me, I just forgot my trainers.'

'Okay, love. Have fun.'

They moved slowly, torturously slowly so no spring in the bed would creak. Another heartbeat had entered the house. There was a risk. His eyes in the dark, in her room, in her bed. Then Mia's voice again.

'Mum?'

'Yeah?'

'You okay?'

It had taken everything Rachel had to modulate her voice, to let a few beats hang before her casual reply. 'Yeah, yeah, just a bit of a headache.'

Mark beneath her, within her, unbearably still. In her bed, the bed she shared with Tim. His breaths on her chest, the sound of his swallows. She wanted Mia to leave, to turn her key in the lock and walk off to her netball practice.

Mark, motionless between her thighs, his hands on her back, her sides, fingers on her skin, not moving.

'Okay. See you later.' The slam of the door, the grate of

the key. Rachel's blood was rigid in her veins. Danger had come so close. So few seconds had stood between her and her destruction, the destruction of Mia's world. But Mark was real and hot and damp, and there with her, bright in her dark. His eyes twinkling with the glee of it.

Mia's room was stark for a teenager's. Each surface held only the objects it needed, her dressing table displaying a rose-gold make-up bag, a hairbrush, and a bottle of the sweet perfume she was devoted to, the baby-blue liquid in a crystal star. Rachel loathed the way the smells she associated with Mia were masked beneath its thick sugary veil. She picked the top pillow from Mia's bed and hugged it to her. It was the closest she'd been to holding her for a long time. If she pressed her face into it, there was something of the bready realness she craved, something that had secreted from her child's pores, not covered them. Rachel rocked the pillow-Mia back and forth, comforting it the way she wanted to soothe her daughter. The girl who used to live in that room was gone now. Rachel's role was all but redundant. She'd assumed it would be gradual; a slipping-away she'd be able to keep pace with, but by the time she felt the moment creeping up, Mia was already gone, even when they were in the same room. She'd assumed it would feel like sadness, a dull ache she'd have to carry with her, but it had manifested more as anger. Rather than mourn her departure, Rachel was furious with Mia for wanting to go.

Mia was so ruthless in her instinct to minimise that Rachel had to sieve through her culls, rescuing the objects she couldn't believe held such low emotional value: the blue melamine bowl Mia had eaten almost every meal from for three years; the tiny stuffed mouse she was given before she was even born. Rachel saved the most precious things, hiding them in a shoe box at the top of her wardrobe. Mia found no meaning in plastic, but she wasn't entirely devoid of sentimentality. A carved wooden box she'd been given for her tenth birthday sat in the middle of a bookshelf.

Rachel lifted it out and sat on the bed. It used to house a few letters Mia had been sent by her older cousins: a silver locket they'd prised open to hold a picture of the cat; a handful of once-glossy conkers. Rachel hadn't opened the box for years, and never alone. She sat for a moment with it on her knee before committing to look. It made her temples tighten, but she needed to know. She needed to know what Mia found important. The box was stuffed now, unfeasibly full of ticket stubs and wristbands and hairgrips. It would take hours to sift through it all, and if she took everything out there was no way it would fit back in, it had been arranged in some fluke of physics that could never be recreated.

But she didn't need to look far. There it was. There they were: a strip, held together by perforated edges, four silver squares, each the size of a circled thumb and forefinger. Rachel held them, their familiar feel, the squirm of something inside, the sharp corners. She knew they'd be there, but that didn't stop it slamming into her like a punch. Four was the wrong number. The packs held three or six. Two were missing. It could imply nothing but bravado; it might be savvy now to carry them in your wallet. They might still be a hilarious curiosity, to be stretched over a banana, a cucumber, thrown into Keira's hair. Or Mia might have used them. They could be a habitual purchase; she could be adept at their primary function. Rachel's teeth clenched. She didn't know her daughter well enough to know. Mia could have closed her eyes in the bed Rachel was now sitting on. Under that duvet, she might have breathed in Aaron's chewing-gum breath and the disinfectant tang of his deodorant. She might have played the roles she'd seen on television, on the internet, coaxing him and cooing, all thoughts on his enjoyment. Mia might have grimaced, pressed to do something, to be something, she didn't want.

Even if she'd been all too eager, it was legally troublesome. Only one of them was of age. Aaron was nudging seventeen, whilst Mia sat months shy of consent. Aaron wielded all the power. His position was not so very far away from Mark's. Not so very far. Rachel squeezed the metal wrapper in her hand until the serrated edges bit into her skin. That blue-eyed bastard was every bit as reprehensible. He had ripped from her daughter something she wasn't able to give.

7

'Mother, it's a party. You don't need to know anything else.'

Mia was packing a bag of make-up, stuffing several choices of outfit into a backpack. It had been agreed that curfew should be extended. The WhatsApp group had been ablaze. Midnight for a house party on a Saturday night was deemed reasonable.

'Mia, I need to know that you're safe.'

'I'll be with everyone else.' Mia spoke slowly, as if her mother might not understand the words. Her tone was flat. 'We'll just be at Sean's.'

Rachel had no choice but to go along with the consensus. Sean Turner's parents were away for the weekend and, in an act of extraordinary masochism, were allowing him to host a party in their empty home.

Mia turned away, tucking into her bag a dress so tiny it could barely be folded. It was as if she couldn't bear to meet

Rachel's eyes. 'Why are you being so uptight? What's wrong with you?'

Rachel kept her voice low, so Tim didn't hear from upstairs. He'd be all enthusiasm for the party. 'I'm not being uptight. I just want to know Sean's home phone number. That's not unreasonable.'

Mia sneered, winding the cord of her hair straighteners around their bulk. 'You're being ridiculous. No one uses a landline. Why don't you understand that? Why is this such a problem for you?' Her words were staccato, her jaw tight.

Rachel felt it as a physical ache that she couldn't follow the girls that night, that she had to let Mia out of her sight. Ella's had been chosen as the pre-party venue, so Rachel could only wave Mia goodbye and wait.

'Why does it upset you so much when I have fun?'

Tim had gone to bed by eleven. His flight was the following afternoon and the jet lag would still be dragging at him when he set off again. These weekends were always swift, always stymied. His sleep made the house precarious. Rachel and Mia had learned where the rebel floorboards were, which steps sent a scream through every room. When Tim was home, they trod softly.

Rachel couldn't sleep until Mia returned. She poured a glass of sweet, pink wine, then another. It tasted of lemonade, of roses. She tried to watch a film, but the images just flickered; the actors' words garbled to nothing. She must have drifted off, resting on the cushions, because when she opened her eyes it was dark beyond the open curtains. Her phone digits were blurred – 12:36 – then suddenly, horribly sharp.

No matter how careful Mia had been, she'd surely have heard her coming in. Rachel crept up the stairs and saw what she knew she'd see. Mia's room was dark and empty. Rachel grabbed for her phone. There were no updates in her messages or calls. She dialled Mia's number. There must be some hold-up. She'd be on her way. Rachel expected the thrum of dials, but there was nothing. It went straight to her automated answerphone. *I'm sorry but the person you are trying to reach is currently unavailable.* The voice was stilted, bloodless. It had no idea what it was conveying. She dialled Ella's phone. The same message monotoned from it. *I'm sorry but the person you are trying to reach is currently unavailable.* They couldn't both be broken. It was implausible. Could the network have failed? Or had they both switched them off? Rachel cursed herself for not insisting that Aaron's number live in her phone. She dialled Keira. Keira would answer. The phone sprang to life with rings. Keira's phone would be trilling. Rachel's name would be flashing. Not her real name, but whatever Keira had logged her as. *Mia's mum. Mia's mum.* The rings continued. But it was ignored. This was deliberate. The girls were following some demand of Mia's. She was hiding something. Sleep was still misting Rachel's eyes, her focus, her reactions. She sent the same text message to them all. *Get Mia to call me immediately.*

The girls knew the rules. They knew what freedoms would be removed if they contravened the agreed code. It wasn't worth it. Rachel rang round them all again, constantly checking the time, checking the door. She didn't know Sean Turner's landline. She wished she had Dominic's number. Dominic would answer. Dominic would take her to Mia. The adrenalin rattled her veins. *I'm sorry but the person you are trying to reach is currently unavailable.* 12:42. 12:48. At 12:50, with no answer, she grabbed her car keys. Then threw them down again. She'd drunk two glasses, three, deep and full. Her blood was toxic. She couldn't wake Tim. He'd be in no state to drive. She left him asleep in their dark room. She made no noise. The shirt she was wearing came off in one motion. Her gym clothes were in a neat pile; she pulled on her already-tied trainers, grabbed her mobile phone, locked the front door and, with one item in each hand, she ran. She ran, not manically, but calmly and evenly, as if on the treadmill. She ran for a regimented twenty-five minutes three times a week. She knew how to pace herself, how to clear a few miles without even feeling it.

Rachel ran out of the cul-de-sac and down the main road, hands full of phone and keys, legs rhythmically pumping. She could feel the asphalt beneath her feet, the distance becoming shorter with every stride. Fear and rage fired her muscles, made her lungs grab the oxygen with ease. The pavement was better than the car. She could peer into corners as she ran, stare at the shadows between buildings. There was no

way a cluster of errant teens would escape her. A glimpse of
pale thigh, or the reflection from a pair of trainers. There was
nothing. The roads were empty, the tarmac bare.

She reached Sean's road in little over fifteen minutes. It
became clear when she ran up Wells Avenue which house
she was looking for. There were balloons on the gatepost,
presumably tied by Sean's parents, still thinking of parties
from six years, seven years ago. The temperature was a little
cooler now it was night, but Rachel was slick with sweat. Her
breathing was calm, trained, but her body bore the strain. No
one was outside the house; no one was visible in the windows.
Rachel dismissed how she must look and flew to the door. She
pressed the bell until her fingers hurt, a constant blaring buzz
that couldn't be ignored. After long, loud seconds, a dishevelled boy opened the door. It wasn't Sean; it wasn't anyone
she'd ever taught. Rachel didn't even say hello.

'Is Mia Collins here?'

He stretched before answering, filling the whole doorway
with his flexing arms. 'Mia? No. That lot left ages ago.'

'Who? Who left?'

Debris from the party was visible behind him, littering the
room: bottles, plates that must once have held food, plastic
cups with cracks down them, a little lacy shawl some girl had
left behind. It had the acrid smack of tequila. 'You know, Ella,
Mia, that lot.'

'Where did they go?'

'No idea, just all left. I can't remember that much.' He

puffed his chest out, pushing the strands of blonde that had flopped over his eyes, so impressed with himself.

'When?'

'No idea. Midnight?'

'Were they going home?'

He smirked, ran his hands over his hair again. 'Dunno.'

Rachel didn't stop to reply. She ran around the corner, slumped onto the pavement and just sat there, wired with hideous energy. Every cell was jangling. She knew she should phone the other mothers, but they couldn't know about this. They couldn't see how far Mia had strayed from her. They were so close to their own daughters. She needed to deal with it alone. She sat on the ground, her shoe tapping the kerb, insistent, unrhythmical, irritating herself but unable to stop. She had to do something.

Marianne. She could face Marianne. Marianne might still be up. She might know where Keira was. WhatsApp felt less alarming than a text. *Hiya*. Casual, ever so casual. *Just checking Keira's home okay*. Non-committal, no sense of urgency. The second tick, to indicate arrival, took so long Rachel worried Marianne's phone was dead, and the message stuck in the ether. Maybe the phone networks had collapsed altogether, shipwrecking them all. Then, as soon as it arrived, the ticks turned blue. The blessed blue ticks that showed Marianne had read it. She replied immediately. *Keira got home about quarter past twelve . . . in lots of trouble for breaking curfew, but asleep now. Hope Mia's okay. Talk tomorrow xx*. Rachel didn't respond, she just leapt to her feet and ran, faster now, no longer pacing herself, no longer taking sleek, measured steps, but pushing her muscles until they screamed, until she was sure she was doing them damage. When she arrived – ragged, burning – at their silent home, she raced to Mia's room, as if she might have been hiding the whole time, playing some elaborate game. Rachel didn't modulate her steps to protect Tim's sleep this time. She knew where Mia was, or at least who she was with. The others had gone home, marginally tardy, but safe. Mia was wherever Aaron was.

There was nothing Rachel could do. If she walked around trying to find them, she might miss Mia's return home. She tried her mobile again, scores of times to no avail. There was still no ring, still nothing but that calm, terrible voice. *I'm sorry but the person you are trying to reach is currently unavailable. I'm sorry. I'm sorry. I'm sorry.* There was no way to contact Mia, no route to get to her. So Rachel sat on the front porch, the door closed behind her, her phone and keys by her side. It was still warm in those early hours. She perched on the stone steps, her breathing steadying, her eyes first on the road that led into the cul-de-sac, then on the alleyway that formed a pedestrian shortcut from the main road. She turned her head between the two every few seconds, watching for Mia to emerge from one of them. There was no other way in.

She watched, but there was just silence and nothing. No birds flew in the sky and no steps echoed. Rachel was entirely alone. Everyone in the cul-de-sac slept. Tim slept in the bed upstairs. Occasionally there was the squeak of an insect, a sound too exotic to be British; then it would vanish and the silence would grow dense again. Rachel hardly moved, hardly swallowed, just waited. The only light was from her own porch and in those lushest hours of dark, she could be anywhere in the world, at any time in history.

She longed for a cigarette. The grate of metal against metal that would take several attempts to spark, to whoosh. It had been years, but her lungs would know what to do. They longed for the fullness of smoke. She'd tremble at the nicotine, the relief of it. She'd devour the whole stick in three drags. But her hands were empty. As she sat, stony as the steps, the backs of her thighs grew numb. Rachel felt her insides tighten. Her daughter was out there in the night, drifting further and further from her. Mia knew how upset she would be. Lily was still missing. Mia knew everyone was on edge. She knew her mother would be in despair. It wasn't just irresponsible, it was cruel. Even with Tim home, it felt tar-geted – an act of malice aimed at Rachel alone. Was this how her own mother had felt on those nights when she'd stood, hands on hips, in the doorway when Rachel had returned home, flagrantly late? She'd apologised back then, but never considered her mother's distress. This was different. Rachel had stayed late because she wanted to be out, not because she didn't want to come home.

Rachel heard Mia's laugh before she saw her. A ripple of giggles came from down the alleyway, and was joined by a deeper voice, Aaron, the source of the hilarity. They came into sight but didn't look towards the house. It wasn't a laugh that indicated mirth; the shrill peel sounded more like mania. They were clumsy on their feet, drunk and unsteady, staggering together. They kissed, long and deep, clinging to each other. They had no thought of Rachel. A minute or more passed before they broke apart, before they looked to where she was sitting. The grin fell from Mia's face when she saw her mother stand up. Had she assumed Rachel would just head to bed that evening, unconcerned, happy to check on her daughter in the morning? Rachel stared at Mia across the empty cul-de-sac for full seconds, then turned, closed the door behind her and walked upstairs.

There would be crumbs all over the bedspread. The room would look bare, with only their two bags of belongings to fill it. In that tiny template of a room, she'd sit on the bed. He'd be able to see her from the bathroom, reflected twice, her image bouncing from one mirror to another, from the dressing table to above the sink. Rachel knew the angles. The sun would be shining just as brightly in France, but they'd rarely feel it on their skin. They'd witness the weather as patterns on the floor formed by the blind's slats. They'd have spent over a week indoors, breathing the same air. Lily would be getting fractious, tetchy in the gloom of that studio.

They wouldn't have devices. Her phone would be nestling in the sand at the bottom of the Channel, a tiny submarine from which no message would ever be able to swim up. His would be switched off, hidden in a drawer. He'd be meticulous. He wouldn't risk a Wi-Fi connection being their downfall. They'd be cast back two decades, before the internet had crept into every home, every pocket. It would smack of nostalgia for him, but be alien to Lily. Her time would feel endless. The TV in their room would look cumbersome to her modern eyes, as fat as a fridge and bulging from the wall. They couldn't buy British newspapers and didn't pack books. He'd rarely be leaving the room, paying with cash, his hat pulled low, and she wouldn't have set foot outside for days. The crackling television would be their only portal to the world beyond that room.

Her year of GCSE French would be too sketchy to follow the local news, the national soap operas. She only knew Mme Cressida's precise pronunciation. *J'habite en Angleterre. J'ai quinze ans. Ou est le syndicat d'initiative?* Or the phrases her friends trilled to each other in dense, foolish accents. *J'aimerais voyager à Surrey. Surrey est plus belle que Marseille.* The voices from the television would be speaking a different language altogether, not chanting classroom dullness or daft mockery, but something swift and liquid. Lily would barely catch a word. She'd try to silence her yawns, her sighs, but he'd hear them. He'd be worried that she was bored, that she was regretting her decision.

Mia should have looked younger. Lying in her childhood bed, with her face pale and her eyes closed, she should have seemed more approachable. Illness usually shrank her, taking her back to the years when she was willing to curl up in Rachel's bed and let her mother stroke her hair, feed her from a spoon. This was very different. She wasn't battling chicken pox or a throat infection, but a distinctly adult problem. These aches made her insurmountably older.

Rachel watched her daughter sleep from the doorway. Her eyes were puffed, with smudges of purple underneath. At a glance, it looked like bruising, like she'd been hit twice, hard, but Rachel knew it was just the impact of a surplus of ethanol and a deficit of sleep. Rachel tried to see the prone figure in the bed as her little girl, as the tiny creature who would snuggle into her, push her face into her mother's stomach and hide. But there were so few traces of that girl left. She wasn't limp like a sick child, but tense in her distress. As Mia's eyes flickered open, Rachel could only see the coldness in them.

'Honestly, Mia, I just hope you've learned something from all of this.' Rachel heard her words as an unbearable cliché. It was absurd. The idea that Mia would eschew all alcohol due to this one nauseating headache. It was just the only thing Rachel could bring herself to utter. She found herself to be a bitter nurse. They'd turned their phones off. They'd ignored her calls. It had been deliberate. *I'm sorry but the person you are trying to reach is currently unavailable.* Rachel held the headache tablets in the palm of her hand, round like sweets with their name printed in tiny capital letters. She wanted to ask Mia about the other pills she might have swallowed recently, wanted to force a confession from her. But she couldn't risk the response. Mia could never know how Rachel had followed her, how she'd watched from the car for so many hours. This stranger dressed in her daughter's pyjamas, drinking from her favourite mug, could turn on her. This girl she'd done everything for. It was too precarious.

Tim found it only amusing. 'Oh, Mia. Oh dear, little Mimi, what have you done?'

Rachel held his arm. 'Don't. It's not funny.'

'Oh, Rach, but it kind of is. I mean, we've all been there, haven't we?'

'Tim, she's fifteen.'

He teased Mia, describing the rich concoctions he was planning for her breakfast, the heavy metal he thought they should play at full volume. She groaned, contorting her face into cartoons of anguish. Rachel had to walk away. She couldn't watch Mia clowning for Tim's attention.

Then Tim's case was in the hallway, his taxi to the airport booked. Another three weeks would begin. Three weeks of missed calls and stilted conversations. Rachel kissed the soft of her husband's mouth, held his face for a moment, stroked that longer stubble, met his eyes. She tried to breathe him in. *I'll miss you.* By the time he returned permanently, the heat would have faded. Rachel blinked hard.

Mia threw herself upon her father, whispering in his ear, so softly Rachel could only make out a low hiss. They waved as the Prius that carried him away left the cul-de-sac.

When they were alone, Rachel tried to muster the cooing softness that might lure her daughter back. She knew how it could be done. Favourite foods served in dishes she hadn't used since she was little, calling her childhood nicknames. *Mimi, Meerkat*. Hours sitting on her bed in the dim light, sympathising, sharing stories of her own reckless teens, even sharing the pictures, laughing together at haircuts and dresses that had once been stylish, watching old episodes of loved sitcoms until she drifted off to sleep. But Rachel couldn't summon it, couldn't even do the impression. The tenderness had escaped her. She could barely look at that girl who was once half her, that toddler whose face she'd studied to see which of her own features would push from the bones. She was all herself now, no more like Rachel than a stranger. Mia had been as much formed by reacting against her mother as by inheriting her traits.

Rachel wanted to punish Mia. She wanted to snatch the palm of Nurofen away, have Mia beg for the privilege of pain relief. She wanted to leave the sink stained with Mia's vomit, and make her clean the sour smell away herself. She wanted to make her answer tough questions whilst she was still weary enough to tell the truth. She tried to drop it in, disguised as concern, but her voice had no chance of hitting the right pitch.

'What else did you take last night, Mia?'

Mia didn't move. 'Nothing more than alcohol, Mother.' Her voice was blank. Her stillness was unnatural. The flame seemed to have burned out. She was usually so hectic, with each emotion – joy, hilarity, despair, horror – smacking into the back of the last before it had even ended. This flatness was new. Without seeming to move anything but her mouth, she spoke again.

'You can hardly criticise me for that, can you? You have "adult headaches" most weekends.' The dullness in her voice, the lack of expression, was far worse than if she'd been shouting. It felt more aggressive.

'But I *am* an adult, Mia.'

Mia just curled her lip. She wouldn't break eye contact. Rachel tried again. 'You have to tell me if you have taken anything else. It is important. Tell me what that boyfriend of yours gave you.'

Mia didn't deviate from her monotone. She closed her eyes, revealing the network of blue veins now showing on the thin skin of her eyelids. 'It's none of your business.'

'That's absurd. Of course it is. It is absolutely my business if my child is in danger.' Rachel's voice raised, clanging in the silent house, but nothing came back. It was futile. Mia rolled a little further into her pillow. Rachel couldn't stop herself. 'Mia, you're being a complete bitch.'

Rachel stalked from the room and down the stairs, aware that the kitchen sat directly below Mia's room, below the bed where her head was resting. She clattered as she heated soup from a carton, no concern for chips or breakages. She thumped the pan down, and scraped butter across toast with force. When she took it up to Mia's room, Rachel slammed the plate and bowl onto her bedside table, satisfied with the jump of Mia's body at the noise. Mia struggled to raise herself into a sitting position. Rachel watched as her eyes focused. The lilac dress still hung like a carcass on the outside of the wardrobe door, still in its grey protective bag. Rachel sweetened her voice to a coo, made it almost sing-song. She leaned in a little.

'I assume you know there's absolutely no way you're going to the Prom.'

He wouldn't allow her to find the English news channels on that lumbering television. He'd know it would upset her too much to see her own face beamed back at her, her mother trying to reach through the screen. Not seeing it would just mean that she imagined it. She'd wake herself with sobs so great she was nearly sick. He'd promise it would only be a few years, no different to if she'd gone away to university. But her mother wouldn't see it that way. Lily would long for the soft pillow of her flesh, pliant and safe. Her mother might never forgive her.

Lily's fingers would be itching, with nothing to click. There was no way to photograph her new surroundings, to scrawl comments over the top with the tip of her finger. For the first time, she'd have no connection to the lives of her friends. The fine chain that threaded them together would be severed. She'd have no route to them: what they were wearing, what they had chosen to do with those days of sunshine. The stories were all cut off mid-flow.

Without her phone, Lily would have no clock, no calendar. She'd be tempted to mark each day out with a line, like a cartoon prisoner. Her birthday was only a few months away. Her mum had already bought tickets to *The Lion King* in London; the girls had already watched the dancers on YouTube, their feet bare on the wood of the stage, fur stoles on their shoulders and iridescent smears on their cheekbones. Lily would fear they'd all go without her or, worse, that the tickets would lie in her mother's wallet for years with their perforations unripped.

She'd have packed her perfume, that little blue star of glass. So much would be unfamiliar that she'd hold it, snug between her fingers, and inhale. Its sugary comfort would fill her lungs and, for a second, she'd be back across the Channel, far from him.

They were supposed to meet at Waterloo at two-thirty that Sunday afternoon. They'd both expressed an interest in the exhibition. Tim had left for his flight, and Amanda wasn't bothered. They were going to stop at the street-food market behind the Royal Festival Hall and buy vegan dosas or artisan croque-monsieurs on cardboard plates. They were going to eat them perched on the stone slabs outside the National Theatre, licking the grease from their fingers, then walk in the sun along the river – maybe with an ice cream or frozen yoghurt – to the Tate Modern. Rachel knew how carefully Graham would have planned it.

It would be chilly inside the gallery. She'd feel the cold from the concrete floor creeping through the soles of her sandals. They'd walk in near-silence – except for the yelp of an occasional child – around each echoing room, pausing in front of the paintings or installations they found most intriguing. They'd breathe in that cavernous building's odd, vinegary smell, that smack of art, pickled and preserved. They'd talk in low murmurs. He'd show her the rooms he loved the most, the works he liked to revisit: Louise Bourgeois's majestic spider-mother, a David Hockney sketch he always found moving. They'd stop for small, bitter coffees after a few hours and compare their reactions, looping back afterwards to see favoured objects. They'd talk until they stepped back out into the blinding light.

Rachel couldn't. She knew what the day would be. It would be lovely. And she couldn't. She couldn't have a day as untroubled and pleasant as that. She couldn't leave Mia alone.

Rachel waited until Graham would nearly be leaving his house to head for the train, calculating the times exactly. She knew he'd check his phone. The text was sent with precision. *Sorry. Not feeling great today. Let's rain check.* She couldn't tell him the truth. When she pressed the button, her phone animated the journey of the words, articulated them with a whoosh. It felt like power. She had made him react. She knew she had. She knew how his shoulders would slump slightly as he read the digital letters. She closed her eyes, drunk on the bliss of impact.

*

HAZEL BARKWORTH

Mia stayed in her room for the rest of Sunday. The hangover fug must have lifted enough to allow for movement, but she remained under her duvet, behind her closed door. Rachel had considered forcing her out for food that evening, but had instead delivered a bowl of chilli and received a curt nod of thanks.

As Rachel headed towards her own bedroom to sleep, she knocked on Mia's door.

'Mmm.' Mia emitted a sound rather than words. Rachel took it as assent, and walked in. Mia didn't look up. She was talking on her phone, her hands cupped over her mouth to keep her words private. She glanced at her mother, her eyebrows raised. It was a question, an accusation. Rachel rose to it.

'I'm just here to say goodnight, Mia.'

Mia looked away, and smiled down at her phone, giggling at the words from the other end. It must be Aaron, cooing his seditious thoughts into her ear. Rachel waited, insistent that Mia acknowledge her. Eventually, Mia looked up.

'Goodnight, Mum.' Rachel turned to leave. 'Oh, and Dad says goodnight too.' Her voice was flint. She was talking to Tim. He could only have landed within the last half hour, and the first person he'd called was Mia. Mia smiled at her mother, eyes unnaturally bright, then whispered again into her phone. Rachel walked out of the room.

Lily would be snatching the moments he wasn't around. She'd be making her voice petulant, purring at him to buy a punnet

244

of strawberries, a carton of ice cream, a circle of the chocolates she loved, just to get him out of the studio. When he was gone, the air would be cooler and thinner, able to slip into her lungs more easily. The tiny room would expand. She'd be able to stretch her limbs the full length of a double bed. She wouldn't have to weigh her words before she spoke them.

She'd be working hard. Even at fifteen, femininity is a phantom. Rachel knew Lily would need time to retreat, to make herself look the way women are supposed to. She'd have to shave and pluck, to stain her lips and pink her cheeks. She'd be living in fear of a blemish, of the way her middle had thickened from the cheese and the bread, from the density of food and the scarcity of movement. She wouldn't have ever done this before. She was a different person now, in a different city, across an ocean. She wouldn't know how women prepared their bodies, the rituals they undertook to make it feel right, move right, smell right. She wouldn't have practised in the mirror, learned the angles that most flattered, that made her flesh hang like a garment. And her blood was primed to betray her. She'd usually make marks in her homework diary, a tiny x next to certain dates, but those marks were over two hundred miles away and she'd lost track. She'd fear the smell it would bring, the pain, the mess. She'd try to reduce her body to something functionless, all decoration. Rachel knew how she'd try to erase every growl, every burble it made, reduce her pissing to nothing but a silvery tinkle, nothing that might put him off.

She'd never be certain of what would delight him, what would make him withdraw. It was a game with no instructions. And he knew everything. She'd have learned to make her eyes lengthen and tighten as he looked into them, but it would be no shield. His eyes would make her feel naked. She'd worry he could see all of her, not just the good, that he could see the things she'd do anything to hide; the embarrassments, the contradictions, the weaknesses, those blasts of humiliation that played on loop through her mind as she tried to sleep.

The Hub was empty, and Rachel sat, blank. She didn't move, didn't even raise her eyes. Sleep had been a stranger for more nights than she could fathom. She'd arrived in the building that Monday whilst everyone else was still at home. Mia had declared that she would walk to school. Rachel had waved no goodbye. The papery wisps of her eyelids were lead. Every blink stung. Her body seemed to be moving by some volition other than her own. She felt automated. Only her thoughts had energy, but every imagined scenario robbed her of something significant.

He could still wake up. In that white-sheeted bed, cold and clammy, he could know in a bolt that what he'd done was disastrous. He could think of the weekend they'd spent together. He could still leave Lily, her face pressed into the pillow, her dark hair tangled. He wouldn't even need to say goodbye, or kiss her on the forehead. He could just leave a note, a stack of euros tucked into her passport. Rachel tried to clear her brain of the images, but couldn't muster the effort.

He'd get back to England. Against all likelihood, he'd get back. He'd do whatever it took to get through customs, to find a boat that would stow him. He'd fly or float; whichever was safer, whichever was more likely to get him back to her. He wouldn't waste a second once he was on British soil. He'd rent a car from Kent or hitch a lift to hurtle down the M20. He'd find a way to send her a text, lighting up her phone, or he'd knock on her door. Or he'd leave a note between pages fifty-six and fifty-seven of Pat Barker's *Regeneration* in the sixth-form library, or on the staff noticeboard just above the sports-hall schedule. Rachel still checked both. He'd ask her to meet somewhere no one else would think to go. They'd stand, facing each other. He'd look at her and she'd fight the deafening rage to listen to him. She was the only person who knew the inside of him, who understood the struggle. She'd listen to him try to explain it. There might still be a way for him to excuse himself. She'd listen to him beg forgiveness for his rashness, his idiocy. His callous treatment of her. She'd see the tears prickle his eyes. It could be okay. They could go back. It could still be pure. Rachel's eyes closed, and she swayed into the salty darkness.

'Rachel!' Graham's voice jolted her awake. It sounded like a yelp of undisguised delight. Rachel made her legs propel her to standing. She couldn't quite remember what delight felt like. Where Graham's voice had lifted, she made her own deepen through the syllables of his name, as if they were reading football results.

'Graham.' It would seem professional. She understood he couldn't show favouritism, couldn't reveal too much of their friendship, even though the room was empty.

'How are you feeling now?'

She'd told him that she hadn't felt well. Of course. Her face would corroborate the story. Rachel slipped a coffee pod into the gleaming Nespresso machine, snapped it shut and pressed the button that made it whir and steam. 'A little bit better. Thank you.'

'We should arrange another day, if you like, whilst the weather holds. The Twombly exhibition is only on until late July.'

Rachel felt her eyes blur. She looked down at the stream of coffee that was filling her mug. 'Absolutely. I'm pretty busy in the next few weeks, but let's see.' Her face and her tone made it clear, even if her words were neutral.

'Oh. Okay. Great.' His gaze stayed even, but his mouth – for a moment – became a smudge. He couldn't hide the sudden softness, the smear of his lips. It gave away the disappointment. Rachel felt heat creep up her neck like an allergy. Her body was awake now, and entirely her own again. This wasn't heat from the sun or the coffee-machine steam; this was heat from within. She knew her chest, her collarbone would be mottled with crimson like an illness from long ago. There was no covering it. No cool air could soothe it away.

He reached over to get his own coffee pod, picking the deep purple capsule that indicated rich intensity of flavour. As he fed it into the device, Rachel didn't walk away. As Graham leaned to turn on the milk foamer, his hand brushed Rachel's arm and, for a single second, their bodies were connected.

They were no longer huddling around a laptop. A flatscreen television had been rigged up in The Hub, with BBC News scrolling silently all day. Its bland authority was calming. Occasionally Mark's face would appear, back in that space where they all knew him, peering down at them. It always sent a judder through the room. He was there, again, in that place where he'd killed time between lessons, where his phone had glowed with Lily's words, where he'd examined foreign streets on Google Maps, where he'd marked her work, leaving notes in the margin with his red pen, drawing tiny smiling faces next to her mistakes.

The same two pictures had been used in every news report. Her school photograph, his Facebook profile shot. Rachel had felt them become uncanny, then meaningless. They became avatars for strangers. The newspapers had used the pictures most days, charting minute developments, printing the same titbits of information over and over. There had been opinion pieces, guides for parents on watching for signs of distress in teenagers, endless quotes from sources close to the school. The television reports were marginally more measured, returning to the story only for new developments, so when the pair of pictures flashed up, Rachel took notice.

The room was filling now, and in one movement cups ceased clanking and conversations ended. All eyes were on the television. Someone found the remote and the stilted words along the bottom of the screen became sound. Foreign streets were shown, bustling with people, shopping and working, going about their day. Rachel had been right about France. She walked up to the screen, so close that focusing made her eyes ache. She wanted to pause the images and zoom in, confirm her suspicion, recognise the jut of a building, a shop or street name, know that it was that town, know that her imagination had firm roots. The voiceover declared that the police were closing in on the couple. The couple. Lily and Mark. Their faces expanded to fill the whole screen. It was as if they'd been away for years. Even their names seemed hollow now. They were characters rather than people. The couple. The police were near them now, smoking them out. They knew where they were, but couldn't mention the town. They didn't want to move in too quickly. They couldn't risk the couple fleeing.

The heat would steal all oxygen in that room. The days would be blurring. He'd be spending longer on the bed; she'd be spending longer gazing out of their single window. As Rachel recalled, the view was only of the building across the alleyway, but that would be enough to keep Lily's attention. There would be a boy there, a French boy in the window opposite. She'd have jumped from sight the first time she noticed him but, as the days wore on, she'd let him see her face. With her brown hair, she'd look nothing like the images online. To him, she'd just be a girl. He'd be so much younger than Mark that he could easily be his son, but would look nothing like him. Mark's features were dark against pale, but this boy would be golden. Lily would wonder how different it would feel to kiss him.

He'd lean his head one way, and she'd copy. He'd lift his arm to hold the cord of his blinds, and she'd do the same to the dusty one in their room. She'd have learned that a tilt of her head could render Mark feeble, but might not have considered that it was universal. Were all men so simple? She had never before wielded that power. The boys at school hadn't noticed, but now the print of sex was upon her, this boy might be able to sense it, even across the passageway and through two panes of glass.

Mark would clock him eventually, register the rival gazing into his domain. His voice would gravel, and Lily would feel his fury for the first time.

'Fuck him, looking at you!'

She'd feel the chill of what would have happened if Mark had seen her looking back, if he'd witnessed their strange semaphore. Rachel knew how the fear would whip through her, take the air from her body. He'd backtrack, try to undo what he'd done. He'd stroke her arm, her neck.

'We can't risk being seen, honey. They're all looking for us.' His accent would twinge with American, like some fantasy road movie. 'Come here. Look at me. You are the light, you hear me, the light of my life.'

She'd been hidden for so many days, she wouldn't have walked on solid ground, wouldn't have had any chance to leave. Her face would be in his hands, his head shaking with disbelief or something worse. He would have grown a beard easily; his was the sort of stubble that cast a shade across his whole face by dinner. It would have felt coarse after a few days, ripping into her skin when they kissed, reddening what was once white, then suddenly soft, like the pelt of an animal, and almost damp, sleek as an underground creature. It would have carried smells like burrs; from the food they'd eaten, cigarettes he'd drained on the balcony. She'd feel that fur in the cove of her neck as he held her. His fingers on her throat. She'd fear anything that could trigger his withdrawal. A flat look from him could slay her. His voice in her hair. 'I don't want those boys to get their hands on you.'

When Rachel reached the drama studio after school, Dominic was there alone. Briony couldn't make it; Ross had football practice. Rachel wanted to go home, tell Dominic to leave it for that day. But he'd turned up. He still believed the play was going to be staged, still believed Lily would come back and everything would return to how it was before. The performances were still scheduled for the last days of term. Rachel willed herself to wake up, to reward that loyalty. Dominic wanted to apply to drama school after sixth form. He longed for dark rooms and dusty lights and faces thick with emotion; he wanted to wear white tights or leather jackets or wigs or sandals; he wanted to carry the words of made-up people.

'Which part do you want to run through, Dominic?'

'With just the two of us here, maybe the Laura and Jim sequence right at the end of scene seven?'

'Perfect.'

Dominic glanced at his copy of the play, found the line he wanted to start from. His eyes were so clear. He still retained the sweetness of a boy. He hadn't yet lost it all to the gruffness of grown masculinity. Boys and men were creatures apart to Rachel. Dominic was teetering on the edge, but – with his undisguised enthusiasm, with his downy cheeks – still fell on the softer side. Rachel read Lily's lines straight, with no attempt to inhabit the character. She spoke them only so Dominic could respond. It seemed to throw him. He faltered on the words, seeming unsure of himself. It was hard to extricate his own awkwardness from the fumbling of his character. Rachel didn't know if he was lost in Jim, or just lost. She stood up, to break his flow and address him as himself.

'It's a tough scene.'

Dominic nodded. 'I'm not sure I get it. I can't work out what he's thinking.'

'Yeah. He's torn. You should remember that Laura is very unusual. She's not like his fiancée, she's not like the other girls he knows. He's totally . . . totally wowed by her in that moment.'

'Is she beautiful? Is that what it is?'

'Um, it's more that she's sort of magnetic. Does that make sense?'

Dominic looked away. 'Yeah. It does.'

Rachel sat down again, folded script in hand. She pointed at the printed words. She tried to make the words all she thought about, tried to be nothing but a teacher. It was her best escape. If she focused, she could cast away the thoughts that smothered her.

'You really have to put yourself in his position. Imagine that she is so lovely that you can hardly bear it.'

It was suddenly too hot. Even in that dark room the sun could never hit. Rachel was sharply aware how close they were, no more than inches apart, as she played both actor and director.

Dominic cleared his throat with a small cough. 'I think I know what you mean.' His voice was soft. He rested his hand on her shoulder.

Rachel froze. She was so brittle that a single finger laid on skin could snap her, and his hand on her shoulder shattered everything. She couldn't hold it in. That little gesture was all it took. She couldn't hold the sob back, and in that second of tenderness, her face was entirely, irrevocably, wet. She tried to hide in her sleeve, tried to turn so far away he couldn't see.

'I'm so sorry. I'm sorry, Dominic. I don't know what's

wrong with me.' She felt panicked. She was showing him something she'd fought so hard to keep hidden.

He didn't move his hand away. 'Nothing's wrong with you. Nothing at all.'

His voice was sweet and low. Rachel didn't have the strength to stand up as his arms moved around her and held her more firmly. It was an act of genuine comfort. She could feel his heart through his school shirt, beating faster than it should. His human heart pumping blood around his body. He didn't let go of her. His warm arms on the bare skin of her shoulders. She should move. She should leave, but she let the sobs continue to rack her, let him continue to hold her, his face next to hers. Rachel closed her eyes against the sting of the tears, screwed them tight, so she could retreat. Then damp. Damp on her cheek, her neck. Her own tears, or something else. The heat of his breath or the heat of his mouth. There, then not there any more. Only fleeting, but definite. Something.

In a second, Rachel was out of the room, bags in her hands, books grabbed, out of the dark drama studio, through the blazing, blinding light and into her car.

Rachel drove without looking, without thinking. She was motivated by nothing but being as far away from the school as possible, as far from that drama studio, from that downy-faced boy with his damp lips. She couldn't process it, couldn't recall the moment, only minutes before, with anything like clarity. Was it the heat of his breath or the heat of his mouth? It made such a significant difference. Her mind wasn't reliable. She couldn't have let him kiss her. It was impossible, unthinkable. But when his arms were around her, when his gaze was on her, when she couldn't see through teared eyes? She wiped at her cheek with the back of her hand, like a child removing the germs from a loathed source. He couldn't have. But she couldn't be sure. Rachel pressed the accelerator harder than she'd ever pressed it on those safe suburban roads, flooring it like she was on the motorway, flying down each stretch, taking the corners wildly. The journey home was only three major junctions, and the home-time rush had faded. Other cars beeped their horns as she swung into side roads without pausing, with only a cursory glance, but she hit nothing; she caused no one to leap or screech out of the way. It was fine. Then she got to their cul-de-sac, their driveway.

She jammed the brakes, left the car where it stopped and ran inside. Their house. Mia wasn't there. She was at netball, the only outing allowed in her grounded state. Rachel ran up the stairs, with no clear sense of where she was trying to get to, just trying to be as far away from other people as possible. She wanted to burrow herself away where no one could see her, no one could make her explain herself, make her deal with her actions, her thoughts. Before she could even get to the bedroom, she curled onto the floor of the landing. A pile of recently laundered towels sat there, and she nestled into them, grateful for their smell. Their fibres soaked up the remaining tears that sat on her cheeks. She breathed through their fabric, slowly and deliberately, her nose and mouth full of their chemical cleanness. When her breathing calmed, when her heart had slowed to a bearable rhythm, Rachel rocked onto her back. She could see only the ceiling, the tops of the doorjambs. The world seemed more serene from that angle, pale and sparse. And then she saw a wisp of lilac chiffon.

Mia's prom dress had been moved from the wardrobe door, and had shed its grey skin. It had been suspended like a hanged woman from Mia's light fixture for days, jolting Rachel several times when it had swung into her peripheral vision. It was there as a message to her, a rebuke against the punishment that meant Mia would miss the biggest night in her social calendar. The dress was ridiculous. Rachel would never have worn anything like it. It was a pretty confection – a little-girl fantasy that had been slashed too low at the front and back. Mia loved the layers upon layers of pale purple that had cost as much as their monthly food bill. Tim had happily paid, and Rachel had smiled in the shop, saintly, despite the disdain she felt. Mia had played it cool, but gripped the woven cords of the bag until her hands turned white.

Rachel had to stand on Mia's desk chair to reach it, to unhook the dress's hanger from the metal light fitting. No longer tethered, it lay across her arms like a swooning heroine. It was heavier than she'd expected, no wisp but something substantial. Stepping back onto the carpet, she held it at its full length, like another person in the room. She and Mia were the same height. Rachel draped the dress against her own body, as if she was wearing it, but her black top and trousers ruined the effect, peeping out from the sides. She slipped her vest off, peeled her trousers down, and stepped into the dress, holding its straps. She didn't imagine she would fasten the zip. It would stick halfway, surely, the dimensions of her daughter's body so different to her own, but if she breathed in, she was able to just close the tiny metal hook at the top, run the zip all the way up. Rachel sighed in victory. It was more structured than she'd imagined; it held her more firmly.

Rachel turned to face the mirror. She didn't look like herself at all. But it fitted. She was encased in the dress her daughter loved. The dress was as much about the flesh it revealed as the flesh it hid. Rachel had witnessed the hours Mia spent scrubbing her skin raw before slathering it with unctions that smelled edible in all the wrong ways, like the crackling on pork. They left her body glowing. Fake tans used to be treacherous, but technology ensured that Mia's limbs had none of those streaks and bruises of orange. It worked. It made her look like she'd returned from a week in the Mediterranean. Mia's skin looked nothing like Rachel's skin, nothing like the skin she was born with.

Mia's make-up bag sat neatly on her dressing table. Rachel unzipped it and spread the contents over the wooden surface. The foundation smeared easily over her cheeks, warm and oily from the sun. She patted it in with the pads of her fingers until it was even. When she sat back, her skin was suddenly uniform, tanned without texture, a blank space to be filled. Rachel's usual style was heavy on black liner, lips that looked bitten, cheeks pinched. Mia's generation required so much more. Everything hung from the eyebrows now, and Rachel's were still the wry arches of the nineties, so she seized Mia's powdery pencil and filled the gaps, thickened the lines, stroke by stroke, into a heavy scowl, as if she was furious with the whole world. Once the brows were brooding, her lips looked wan, so she pasted on red straight from the stick. A glossy, cartoon mouth that could only say provocations, only shouts or whispers. The gap between her eyes and lips now seemed empty. There was a flat-headed brush, and a palette of eight varying skin tones. The darker ones scooped the flesh out; the lighter ones added shimmer to the bones. Rachel brushed new hollows into her cheeks, carved a new structure. With powder and paint and a dusting of mica, she turned her face into a version of her daughter's. Only her hair was wrong. Rachel unhooked it from the rough bun she'd worn all day and shook out the kinks. Mia's straightening brush heated up almost instantly, and a few minutes of deliberate strokes turned Rachel's hair glossy and obedient. The effect was complete.

Rachel turned to the full-length mirror. She looked younger, but not her own younger self. Her hair was silky, her face so painted it had become static. Only profound movements registered; the tiny flickers of brows or lips were smothered; the creases around her forehead and the puckers beneath her eyes had vanished. The lilac dress draped over her forty-year-old body, hiding the parts that had aged, had lowered, had widened. It scooped right down her back, but the structure of the front kept her breasts high, her waist tight. Staring at herself, Rachel wondered if this was how they looked, if this was how they felt. It seemed impossible that a swathe of material and a palette of shimmer could rub out twenty-five years, erase two scores of summers. Yet she could now walk into the Year 10 and 11 Prom and mix with those teenagers undetected. She turned to face her reflection at the angle she'd seen them all create, twisted so their chest and bottom stuck out and their middle whittled to nothing. She pouted her lips the way she'd seen them do so many times and, as her skin pulled taut and her cheekbones sharpened, she understood why. She slit her eyes until they were nearly closed, and tilted her chin forwards, lips puckered, until she was Marilyn Monroe, until she was Miley Cyrus, until she was Lily Dixon.

It took an audible gasp for Rachel to realise that Mia was standing in the doorway.

Every sigh of that old building would terrify them. Every creak on their stairs would convince them that it was all over. He'd have stopped leaving the flat, and the shutters would now be closed tight. He might have glimpsed news reports, or just known that with every passing day their fate was growing imminent.

When the moment came, it wouldn't be quiet. There would be no dignity. It wouldn't be a knock on the door, then a respectful exchange. Black-clad police would burst in, destroying their door, those white shutters, sending their things flying, muddying the bed they'd spent their nights in, dragging them apart. The world they had created would be shattered. They would slam Mark against the wall, roughly binding his wrists with metal. He wouldn't be able to reach out to her, wouldn't be able to touch her one last time.

She'd scream his name into the night, into the foreign streets, not caring who she woke. *I love you, Mark. I'll always love you.* She'd need him to hear her. She'd scream herself hoarse with declarations, physically restrained by more than one officer, so she couldn't get to him, couldn't attach herself to him and refuse to let go, couldn't grab a shard of the smashed mirror and threaten to slice her own throat unless they released him.

Their last moments together would be hideous: heads twisting painfully to glimpse the face of the other before they were wrenched apart, before they were taken away from their sanctuary to endless grey rooms and questions and wretched people who had no idea what it had been like.

In those moments, Lily would feel the brute strength of men's arms on her body. She'd scream with outrage, telling them to get their hands off her, off her now.

*

'Oh my God.' Mia shook her head. 'Oh my God, what have you done?' Her hands were over her mouth, but her words were still clear. 'What have you done? You're such a freak.'

Rachel flashed cold.

'I just . . .' There was no way to explain it.

'What's wrong with you? Why are you like this? You're absolutely twisted.' Her voice wasn't raised, but slow and calm, like she was stating nothing but fact. She was looking at her mother with naked disgust. Her tone held the violence that can only arise between people so close. It was brutal. If Rachel moved her head, she'd see her reflection again. She'd see herself in that floaty dress; she'd see the make-up she'd layered on. 'I can't believe you took my dress.' Still calm, still quiet. 'I can't believe you've done this.'

'I'm sorry. I really am. I just . . .'

'You banned me from the Prom and then you took my dress – you put it on and posed in it. What's wrong with you? You didn't even ask. You hardly speak to me any more. You've barely even seen me since Lily went.'

There was no way for Rachel to tell her how false that statement was.

'Dad's been there for me more than you have. And he lives in America. He's tried to understand at least. He calls me all the time.'

Rachel felt the words as solid blows. 'Mia, I've tried too. I've tried so hard to be there for you. You just dash away every time. You don't give me a chance. This dress is the closest I've been to you in months.'

'If you knew how stupid you sounded. Honestly, you're ridiculous. You don't even want me around. You wish I was still a little kid; you wish I still did whatever you want. You hardly talk to me. You hardly even think about me.'

'*All* I do is think about you, Mia.'

'Mother, that is, quite frankly, total bullshit. All you think about is him. It's pathetic. You're pathetic. You're just as pathetic as Lily, as that fucking drama queen. I honestly hope she never comes back.'

Her voice was slow now, little more than a whisper, talking to herself as much as anyone else. 'I can't bear it.' She shook her head again, slowly, disbelief rather than disagreement. 'You're just as obsessed with him as she is. The pair of you just let him do whatever he wants, no matter how idiotic you become. All because of Mr Webb. Mr Webb? Really? It's repulsive. I can't stand to look at you.'

Rachel was stuck on a single beat of the conversation. It was all she could hear. Mia knew. Mia knew about her and Mark.

'How do you know?' It was all she could think, all she could say. 'How do you know? How do you know about us?'

Mia's eyes lit with a terrible smile. 'I can read your phone too, mother, just like you can read mine.' She nodded. 'It took me a while to get the passcode. But then you just said it out loud. 1994. You told Aaron. "A hell of a year."' Her eyes were still abnormally bright. 'I've read every message you haven't sent to him. The ones in your outbox. He doesn't message you much, does he? I saw your tickets to Rouen. Your little weekend away.'

Rachel's blood stalled in her veins. Mia just stared, unblinking, her thoughts visibly processing.

'And you knew, didn't you? You knew about them. You must have – you were obsessed with him – you must have known. You knew, and you did nothing.'

Rachel couldn't reply.

'I'm not blind, Mother. I'm not stupid. I can see what's in front of me.' Rachel watched her daughter's face tighten as she added up the words she'd just spoken. 'I'm not like you.'

8

For the hours after Mia left – after she turned around and walked back down the stairs, out of the door, away from the house – Rachel didn't move. She sat on the carpet, slumped against the bed, staring at the wall. There was nothing to do. There was no way of making it better. Her ears buzzed, as if her brain was providing itself with white noise. Mia had known. No matter how careful Rachel had believed she was being, Mia knew. Mia had carried that knowledge with her for days. It would have tainted every word her mother said. It would have sullied everything. She'd sat there, never voicing it, getting on with whatever else her day had thrown, but knowing what her mother was. Knowing what she'd done, and what she hadn't done. It took hours before Rachel had the strength to remove the lilac dress.

*

The following days blurred. Tuesday swiftly became Wednesday. Rachel phoned work each morning to say she was ill. Inflamed throat. Some sort of summer flu. She sat instead in darkened rooms, only flicking on the television when she couldn't bear the silence any more. In the silence she thought of Mia. There was no way to reach her, and no way to know what she was doing. No way to see how she was wielding the knowledge she held.

It was Thursday afternoon when Rachel clicked the remote control and it flashed automatically to BBC One, the six o'clock news in full flow. Rachel had no idea how it had become so late. The room was suddenly alive with brightness, with sound. The images themselves took a few seconds to penetrate, but when they did, Rachel sat upright.

Lily, walking up the steps of an aeroplane, the arms of a woman in uniform around her, shielding her from the cameras. She had a hoodie on, was looking down at her feet on the metal steps. Lily looked unbearably young. Not a femme fatale, not a wild delinquent, just a pale fifteen-year-old who wanted her mum. She glanced up for a moment and it was possible to see the tearstains on her face, the shock in her eyes. The footage of Mark was no more than a flash, a split second of a face in the back of a police car. In the grainy image, he looked pale.

The report was interspersed with footage of where they had stayed. A budget hotel. The type with packaged biscuits and sachets of hair conditioner. Rachel had been right about

France, but not about the town. They hadn't gone to Rouen. They'd driven to Lille. They hadn't been near that ramshackle apartment. They'd been far from the cobbles she and Mark had walked on together. He hadn't retrodden their journeys, relived their days together. He might not even have thought of them. He hadn't ordered the meals they'd enjoyed, savouring the memories as well as the flavours. He hadn't lain in that bed, recalling how she'd sprawled on it, how they'd lingered there all day.

Rachel paused the television mid-flow, stopping time. She rewound until Lily's face filled the screen. It wasn't Lily's grinning school photo, not one of her Instagram selfies, not the painstakingly created poster, but her caught off-guard. This was Lily as she was with her friends, as she was alone. Her hair was still blonde. She hadn't holed up in a motorway service station toilet for thirty minutes, waiting for the dye to take. It was still golden.

The anger hit Rachel like a noise, like a roar coming from within. It was as if it had been waiting there, poised, ready to deafen her when the moment was right. Rage coursed through her, tingling her legs, her fingers, her scalp with its furious tinnitus.

She got to her feet and stumbled out of the room. Her bag was on the carpet, where she'd dropped it days ago. She knew exactly where to look; there was no rummaging. That picture of Debbie Harry. She unfolded it, smoothed out its lines. The blonde woman reached out to her, fingers stretched, pleading, goading. He had snipped this image from a magazine, a back issue of *Mojo*, and with every slice of the scissors, he'd thought of Rachel's face. She'd carried the picture next to her body for nearly five months. It didn't rip easily; the paper was too worn, too soft to tear with any traction. She had to pull it apart, tugging scraps away from the bulk. It was pointless, but it was the only violence she could enact upon him. With every tug, a part of the pictured body broke away; the feet in her T-bar shoes, her naked legs, the waist beneath her studded belt. Each of them falling like confetti to the floor. The breasts tight underneath her T-shirt. The head of messy blonde hair so similar to her own. Soon, it was all gone. The picture had been her treasure. The only thing he'd ever given her, crumbled now to nothing.

The lilac dress was back on its hanger, suspended from the wardrobe in Mia's room. It had come away miraculously unscathed. It had no idea of the emotions it had triggered. There was no visible sign of the humiliated body that had been encased so tightly within it. It was blank and pure, and would never get to experience the event it was created for. It wouldn't get to cover the body it had first known, that it had been altered to fit, the body that had loved it so fully she'd wanted to wear it home, who'd hung it outside her wardrobe for a week, just to admire it.

Mia was staying with Keira. Marianne had called every

---

morning, liaising between them. The humiliation crushed Rachel. Marianne knew how far Mia was from her. Mia had made no contact for days. It was Friday now, and so many hours had passed since Rachel had last spoken to her daughter. She had no idea what Mia was thinking, no control over what she did. Mia could have told Keira and Dominic, told Marianne what she'd learned. They could be steeped in the horrifying knowledge of who Rachel was, of what she'd done with him. All of her shameful secrets could be spilled. The impact on her life, on her marriage, could be imminent. Rachel burned at the thought. But Mia would be mortified as well. They shared that trait. It would keep her silent. Surely, it would keep her silent. Rachel needed to talk to Mia. She'd listened as Mia's phone rings bleated out, but there was never an answer. She'd sent texts, emails, WhatsApp messages, all saying the same thing.

Keira would be getting ready for the Prom the following morning. It would take them all day. Dominic would be picking up a hired tux, invited as Keira's guest and quietly thrilled to be included. Marianne knew Mia was forbidden to go. Mia would have to watch them all. She'd sit on a wooden kitchen chair, furious, whilst Keira's hair was primped and shaped, whilst plastic fingernails were glued to her hands, extra lashes stuck to her eyes. She would take pictures of them all before they left. The lilac dress rippled in the slight breeze from an open window.

*

Tim answered his phone after only three rings, even though it was the middle of his working day. Rachel barely let him greet her.

'We have to let her go to the Prom.'

'Rachel, what on earth do you mean. What is this?'

His voice held the tension of someone being overheard. He'd be hunched at his desk, or facing the wall of a corridor, trying to keep his tone low and impenetrable. He and Mia spoke regularly. She'd said it. One call, one tumble of words is all it would take, one moment when Mia believed it was the right thing to do. Her daughter held the power to shatter her marriage. Every time they spoke, Rachel braced herself for his tone to turn icy.

'Rachel?'

He never used her full name.

'Have you spoken to her today? Is she okay?'

Rachel heard him inhale, exhale, swallow. She closed her eyes, and counted the beats before his response. The lag between their phones created so many seconds of silence. 'No, she's not.'

Rachel's stomach tightened further. 'No?'

Every muscle in Rachel's body was clamped firm. She was poised for her world to shift on its axis. She had no idea what would come after those words.

'Sweetie, you know she's not.'

Mia hadn't told him. The term of affection sealed it. He remained unaware. She was safe.

'No?' Rachel's ears were buzzing. Nothing could relax.

'She's pissed off with you, she thinks you were too harsh about the party. I've explained it to her, you know that, but she wants to stay at Keira's for a bit longer. I think we should let her take whatever time she needs. She'll come round.'

'We have to let her go to the Prom.'

'Rach, you can't mean that. You made it very clear she shouldn't be allowed to go, so of course I've stuck to it. United front and all that.'

'She should. She should go.'

'But she's being punished. I've been really harsh, really hard-line with her. It's been horrible.'

'I was wrong.'

'So, wait, let me be totally clear: you want to go back on it?'

'Yes.'

'Why, Rach? What's she said? What's possibly changed? If we go back on it, we'll lose all credibility, all sense of—'

'Tim, I know. I know. I know what I said. But I was wrong. You're not listening to me. She has to go.'

He seemed to clock that the urgency in her voice wasn't dissipating. 'Okay, if you're totally sure.'

'I am.'

'Rachel.' Her whole name again. His voice was deeper now. 'What's going on with you?'

He knew something was wrong. Of course he did.

He cleared his throat. 'I feel like you're . . .' He paused:
'. . . Not really there these days.'

She couldn't let him talk any more. 'I know, Tim, I do. And
I'm sorry. It'll get better. Please just do this for me. Please.'

He spoke slowly, as if measuring every word. 'Do you want
to tell her, or should I?'

'Tim, I'd love to, but you know she won't speak to me. Just
make sure you tell her it was my decision.'

The car's air-con was a blessing. Rachel sat in the driveway
for minutes, letting it chill her. The hairs on her arms rose up
and tickled as they trembled in the artificial breeze. Being cold
was a treat. She pushed the slats upwards so the air blasted her
face. Make-up hadn't been an option that Saturday afternoon.
Nothing would stay on; nothing would calm the red of the
blood pulsing just below her skin. She hadn't even looked in
the mirror.

Rachel closed her eyes. She had to move at some point, had
to drive the familiar roads to the school. The evening would
involve so many people. She'd seen almost no one for days.
There would be so many reactions to negotiate. If Mia had
told, the night could change everything. They'd know how
she'd touched him, how she'd kissed his mouth. They'd know
what she'd risked for him. They'd know someone like him
had wanted her. Everything she held could crumble. Rachel
drove slowly, lingering at each junction, turning ten minutes
into twenty. She didn't want the night to start, not yet.

She parked in a road opposite the school. The car park was out of bounds; the turning space was needed for the elaborate drop-offs that were planned for later. There was a patch of road with some shade. A laburnum tree, drooping its golden fronds, managed to block out most of the sun.

Rachel wound down the car window. Rather than breeze, it let in the heat, negating the work of the air-con. But it let the smell in too. It was sweeter than she'd expected. The garden in whose shade she'd parked was startling. There were abundant clusters of roses, buddleias in shades of pink and purple so vivid they must be artificial, clouds formed by masses of tiny white hawthorn petals. It looked nothing like a sub-urban garden; the colours were too rich. It couldn't possibly be steps from a school gate in this small corner of Surrey. Rachel wished she could climb from the car and lie on that thick grass. Even in the heat, there would be a lush coolness within that green. She could rest there; she could sleep. She felt her muscles melt at the idea of it. The soil could be her mattress. No one would notice. She could stare up at the blue of the sky until her lids closed. She could cover her eyes with the rose's petals, to heal them with soothing oils. No one would find her. She could rest her head on the hydrangea's plush pompoms, breathe in the thick scent of jasmine, be hidden from the world by those tangled vines of honeysuckle.

'Rachel! Thank God!' Sam threw herself towards Rachel as she stepped through the door, arms around her shoulders, face against Rachel's neck. As quickly as she hugged, she pulled away. There was no time to waste. She was wearing a flared dress made entirely of sequins, that seemed to writhe of its own accord, rippling like water when she moved, and she moved a lot.

'I'm so glad you're here. There's so much to do. Are you feeling okay now?'

The dress Rachel had chosen was navy. It had a high round neck, a hem that sat on her knee. 'Yeah, thanks, I'm feeling much better, just a nasty bug, I think.'

Sam was taking her role as the head of the PTA seriously, glowing with the hectic responsibility. Rachel was grateful for her energy, for the slipstream she created that could drag her along. Sam stormed around the room, with Rachel in her wake, spinning every plate. The event was all Sam's. When Graham had proffered the idea of a Midsummer Ball, it was Sam who had taken the helm, immediately declaring they should extend the event to Year 10 as well as Year 11, making it not just a leavers' party, but a new punctuation to the school year. Graham's idea of the Ball had become swiftly lost in Sam's sparkling vision.

Sam stopped suddenly by a table full of paper cups. She leaned in again, lowered her voice, quiet but emphatic. 'God, it's so good they caught him, that she's coming home, isn't it?'

Rachel found herself able to answer. 'The timing is spot on. The kids can enjoy tonight properly. The girls will be so delighted.' She couldn't betray that she had no idea of

Mia's reaction, that she hadn't glimpsed her since before the news broke. Sam squeezed Rachel's arm, pursed her lips and nodded.

'We're going to make it a bloody great night for them.'

Rachel looked up, took in the space. The room had already been transformed. Rather than pay for a venue, they'd enchanted the assembly hall. It was not the same room as in those long mornings, listening to a trudging speech by the head of Year 10. The orange-varnished floor was chequered with black and white tiles. The walls had vanished. The ceiling of panels and strip lights was hidden. They were covered with swathes of draped black material, a marquee that had been miraculously erected inside, turning the room from municipal to grand. Despite the darkness, the space looked endless.

'*A Night at the Oscars*.' Sam read proudly from the glittering sign that Marianne was propping up on an easel by the entrance. Marianne smiled over. Rachel stared, trying to discern any new tension in that smile. She wanted to grab Marianne, to see if her friend could meet her eye, to see if her view had changed. She wanted to grill her for details of Mia's day. Marianne had sent a steady flow of texts all morning. She knew Mia was suffering more than just a teenage strop, but she hadn't questioned. She'd simply kept both parties informed, somehow managing to update Rachel without enraging Mia. It didn't sate Rachel's hunger.

'It looks unbelievable, Sam. I don't know how you've done it.' Rachel wasn't lying. 'How can I be useful?' Useful was exactly what she wanted to be. There was plenty to be done. Graham was already up a ladder, pinning something to something else, gracefully conceding his expectations of a refined evening on dappled grass. Tina was hurrying behind Sam, scribbling onto a clipboard. The soft-drinks stand had to be set up; signs for the different attractions – photograph booth, candyfloss machine, full-size Oscar statue – had to be positioned; the DJ booth had to be stocked with request cards; lights had to be moved so they hit the glitter balls at alarming angles.

Rachel chose the most tedious job, the one that involved walking to and from the van in the car park, carrying bottles to the drinks stall. It meant endless trips with two-litre bottles – of Coke, of Lilt, of Tango – in each hand and one under each arm. Rachel's fingers throbbed from the effort, but every pulse of pain captured her attention. She narrowed her focus to those bottles, to the sweat between her breasts, to the reddening flesh of her fingers. There was hardly a chance to chat to the others. She raised her eyebrows to Graham in greeting; he docked his palm in a neat salute back.

Despite the endeavour, Rachel's thoughts couldn't be kept at bay. Mia would be there in a matter of hours, full of her anger, full of her knowledge. She would have collected her dress from the empty house and zipped it up so it held her firmly.

The first car to arrive was a limousine. Rachel had expected nothing less. They'd learned how to conduct a prom from

American films. Other parents were prepared to spend the price of a family holiday on dresses, on grooming, on cars driving no more than three miles. Mia would be in one of those cars. Rachel couldn't take her eyes off the school gates.

Limos were the default option. Boxy, stretched-out Hummers with ten or twenty teenagers jammed in. Once they clambered out, each group stood in the car park, on the strip of crimson carpet Sam had insisted pave their way. Their choice of transport marked them out from each other. The stream of vehicles blurred to Rachel's eyes. A handful of vintage convertibles. Two Year 11 boys on a tandem. A decorated tuk tuk. There was only one car she wanted to see.

The teenagers didn't look like the pupils Rachel knew. The boys seemed lost in rented tuxes, but the girls were the main event. Their dresses were all the same. Unvaryingly full length, with no backs to speak of. Bare arms, décolletage and shoulder blades open to the world. Tight bodice, nipped waist, flowing skirt. Each one had a different girl inside. None of them were Mia. Variations seemed allowed only in the straps, neckline, the level of embellishment, the colour. Their hair was equally identical, all sculpted to the same tumble. In floor-length gowns, glittering with rhinestones, the girls looked like women decades older, decades ago. Their glamour was rigidly traditional, as if, at any moment, they might push someone into a swimming pool.

Rachel watched car after car, girl after girl. Eventually, the bubble-gum Jeep arrived. Rachel's breath stopped in her chest.

It was a perfect replica of Barbie's car. That toy the girls had all loved so much was now life-size with a real, thrumming engine and a driver and wheels that turned. They took their time climbing out, one by one, each taking a moment in the spotlight. Their colours were brighter to Rachel than the other girls. Keira in plunging red, Abby in pale pink with shoestring straps, Ella in a daring canary-yellow halter. Their saturation was turned up higher. Rachel waited for the flash of pale purple.

She knew Mia would let the others lead the way. But, after three shocks of colour, the Jeep door closed, and the girls walked together, arms linked, the boys straggling behind. There was no Aaron. No Mia. Rachel swallowed, tried to keep breathing.

The rainbow of girls reached the end of the red carpet and gathered to watch the next arrivals. Rachel could barely move her head. Mia had to be there. A vintage Bentley. A soft-top MG. Then a black London cab. The cab pulled up; another boy in another tuxedo climbed out and held the door. Aaron. Mia stepped out carefully, holding onto his arm, looking only at him. There was no wisp of lilac. She hadn't gone back home for her beloved purple dress. Instead, she was in black. Not floor-skimming, not princess. Fitted, calf-length, not a flicker of embellishment. No frills, no froth.

Rachel's mouth was dry. Mia must have bought a new dress. This sleek number hadn't been sitting in her wardrobe. Mia looked devastating. She seemed a clear ten years older than her real age, but not like the girls in their Dynasty frocks. She looked sophisticated. This was not Rachel's daughter, but a woman she barely knew. This woman was composed and fearsome. She knew her own mind, and could rise above the children in the car park. Mia's hair didn't tumble down her back, but was swept into a neat chignon. Rachel had never seen Mia look so beautiful. She didn't know she could look so cool. Her face was pale, with sharp eyeliner flicks.

The dress and the styling were signals aimed directly at Rachel. They said that Mia no longer needed her mother. That she couldn't bear to wear the dress that had been sullied. That she had moved far beyond Rachel now. Mia and Aaron glided down the carpet, unaware of anyone else, not stopping to pose.

The group suddenly moved as one, sensing that no more class-mates were due, that the evening could begin. Rachel saw the mass of faces, of bodies, of dresses crowd towards her. She stepped back in the hall, where Sam had formed a greeting line of teachers and PTA members, like a wedding. The most confident girls hugged them; the more daring boys risked a cheek kiss with female members of staff. Rachel watched each face light as they saw the transformed assembly hall. No one had expected it to look so good.

Rachel took her place in the line, embracing each of Mia's friends, kissing the air near their faces, greeting them in a way she would never dream of in the corridor. She enjoyed the strange ritual. It meant she'd be able to hold Mia; she'd be able to clutch her daughter, under the guise of a formal greeting, and whisper right into her ear.

Every other girl blurred into one as Rachel waited for the familiar feel, the familiar scent of her daughter. She wanted to hold that poised and beautiful woman, and make sure Mia was still there inside her. She wanted to look in her eyes and see how she was coping now she knew everything Rachel had longed to protect her from.

Rachel could see the black of Mia's dress, so bold in that mist of coloured chiffon. She could sense her daughter stepping closer, could see her hugging Sam, tilting her head in coy thanks at the compliments given. Rachel's pulse thumped in all the wrong places as her arms readied to reach for Mia. But Mia didn't stop. She walked on, ignoring the rest of the greeting line. She didn't hesitate, didn't stop to see Rachel – just walked, her eyes never lighting on her mother's face.

The teenagers did what teenagers do. Rachel found a space on the side of the dark room and watched as they moved in their little groups. Mia's friends were unassailable in their power, their confidence to dance on the empty chequered floor. Mia was not with them. She was nowhere in that room. Rachel scanned every corner, but could see nothing of Mia's black dress.

As Rachel stood, Graham walked over, handed her a glass of the sparkling elderflower they'd kept for the adults. He was in a tuxedo now. She mouthed her thanks. He smiled, but said nothing.

Rachel leaned in. 'It's an amazing night, isn't it?'

Graham only nodded. Rachel was grateful for the company, for the silence.

Rachel couldn't help but imagine Mark in that room. He wouldn't have rented a tux; he'd have insisted on something more casual. He might have stood with her. He might have pressed his arm invisibly against hers, held her hand behind her back. They might have snuck to the empty parts of the building and done what the teenagers weren't allowed to. Would they have danced? Would he have held her lightly in the slow songs, swayed them in circles, no more than colleagues? Would anyone have noticed? The thought of his hands on her waist twisted something inside Rachel. Some muscle in the very centre of her went into spasm. His breath on her face, his hips nudging hers as they moved. Would he have surveyed the room? That room full of teenage bodies, unsure of themselves, unused to their own reactions. The contraction at Rachel's core knew the answer.

But he wasn't in that room. He was somewhere else. According to the news, he was back in the country, being held in police custody until the trial. He'd be in the sort of room Rachel had only ever seen on television. A single bed with a thin, stained mattress. A window too small and high to provide enough light. His hair would be hanging in strings. His skin wouldn't have seen sun, wouldn't have been plumped by sleep. There would be no one for him to talk to. He was locked alone, to face his darkness unaided. The bars and doors and wire mesh were not just to keep him in, but to keep every other person out.

On a single beat, the dancing stopped. The music continued, but no one moved. Some other rhythm had taken over. The adults looked at each other. Something had happened that was far outside their authority, their understanding. Rachel watched as every teenager suddenly addressed their phone: the boys plucking them from the inside pockets of rented jackets, the girls fishing around in tiny clutch bags. In one movement, in a buzz of energy, they swarmed outside. The teachers followed, exchanging frowns. Sam seemed to be the only adult aware of the news, pushing herself to the front of the surge, sequins swimming.

As the group spilled into the car park, Rachel saw that the red carpet was still there, as if it knew it might still be needed. Only seconds passed before a single car pulled into the driveway. Not a vintage car, not a convertible, just a standard family saloon. Rachel stopped. Her feet suddenly rooted to the floor. She was jostled from all sides as the crowd continued to swell. It was Gary's car. Gary and Debbie's car. Their red Vauxhall Insignia. The same car that had driven to Rachel's house countless times to pick Lily up, to drop Mia off.

Sam was talking to Graham, her voice so loud that every word was clear across the crowd. 'I think it is absolutely the right decision. It's not fair to punish her, she's been through enough. She should be with her friends.'

Lily had, apparently, sent a message to her closest friends, which Ella had forwarded to the whole year, so every mobile in the room had shuddered with the same exquisite gossip. Rachel wanted to halt time for a moment, to give herself the chance to catch up before the inevitable ordeal ahead. Lily had been back in the country since Thursday morning. She would have spent two endless days in police interview rooms, giving statements, confirming details. She'd have been urged to condemn Mark, to tell them what they needed to convict him, but she'd have stayed loyal. No question. She'd have refused to cry, kept her chin held firm and declared nothing but devotion. She would have insisted, in a steady voice, that everything had been her choice, but her fingers would have shredded an empty Styrofoam water cup under the table. She'd have wanted to make him proud.

Lily stepped out of the car alone, and stood facing the crowd. The seconds dragged as they all took her in. It was a muggy night, and the air felt thick. She was wearing the dress she'd bought months ago. The dress she'd chosen when she was still a child. It was silver – the same tight bodice as nearly every other girl, but with a full princess skirt that stood whole feet out from her body. It was a Disney dress, the sort of dress a little girl would weep over. She was too old for it now. Her last three weeks were still with her. They were unsheddable. She knew what the others might take decades to learn. She'd squeezed into the dress she'd chosen before she'd chosen something else altogether.

No one seemed to move. Rachel's head felt too heavy for her neck to support. Ella finally broke the moment, rushing forward out of the crowd in her bright yellow dress, to hug Lily, smushing her tight, then taking her by both hands and leading her towards the others. Only a few weeks before, Lily had faded beside her flashier friends; now she was the centre of everyone's gaze, the subject of every photograph. Rachel could see from across the car park how pink her cheeks had flushed. The crowd was now babbling. Everyone had a question for Lily. *Where is Mr Webb? Do you love him? Do you love Mr Webb? What did you do? What will happen to him now?*

Lily's voice rose above the others, her brief stage training coming into its own. She spoke the words like they were lines. 'Of course I love him, of course I'm going to wait for him. I don't care how long it takes. They can't lock him up for ever.' The crowd looked at her with bright eyes.

As the teenagers flowed back into the hall, Rachel stepped behind the door. The girls stopped just in front of her. They were fussing with Lily's hair, straightening her tiara before she faced her public. Rachel could see them clearly from the shadows. Lily was the centre of the group, the others flocking around her, but she was still somehow on the edges. She was strange to them now, something they couldn't quite understand. They treated her with reverence. Rachel watched as

Abby used the curve of her thumb to neaten Lily's lipstick, as Ella adjusted her straps.

Mia was there; from nowhere she was there in her immaculate black dress, just steps away. Rachel hadn't seen her arrive, but could see her lean in towards Lily's cheek, to blend the highlighter a touch more. She could see her daughter's fingers on the other girl's skin, and then could see as Lily pulled away. Lily turned her head so she was no longer facing Mia, rearranging her body, her dress, so Mia was firmly behind her. It was no accident. Rachel's chest ached as she saw Mia's reaction. The others were all focused elsewhere, but Rachel had sight of her daughter's eyes as they crushed closed, of the philtrum of her lip as it curled upwards, a sure sign she was trying to stop herself from crying. From behind the door, Rachel could do nothing but watch as Mia stiffened, then turned and walked back into the hall alone.

The rest of the girls bustled past, no sense of Mia's departure, not an eye on Rachel. Except Lily. As they bundled back to the party, Lily seemed to spot Rachel in the shadows. Her lashes widened. She was pushed along with the group, but turned her head, as if to stay looking at Rachel for longer. Their eyes locked.

A flash of fear coursed through Rachel, chilling her veins in the warm night. What did Lily know? What had Mark told her? Rachel felt naked. Lily's face was just feet away. That face Rachel had seen in newsprint, on screens, on posters, but not glimpsed in moving flesh for weeks. That girl Rachel had imagined so much it was like she'd lived inside her. Rachel could see the pores beneath Lily's thick make-up, beneath the moonglow shimmer she'd smeared on her cheekbones, beneath the pale pink lipstick and the eyelashes that stuck out like stars. The muscles of Lily's face were taut. Rachel recognised it from the mirror, the tension around the jaw and eyes. She knew how that brittleness felt from within. The bravado was every bit as painted on as her foundation. Lily wasn't triumphant; she was terrified. Close up and round and real, she was a frightened child.

Rachel wanted to reach for her, to circle her fingers around the girl's wrist and pull her close, to recognise their horrible kinship. She ached for Lily's distress, the experiences she'd never quite work through. But she also envied her. Those days she'd spent with him. Rachel wanted a moment together with Lily, with no one else, where they could see his finger-prints on each other's skin. She wanted to examine Lily's body, to see what damage had been done. The police medics wouldn't know where to look. She wanted to gently press the bruises that must crush her ribcage, the faint ones on her upper arms. She wanted to probe the hidden places that might not hurt for years. His unavoidable brutality would have left its scars.

Rachel wanted to look into Lily's blue eyes and see if he would haunt her too, if he would also hang inside her like a never-fallen drop. Lily might be luckier. She might forget him within months. Rachel wanted to hold Lily and ask for forgiveness. She wanted to atone for not doing more, for not protecting her. She was the only one who could have. But she couldn't apologise with sincerity. She knew she'd do the same thing again. She would always put Mia first.

Lily was beset. She was swarmed from all angles. Drinks were brought to her; her dress was admired, photographed; she was in so many selfies she had only seconds between smiles. Her gang basked in the light of it. They had never been more in demand. They moved in formation around Lily, flitting and preening, like bees to their queen. Mia was not with them. She hadn't returned. Rachel scanned the dark hall, the small round tables scattered cabaret-style by the stage. No sign. She walked around the edges, expecting to find Mia in a clinch with Aaron, to back away before they saw her, but they were not in any shadows, nor behind any fold of the marquee. She must be outside. Little groups had wandered out to get fresh air.

It wasn't until the door closed behind her that Rachel realised how densely the music throbbed in the hall. The heat outside was as oppressive as in the daytime, with the kind of heaviness that aches for thunder. A few clutches of friends hung around the car-park gate, surely sharing a contraband cigarette and feeling outrageous. Rachel turned away. There was no need to stop them.

Mia was nowhere in sight. Rachel hurried in her wobbling

heels around the edge of the hall to where the building met a low wall. As she turned the corner, the figure sitting there startled her. Not Mia, who she was desperate to find, but Dominic, who she'd dreaded having to face. Rachel could conjure no more memory of that terrible rehearsal. She'd tried, but it was still only a tangle of tears and skin. They might have simply hugged. It might be nothing. As he looked up and registered her face, Rachel tensed. The pulse from the hall set her blood's rhythm, the electric beat too fast for a human body. So much of her life hinged on the responses of teenagers. She was so often held hostage by their whims.

Rachel switched her tone to bright. 'You look very dashing, Mr Taylor.'

Dominic smiled, and Rachel felt herself ease a little, but then his grin faltered and faded.

Rachel kept her bravado and sat on the wall, dismissing any concern for her dress. 'Is everything alright?'

She didn't move any closer to him, although he was visibly upset. His face didn't stay in one expression, but seemed to move between several. It couldn't be what had happened – what might have happened – in that stuffy drama studio a few days ago that was upsetting him, that had made him sit alone on a dark wall outside rather than join his friends. It couldn't be.

Rachel tried again. 'Why on earth are you out here? Why aren't you ripping up the dance floor?'

'Don't really feel like it.' His usual puckish charm had vanished. Had he told Mia everything that had happened that afternoon? It couldn't be that. It would be some overblown drama, some minor teenage heartbreak. She couldn't have let his cheeks touch hers, his lips touch her skin.

'Do you want to talk about it?' Rachel perched on the far side of the wall, keeping several feet between them.

'Well. It's just. It's Mia.'

Rachel was glad for the bricks beneath her. She gripped them so hard it bent her nails backwards. If he'd told Mia about that rehearsal. If Mia had told him about her mother and their physics teacher. How would they have reacted? Rachel might never get close to her daughter again.

Rachel knew not to panic in front of him. It took all the strength in her diaphragm to keep her voice even. 'Mia?'

'Yeah. She . . . I just don't know if I should . . .' Dominic looked in genuine distress.

'Dominic?'

'It's not mine to tell.'

Rachel let one moment go, two, three. She lowered her voice, softened it. 'Dominic, if you know something about Mia, you really do have to tell me.'

He paused, evidently teetering on the brink of something.

Rachel pushed one more time, but gently. She had to hold herself back. 'It's not your choice, I'm afraid.'

This seemed to unlock something within him. He closed his eyes as he spoke. 'Mia knew.'

Rachel's hands still gripped the wall; they still throbbed with every pulse. Did Dominic know her secret? She couldn't ask the question.

'She knew about Lily and Mr Webb.'

Rachel swallowed, but moved no other part of herself. She didn't want to disturb him, to ebb his flow. She let the silence hang and waited until he was ready to speak. He raked his hands through his hair. It was longer than the other boys' and stood out from his head in tight black curls. 'She knew where they were.'

Rachel didn't move. She didn't even blink in the dark.

Dominic took in one shaking breath, then spoke rapidly. 'Not when they first went, she just knew that they were together then. Well, she didn't know for sure, but she suspected. Then she worked out where they were. Lily used to write her little notes, on special paper, you know, and she'd fill it with that silly French they all do.'

Rachel recalled the notepaper from Lily's room, the turquoise filigree borders.

Dominic didn't stop. 'She wrote the name of the town. It looks like her name. Mia looked at all the bits of paper again, and saw it. Lily must've thought Mia wouldn't pick up on it, wouldn't understand, but of course she did. It's Mia. Mia's sharp. Mia gets everything. She knew Lily was writing the name because she was excited.'

It was as if he wanted the words out of his mouth, as if

they'd been in there too long, as if they tasted bad. But he wasn't finished.

'And it was Mia who told the police.'

Dominic kicked the heels of his shoes against the brick wall, scuffing the black leather, letting them rebound before slamming them back again. It was the action of a boy years younger. He was struggling. Mia would have sworn him to silence. His confession had been a betrayal.

Rachel couldn't focus on him. Mia had called the police. She'd known the name of the town they were in. Lille. The town so much like Lily's name. It must have been by telephone. Rachel had been there in the face-to-face interviews, when Mia had claimed to know nothing of her friend's whereabouts. She might only have put the pieces together later. She must have walked somewhere alone, or closed her bedroom door and dialled the number that was on so many posters around the school. The same number that Rachel had tried to dial so many times. Mia would have typed in all eleven numbers with her thumb, and listened whilst the tone bleated. Then, unlike her mother, she'd spoken. When the call was answered, Mia had spoken the most enormous secret she'd ever known, the heaviest words of her life. She'd been able to do it. She'd cared enough about her friend to do it. Where Rachel had hung up every time, Mia had spoken. Mia had been brave enough to put Lily first. She'd said the name of that town. She'd risked ripping her friendship group apart.

She'd held her mobile in one hand and in one sentence had endangered everything she held dear.

'Should I have told you?'

Rachel nodded slowly. 'Absolutely. Yes, Dominic. Yes, you should. It was absolutely the right thing to do.'

'She hasn't told the others, not even Keira. She doesn't want them to know. It was just because she was worried about Lily, and wanted her home, you know. She started to worry that Lily would get hurt.' Rachel remembered the conversation in their back garden. The garish orange fizz, the fear she'd instilled in her daughter. 'She didn't mean to tell on her.'

Everything Mia had said, every reaction that had passed over her face, had been a disguise. The weight of it must have been unbearable. She hadn't been simply reckless or self-centred; she'd been dealing with incredible responsibility. She'd been valiant, and her mother had done nothing but punish her. Dominic's voice cut through Rachel's thoughts.

'She's so scared the girls will find out what she did. No one else can have known where they were. She's really worried. She's only really seen me and Keira. She didn't even get ready with the others today. My mum lent her an old dress and did her make-up.'

Marianne. It was Marianne's dress. Marianne had been there for her child when she needed help. She'd brushed Mia's hair and stroked foundation onto her face. She'd been there when Mia found herself motherless. She'd delved in the back of her wardrobe for a long-forgotten gem. The dress wasn't a signal to Rachel at all.

'When that message from Lily came through, I thought she was going to be sick. She looked awful.'

A sudden thought flashed through Rachel. 'Did she only tell you?'

Dominic kicked his feet against the wall again before saying more quietly, 'No. She told Aaron tonight.'

Rachel stood up. 'And what did he do?'

Dominic seemed to have shed several years. His voice was only just audible. 'He was angry. They broke up.'

'He broke up with her?' Rachel's voice was loud, ringing out above the thump of the music inside. She was practically shouting. 'He dumped her because of that? Where is she now?'

Dominic looked like he was fighting the urge to cry. 'I don't know. She was upset. She ran off before I could stop her.'

Rachel walked as fast as she could. Mia was there somewhere. Rachel needed to find her. Dominic was certain she hadn't gone. Mia was in the school, full of her secrets, full of her misery. Rachel had left Dominic on the wall as a lookout, guarding the main doors in case she came out, trying her mobile every few minutes in case she answered.

Away from the main hall, the school was nearly dark. Only the security lights buzzed their dim orange glow, barely enough to navigate by. The school was treacherous at night. Every thud echoed, and every corner seemed to conceal something terrible. Rachel scoured every shadowy corridor, her eyes flashing into their depths. No Mia. Their dimensions seemed to have shifted. The walls seemed taller, looming more heavily above her. The glass of every safety door was black.

Rachel searched the toilets first, but the ground-floor bathrooms were empty. No Mia. Next were the corridors. She tried every door handle, jerking them with force. Some opened; some stayed firm. There was no clear logic. The building wasn't on her side as she hunted. She didn't know its quirks and laws, couldn't decipher its codes. Rachel flung wide every door that let her, braced for something terrible. But each time the room was empty.

Mia was out there somewhere. The bassline thud from the assembly hall pounded at one end of each corridor, fading to nothing at the other. Those thumps gave the building a frenzied pulse. Rachel stamped her feet with every step, faster than the music, as fast as she could go. She coursed through floor after floor, department after department, finding nothing. Mia wasn't behind any door. She wasn't around any corner.

Rachel's ragged breaths echoed down the corridor. Mia was nowhere. She was nowhere in that empty building. Dominic. She had to go back to Dominic. The back stairwell was direct, so Rachel ran. Flight after flight of thirteen stairs. The light was too dim; the spinning made Rachel dizzy. She counted her steps – *eleven, twelve, thirteen* – looking at her feet – *eight, nine, ten*. As she reached the ground floor, there was someone in front of her. Rachel stopped dead. Aaron. He was hidden by the gloom, then suddenly visible. He seemed to leap out despite not moving. Rachel screamed. He seemed just as shocked to see her. In the half-light, he looked like a hologram. They were alone.

'What are you doing here? Where's Mia?' Rachel was alarmed by the venom in her own voice, but couldn't hold back. 'Why are you creeping around? Where is my daughter?'

'What do you mean? I was just, you know, sitting here for a bit.' Something about him was askew. His eyes were wider than usual, his movements jumpy.

'Where is Mia?' Rachel couldn't waste time on him when Mia was out there. 'Get out of my way.'

He stepped towards her. 'No. You don't understand. It was Mia that told. It wasn't me.'

Rachel could only stare. He had utterly misunderstood her anger, jumping to his hair-trigger response of denial. He was instinctively blaming Mia, accusing her to her own mother.

'She told on Lily. She got all up in their grill, and told the police. I had nothing to do with it. It was all her, she didn't even tell me until tonight.' His words were garbled. 'If she'd told me before, I'd have said to leave well alone. It's nothing to do with her. She's always such a good girl, always got to be right about everything, couldn't just be cool . . .' Spit was forming around his mouth. 'I think, at the end of the day, she was probably just jealous. She kept bitching about how it wasn't fair Lily was getting all the attention. I think she just wanted it to stop, so . . .' He took a long-overdue breath. Sweat was beading on his temples and over his scalp, where the hair should be. His feet were jittering, his hands dancing. Everything about him was sped up. 'She was totally out of order. It wasn't her business, she should've let it go, not got all pathetic and grassed them up. It's childish. If she'd told me back then when she did it, I'd have made sure she kept her mouth shut, made sure—'

Rachel slapped his face. The action seemed to come from outside her body. She felt the impact of the flat of her palm against the skin of his cheek. Hard. Far harder than she realised she was capable of. It shut him up. It silenced those manic words. She'd slapped him like she might slap someone hysterical, but also like she might slap someone she loathed. Her muscles had reacted before her brain, but they'd nailed it.

The silence stretched into seconds. Aaron held his hand over the place where her hand had hit. His mouth was hanging open in a dumb circle. Rachel let herself taste the satisfaction for a moment. It couldn't possibly last. He'd be able to form words again, and it would all turn to horror. She tensed herself for the outrage that would come bellowing out, the threats that would flow. He'd have every right. She'd done a terrible thing. She'd hit a pupil on school grounds. But he said nothing, just gaped at her, silent, hand over the skin she'd hurt, his pupils black and massive. She'd done something so terrible that if he told she could lose her job. She should lose her job.

But he was frozen. Something was stopping him. Rachel

tried to look in his eyes, to read what was there, to unravel him, but they were still skittish. Something was making them roll in their sockets. It became searingly obvious. He couldn't destroy her. Her harshest judgements had been accurate. Whatever was making his blood hectic was every bit as inappropriate as her action. Whatever chemical was racing through his veins would indict him before he even began. But there was something more in the black of his eyes. Mia. It was Mia. Whatever poison was hurtling through him was in her as well.

Rachel didn't give Aaron another look, just flung herself round and back up the stairs. Mia was out there somewhere, and she needed her mother.

Rachel moved more slowly than before. She had to be thorough. She found the flashlight on her phone and aimed it into every corner. Mia was somewhere. She was hidden in some nook; she just had to be found. Rachel examined classroom after classroom, with nothing but the sound of her own blood thumping, her own breaths shaking. Room after room. Geography classrooms with wall maps that could be crept behind, computer labs with tangles of cables and wires that seemed to writhe in the shadows, English rooms where handwritten poems rustled on walls in no breeze whatsoever. In the science block, only one room was open.

Mark's classroom. It was still being used. Classes still needed to be taught. Electrons still carried negative charge. A body in uniform motion still stayed in that state unless acted upon by an external force. A stream of supply teachers was watching over classes as they ploughed through their work-books. Everything of Mark's was still in there: the framed infographics were still on the wall, the wooden in-tray still sat squarely on his desk, the metal pen pot, the Einstein quote above the whiteboard. *Nothing happens until something moves.* He had always been a good teacher. The faint smell of him persisted. Lemony and fresh, with a hint of something darker. Nicotine or tar. He was still in there. The ghost of him hadn't faded. Rachel's hundred days with him still had the power to destroy everything else.

Mia would be here, of course she would. Rachel called Mia's name into the air. Those two neat syllables. *Mee-ahh. Me. Ah.* Nothing.

There was no hint of Mia anywhere, but particles of Mark must litter every surface. Invisible flakes of his skin, strands of his hair. The memory of his movements, of how he paced in front of the whiteboard, of his voice making the complex simple, decoding equations so they were clear. Every eye would have been on him. He would never enter that room again. He was behind steel doors and wire cages. A prison sentence was inevitable. A minimum of two years, surely, if he was lucky, if he kept his head down. If no one provoked him. It would be twenty-four months before he could walk out of there, before he could scream on a fairground ride or dance in a darkened room. Before he could dip his toes in a river. He would spend years only able to talk to his loved ones with supervision, clutching fingers, but not allowed to embrace, every action watched by someone primed to intervene.

Rachel would never go there. She would never drive the thirty-four minutes Google Maps estimated it would take to arrive at Banstead. It would surely be High Down. It was the right level of security; it was mercifully close by. She would never sign her name in the official books, and be escorted to see him in whatever secure space was given to visitors. She would never see him across the room, seconds before he noticed her, and take in his diminished frame, the pallor of his skin, the thinness of his hair. She'd never watch as he stood awkwardly, stunned at her presence. She'd never see the relief flood his face, never hear him whisper how sorry he was. She'd never lock eyes with him as she sat down. She would never reach across the pocked and pitted Formica table and grab his fingers in her own.

There were fewer rooms on the ground floor. When Rachel reached the main corridor, the busiest part of the school, the point where every thoroughfare crossed and every route intersected, she saw a light. The girls' toilets. Not the flashy new ones near the main entrance, but the old ones near the walkway that led to the dinner hall. She'd looked there, briefly, and found them empty. But now, in the dimness of the corridor, light shone around the edge of the door, glowed like an alien craft. Rachel ran. She ran as fast as she was able in her stupid, spindly shoes; she ran down the full length of the hallway. She knew it was Mia. She knew Mia's fingers had turned that light on. She knew her daughter was behind that door.

She was on the ground. As Rachel threw the door open, she saw Mia slumped beneath the sinks, her head on the white tiles, her hair no longer neatly styled but covering her face. Her legs were splayed at startling angles; Marianne's black dress had ridden up around her thighs, her skin and the fabric both soaked.

'Oh, God.' Rachel was instantly on the floor, shoes off, kneeling, cradling her daughter's head. Mia's eyes were closed, her lips damp with frothy saliva. Rachel smoothed the hair away from Mia's forehead.

'Mia. Look at me. Look at me, Mia.' Rachel tried to lift her eyelids. Mia opened her eyes briefly, but didn't focus. Her body was heavy and limp.

'Come on, darling. You need to get up. Sit up now.' As Rachel heaved Mia upwards, her hand fell open. In the crook of her palm was a tiny, rainbow-striped pill. An unswallowed version of what she had surely ingested, of whatever Aaron had given her. Rachel steeled herself, cleared the foam from her daughter's lips, made sure she could breathe freely.

'Come on, Mia. Come on, love. I need you here with me. How many of these have you taken, Mia? Mia? Sweetie, how many did he give you?'

Mia was breathing; her mouth was moving, contorting into

the shapes of words. She seemed to rouse herself. ' . . . hates me so much now.'

Rachel hoisted Mia until she was sitting upright, her back against the cool tiles. She kneeled in front of her, and held her eyes open, her fingers on her daughter's lids. She tried to discern the danger. Mia had poison flowing through her veins. How much damage was it wreaking? On that damp and filthy floor, their faces were at the same level. They could look straight at each other.

Mia's make-up had rubbed off; sweat or water had washed it away. There were no heavy brows, no sculpted cheeks, just Mia's face, damp and pink. Rachel could see her daughter for the first time in months, and Mia could look right back. Neither was what the other had expected. Those hot days had contorted everything; melted it down and reset it into odd new shapes. They had no secrets left to tell. Everything was on the outside. There was no going back.

Mia tried to speak again. 'Mum?' Rachel felt her throat tighten. Slumped on the floor, Mia's guard was down. 'Mum? What will happen when I . . .?' Rachel swallowed. She stroked her daughter's sweat-soaked forehead. This broken girl still had the power to destroy her. Mia reached out and touched the ends of her mother's hair, the blonde tips that fell near her hands. She twisted them in her fingers, stroking them with her thumb, as gentle as with a pet. When she spoke again, Mia's words were thick and jumbled. 'I'm so tired. And I just, I don't know . . . I need you to . . .'

Rachel leaned in closer, her arms around Mia's shoulders, her ear next to her mouth. 'What do you need, my love?'

'I need you to . . .' Her words were choked by a sob.

Rachel held Mia against her, rocking her gently. She understood what Mia was trying to say. 'I know, sweetheart. I know. I need that too. I promise.'

Mia's eyes suddenly grew glassy again, and her head lolled on her neck as if it wasn't fully connected. Rachel wanted longer to talk, to grab at the tangles of her daughter's thoughts, but there was no time. As her head rolled forwards, Mia's hair fell across her face again. Her limbs were loose, her joints fluid. Her hands and feet seemed too heavy for the bones that held them. Not a single muscle seemed tensed.

'Shit.' No one was around. Rachel lifted her head, tilted it backwards and yelled. 'Help! Help!' There was no point in calling out; her voice was swallowed instantly by the music coming from the assembly hall. Rachel's mobile had no signal in that deep part of the school. Mia needed help now: there was no time to waste, no time to run, to find someone, to explain quickly enough. Rachel didn't know what Mia had swallowed, didn't know what damage it was inflicting as it tore through her body, but she knew that every second Mia didn't open her eyes was dangerous.

They were almost the same height, the same dress size. Rachel hadn't been able to lift Mia for nearly five years. But she had to. Resting Mia back on the floor, Rachel got to her feet, bent her knees and heaved her daughter's body onto her own. It should have been impossible, but Rachel's muscles, her sinews, seemed to understand. Rather than scream out, they stiffened, enabling her to take the weight. Strength Rachel was unaware of came to the fore, strength that must have been dormant, poised for the moment it was most needed. Rachel held Mia as though she was a fairy-tale damsel, supporting her middle over outstretched arms, whilst her limbs flopped towards the ground. Like that, Rachel staggered outside, kicking the doors open as she went, her steps wobbling, each one risking a fall. She was grateful for every metre she'd ever covered on the treadmill, every second that had built her to be just about robust enough. Rachel reached the fire door that opened onto the car park and backed into it with enough force to push the bar down and blast it open.

It was darker outside than she'd expected. The sky was already milky. Rachel tried shouting again, hoping the cooler air outside might carry the noise better, but her lungs had little power left. Her arms were beginning to roar with pain, beginning to give way. She couldn't hold Mia much longer. Her car was three roads away, tens of metres, hundreds of steps. It was impossible. Then the crunch of feet on gravel, a voice.

'Here, let me take her.' Graham. He reached down, knees bent, back straight, and lifted Mia from Rachel's arms, carried her easily in his solid grip.

'This way.' He walked decisively. He knew exactly what to do. Rachel followed, scanning the car park. Mia would be mortified if she was seen, if her friends witnessed the state she was in. There was no one around. Even the wall Dominic had been sitting on was empty. They would all be inside, dancing with their arms raised above their heads, taking photographs of each other, laughing so everyone turned to look. Lily would be twirling in her silver princess dress, letting the others try on her tiara.

Graham was pounding across the tarmac, already planning their route. Rachel jogged after him.

'If we call an ambulance it will take longer, the hospital is only a few minutes from here.' He was opening the door of his car, gently lying Mia on the back seat. He knew what to do. 'Get in the back with her, Rachel.'

Rachel watched her daughter. Mia's head was in her lap. Rachel stroked the hair out of her face, tucked it behind her ears, stroked the skin of her forehead. All of Graham's attention was on the road. He was driving fast, too fast, but with a determination that felt safe. Without shifting his eyes, he spoke.

'Is she okay? How are you doing?'

Rachel looked at Mia. Her head was tilted so that her now-unclipped metre of hair waterfalled over the edge of the seat. There was no space for her to stretch out full length, but her limbs sprawled over the upholstery. Her crimson-painted toenails. The wingspan that seemed impossible. Her skin was smooth, as warm as honey, and there were no hairs on her legs, not even little golden ones that might glint on her thighs. Her dress was wet and wrinkled. Her hair was tangled. She looked perfect. Mia's eyelashes fluttered for a second and she opened her eyes. This time they didn't swim, but focused on her mother. She didn't say anything, just looked.

'I think she'll be okay. I think so.'

'We're nearly there. They'll be able to treat her, Rachel. She'll be absolutely fine.' She was more than fine. She was incredible. She was braver than Rachel had ever guessed. Rachel held that body she'd known so well. The clavicle she'd kissed so often. The ribs she'd once xylophoned.

Rachel pressed the button to wind down the window. The air it let in had texture. It was beginning to rain for the first time in weeks. Just a smattering, just a mizzle, but Rachel could feel it on her face. She pushed her head further out of the window, watching the houses speed by. They were no more than three roads from the hospital now. Only minutes at most. The rain became more insistent, drops fatter and faster. Everything, suddenly, was wet and clean. The tarmac reflected; the front windows were slick; the plants growing around the doorways were dripping. It all looked different. Light fell in new angles. When the pressure in her lap shifted, Rachel moved back into the car.

'Mum . . .'

'Darling, don't talk, just rest. We're nearly there, we're nearly there, Mi.' Rachel leaned over to whisper right into Mia's ear, into that soft whorl of flesh. She stroked her hair as she spoke, breathing in the warm salt of her daughter's scalp. 'I'm here. I'm here, Meerkat, and I'm not going anywhere.'

The breeze from the window was bolder now, filling the car with cool air. Rachel sat up straight and turned her head to the outside, breathing great lungfuls of the earthy petrichor that rose from those familiar pavements.

Acknowledgements

Many magnificent people have helped me in the journey to creating this book. I am grateful to every one of them.

First, thank you to the incomparable Lucy Morris, who sent the email that changed my life. Thank you for your brilliance, vision and determination. There is no one I'd rather have on my side and by my side, and no one I'd rather do 'Let's go down the disco!' dancing with.

Thank you to Luke Speed, and everyone at Curtis Brown, for your spirit and hard work.

Thank you to the extraordinary Frankie Edwards, for your incisive intelligence, sharp wit and deep understanding of what I am trying to do. It has been such fun to build this book with you. Thank you for always pushing me to be bolder.

Thank you to Jessica Farrugia and Jo Liddiard for your incredible ideas and energy. Thank you to Yeti Lambregts for such a striking and beautiful cover. Thank you to Bea

Grabowska, and the whole team at Headline, for your enthusiasm and support. I couldn't imagine a more fantastic team to guide me through my first novel.

Next, thank you to the Unruly Writers for your fierce brilliance. Especially the London contingent, without whom I would have abandoned this book long ago: Susie Campbell, Shahla Haque, Sarvat Hasin, James Ellis, Imogen Harris, Kiran Millwood Hargrave and Daisy Johnson. Your work inspires me every day.

To Curtis Brown Creative, where I realised what I wanted to write. Especially to Anna Davis for your constant support, and to Erin Kelly for your wisdom, perception and belief. Thank you also to my wonderful course mates who tirelessly read my words and gave such invaluable advice.

To those who taught me how to love words and how to shape them: Jude MacAdam, Sue Tomlin, David Bean, Stuart Pickford, Anna Beer, Julian Thompson, Clare Morgan.

To the friends who have shared my love of stories, and provided me with enough gossip to fuel my own: the Dunblane friends who shaped the glory of my early teens, the Harrogate drama queens, my magical Regent's Park comrades, and the What If Wonders. Thank you to the Cultural Insight team, who had my back whilst I wrote this, and made me laugh and learn every day: Francesca Simon-Millar, Jessica Parr, Hannah Robbins, Lyndsay Kelly, Hari Blanch Bennett, Laura Tarbox, Tom Pattison, Ophelia Stimpson, Sarah Neary, Claudia

Bhugra-Schmid, Eleanor Lloyd Malcolm, Helen Firth, Izzy Pugh, Cato Hunt and Paul Cowper.

Thank you to the friends who have loved me with such kindness and gusto. To Ruth Brock for simply being magnificent. To Carli Bean for your dramatic soul and those splendid days lost in words. To Mary Groom for sharing glittering nights, and for reading my words for so long. To Eiluned Jones for your luminous support. To Xavior Roide for sparkling conversation and total belief. To my Lincoln friends, especially Rose Mortimer, Shazeaa Ishmael and Tallie Samuels, for celebrating so generously with me. To Laura Wright, Beatrice Montedoro and Will Brockbank for thrusting me into whole new stories, and for making Oxford home.

Thank you to Katy John. For sparking my desire to write and for constantly fuelling it. For believing in me and pushing me. I couldn't have done it without you.

Thank you to my family. To Elaine and Andy, and Wendy and John. To Ellen, Nathan, Christopher, Joshua and Henry. To Janet and Norman. For such inspiration, joy and belief. To Harry, and to my wonderful in-laws, Muriel, Bill and William, for support and love despite my lack of a decent service game.

To my parents, Linda and Glen, for teaching me not only how to read but, more importantly, why. Your enormous love of stories in all their forms is one of the greatest joys of my life. Thank you for believing I could create my own.

To Paul. For being there for every word. For holding my hand through every step of our strange and beautiful adventure.

Hazel Barkworth grew up in Stirlingshire and North Yorkshire before studying English at Oxford. She then moved to London where she spent her days working as a cultural consultant, and her nights dancing in a pop band at glam rock clubs. Hazel is a graduate of both the Oxford University MSt in Creative Writing and the Curtis Brown Creative Novel-Writing course. She now works in Oxford, where she lives with her partner. *Heatstroke* is her first novel.

 @BarkworthHazel

 @hazelbarkworth

Reading Group Questions

- We experience *Heatstroke* entirely through Rachel's eyes. Do you think she is a reliable narrator? Why?

- **'Rachel felt suffocated by the neat rows of buildings that inevitably spread out over every hill's real prow.'** Discuss the presentation of suburbia in the novel. Could the same story have been written in a different setting?

- *Heatstroke* is a female-led narrative in which male characters generally appear only on the periphery. Did their absence impact on your reading of the novel?

- Throughout the novel, Rachel takes on various identities: mother, wife, colleague, teacher, lover. How do these roles interact with one another?

- **'Act like you give a shit. This is real. Do you understand that? And if you just sit there and keep quiet, you are part of it. You are responsible.'** To what extent is Rachel complicit in Lily's absence? How did you feel about her staying quiet?

- How does *Heatstroke* engage with questions about consent?

- **'Suddenly, there were two women in the house.'** Mia and Lily are on the fringes of womanhood, trying to break free from the 'restraints' of being teenagers. How does the author play with notions of power and agency through her characters?

- *The Glass Menagerie* is known as a 'memory play', in which events are drawn from a lead character's memory. How do Rachel's memories impact the structure of *Heatstroke*? And do you think Lily leaving is in any way informed by her starring role in the school production?

- **'They still knew the mothers who'd borne sons, but the connection was weaker.'** Do you think your life experiences – including the roles you inhabit (e.g. mother, daughter, father, friend etc.) – affect how you engage with *Heatstroke* as a reader? Do you think you'd feel differently if you'd come to this book at a different point in your life?

- How did you respond to the heat and claustrophobic atmosphere in the book? What effect do you think those hot summer weeks had on the characters? Would they have acted in the same way under different conditions?

- Did your understanding of Mia change over the course of the novel? Why?

- **'I suppose she was just destroyed by her daydreams.'** Do you think Rachel's life is what she wanted? Or has she found herself disappointed by her reality? Discuss.

- How does Hazel Barkworth's novel explore the idea of shame – in particular, women taking on male shame?

- **'It all looked different. Light fell in new angles.'** What do you think the future looks like for Rachel and Mia?